VANISHED ON VACATION

An Agent Victoria Heslin Thriller, Book 6

Jenifer Ruff

Greyt Companion Press

VANISHED ON VACATION

An Agent Victoria Heslin Thriller, Book 7

Written by Jenifer Ruff

Cover design by Rainier Book Design

Copyright © 2022 Greyt Companion Press

Ebook ISBN: 978-1-954447-28-8

Paperback ISNB: 978-1-954447-22-6

Hardback ISBN 978-1-954447-23-3

Visit the author's website for more information. www.Jenruff.com

ALSO BY JENIFER RUFF

The Agent Victoria Hesin Thriller Series
The Numbers Killer
Pretty Little Girls
When They Find Us
Ripple of Doubt
The Groom Went Missing
Vanished on Vacation
The Atonement Murders
The Ones They Buried
THE FBI & CDC Thriller Series
Only Wrong Once
Only One Cure
Only One Wave: The Tsunami Effect
The Brooke Walton Series
Everett
Rothaker
The Intern
Suspense
Lauren's Secret

VANISHED ON VACATION

V ANISHED ON VACATION is the sixth book in an award-winning series of standalone mystery thrillers featuring FBI Agent Victoria Heslin. You can find a list of those books and others by Jenifer Ruff at the beginning of this novel.

PROLOGUE

U nder the night sky, the vast ocean appeared inky black at every depth.

The perfect place to hide a body.

But they didn't always stay hidden.

The mutilated corpse floated face down in the water, hands secured together in back with yellow nylon rope, long hair twisting with seaweed tendrils in the rolling waves. A slight pull back to the horizon followed each movement toward shore. With practiced patience, the current's rhythm persisted. In no rush but determined to deliver the body home.

CHAPTER 1

The first two days of the vacation passed in a blur of sun, sand, frozen tropical drinks, and dancing into the early morning hours. With only one night remaining, Avery Jennings planned to relish every minute. Tomorrow morning, she and her friends had to wake up crazy early to catch the first flight back to Virginia. They'd be hungover but sun-kissed and ready to embrace the final weeks of their college senior year.

Wearing her workout clothes, Avery tied up her shoelaces, tucked her water bottle into her bag, and headed for the door. Before she got there, it swung open and her friend Brie burst inside, waving a piece of paper through the air then holding it against her bikini top. "I'm negative! Yes!" Brie shouted.

Of the three friends, Brie had been the most anxious about testing positive for Covid and getting stuck in Mexico. She had two job interviews lined up for the following week and didn't want to miss them.

"Whew. I can finally relax now that I've got this." Brie slapped the paper down on the desk. "I love it here, but...you know...I have to get home. And if I don't have Covid, then none of us should."

Brie took out her phone and typed away. A second later, a new text popped up in the *Azure Cove Babes* group chat on Avery's phone. It said, *Negative Covid Test!* followed by heart and smiley face emojis.

"I'm totally going to party now," Brie said, opening the closet and removing a silk pouch from under a pile of folded clothes. She uncinched the pouch and shook out colored pills. Some mint green, some white. "Want one?"

"No, thanks." Avery wasn't even tempted. "Where did you get your test result?"

"At the registration counter. We need the paper to get through customs. I tried to get all of ours when I was there. They wouldn't let me. Confidentiality and all that."

As much as Avery wanted the reassurance her negative test result would bring, the reception desk was in the opposite direction from the exercise area where they held the group classes. "I'll get mine after Zumba," Avery said before waving goodbye to Brie.

Walking across the beautiful resort on a path lined by lush flowers and palm trees, Avery cringed as she thought about her recent nasal swab. It had been unnecessarily brutal. She'd taken countless tests by now. Random selection tests throughout the school year, and almost every time one of her good friends had tested positive. Another test when she was so sick, she couldn't get out of bed for two days, which ended up only being the flu. Yet none of those compared to her experience yesterday in the resort's health office. The woman administering it stuck the swab so far up Avery's nose, she was certain it pierced her brain. If that wasn't bad enough, the woman twirled the swab around for what seemed like forever. It was almost as if she was desperate to find a trace of the virus and keep people from leaving. Avery stumbled out of the health office with tears in her eyes. Thank God that was behind her.

As she neared the water sports pavilion, the launch area for the sailboats, paddle boards, and kayaks, she slowed to a stroll. The young men who worked at the resort were handsome and charming and they knew it, but none of them caught her attention like Henri, a hottie from France with piercing blue eyes who worked at the pavilion. When he flashed his sweet and seemingly shy smile, Avery almost forgot about her no-random-hookups rule. On her second paddleboard excursion, Henri had carried her board down to the water and given her some pointers, totally flirting with her. Flirting was okay. And maybe it wouldn't hurt to kiss him later that night.

Under a huge gazebo next to the paddleboards, the Australian woman with long blonde hair and an impossibly tight, tan body—Avery couldn't remember her name—was handing out life jackets to a pale-skinned couple.

Avery's gaze moved to the sailboats by the water. They looked picture perfect against the blue sky with *Azure Cove* stitched into their brightly colored sails. There was no sign of Henri there, and she hadn't seen him earlier in the day either. Perhaps Sunday was his day off. Huge bummer.

Avery pushed aside her disappointment and continued to the outdoor exercise area where she joined other women in sports bras, tiny shorts, and even bikinis, and a guy wearing a hoodie, despite the heat. Some of their faces were now familiar, including Teresa, who attended the exercise class every day. Teresa stood dead center in the front, only a few feet away from the instructor, and kept up with the dance moves well, considering she had to be at least seventy-five years old and didn't weigh much more than her age. Maybe she'd been a dancer when she was younger. As much as Avery admired the woman, Teresa also acted like she owned the place and could boss everyone around. With this being Avery's last day, she didn't want any more trouble from anyone. She made a point of finding a spot on the floor as far from Teresa as possible.

For the next forty-five minutes, Avery danced along to energizing music, following Nicole, an instructor from Brazil whose hips could move in ways most people's, including Avery's, never would. The fun outdoor class was exactly what she needed to sweat the alcohol out of her system and detox before they started drinking again.

When the class ended, Avery dabbed her face with a towel, swigged from her water bottle, and headed back to her room thinking about how to make the most of the evening. She still had to try the Dirty Monkey cocktail Haley raved about, bananas and chocolate and three different liquors, and the Caribbean Rum Punch Brie swore was her favorite. But first a shower, maybe a quick power nap, and then dinner.

A resort employee wearing the light blue uniform shirt walked toward her on the path. Impressive muscles bulged from his arms and under his tight shirt. He stared at her for longer than normal.

"Hey." She offered a smile. The guests didn't have to wear their masks outside, but the staff wore them everywhere. Even with masks, a slight crinkling of the skin beside the eyes usually indicated a smile. If this man had smiled back at her, it didn't show. Feeling a little uncomfortable, Avery looked away.

"Avery Jennings?" the man asked.

"Yes."

He stopped in front of her, blocking the path. "I was looking for you."

"Why? What's wrong?"

"Uh, sorry to tell you this. Your Covid test came back positive."

Avery felt blood drain from her face. "Are you serious?"

"Yes. It could be a false positive. We'll do another test for you."

"I...yeah, let me take another test. Because I'm vaccinated and boosted. And my friend, one of the girls I'm with, she already got her test result back and it was negative."

"We always retest. But first you'll need to get your belongings. If the second test comes back positive, you'll have to go to our quarantine area."

Avery wiped away a single tear as they walked to her room. False negatives weren't uncommon, but false positives were rare. She didn't have any Covid symptoms—no cough, runny nose, sore throat, nor fever—but she suddenly felt sick to her stomach. She'd known this might happen and she'd mentally prepared for it, but it still rocked her world and it scared her that she was no longer in control of her plans or her life. She might be stuck in Mexico while her friends got to go home.

As she followed the employee back to her room, she sent a message on the group text. *OMG! Positive test!* followed by a long line of crying face emojis.

CHAPTER 2

Working on a fishing trawler in the Pacific for a few months had sounded a lot cooler than it was in real life. After only two days toiling and sweating like crazy on the bare-bones ship, Trevor's whole body ached. He had thought he was tough and the muscles he was sure to develop would look great under deeply tanned skin, proof of his awesome experience. Instead, he'd gotten the worst sunburn of his life. His mother hadn't helped one bit when they finally had cell service and he called her. She reminded him his grandfather had died from skin cancer after having lots of disgusting lesions removed from his face and shoulders.

The captain and the other crew members had a good laugh about the zinc oxide Trevor slathered over his peeling nose. He didn't care. He was going to quit this awful job as soon as they returned to shore. This filthy drudgery was not for him. McDonalds and Wendy's seemed more appealing now. They had air-conditioning and scheduled breaks.

With a cigarette hanging from one side of his mouth, and the sun still baking his skin, Trevor cranked the winch around. The heavy fishing net rose out of the ocean with a shrieking grind of metal. Sargassum, a brown seaweed, dangled from every haul, and this one was no exception. Trevor could also count on a surprise or two. Yesterday he'd reeled in a squid. It wasn't Squid-versus-Godzilla sized, but it was freaky enough to provide a few much-needed minutes of entertainment on the ship.

Trevor scanned the haul. Within the confines of the slimy ropes, brown and silver fish thrashed around a red piece of something large. Really large.

He guided the net into place and pressed a button to release its contents over a giant trough.

The slithering fish tumbled out. And with them...a girl.

Trevor froze.

The girl wore a red shirt and nothing else. The shirt was twisted around her torso, exposing one breast. She looked like she could have been Trevor's age, though he wasn't sure how he knew that. Her body was crumpled into a grotesque form beneath the writhing fish. She was definitely dead. But that wasn't the worst of it. Her hands were tied together. And something wasn't right with her face. Her ear...

Trevor had just enough time to shout for the ship's captain before vomiting on the deck.

CHAPTER 3

On Monday afternoon, FBI Special Agent Victoria Heslin sat on her back patio with her boyfriend, veterinarian Ned Patterson, and a glass of chardonnay. The glow from the flames in the firepit illuminated his face as he looked out over her expansive property at the long-range mountain views. Ned had the lean build of someone who ran, biked, and swam as often as possible for the sheer joy of it, and Victoria couldn't help but appreciate that. She'd never been preoccupied with looks, her own or anyone else's, but having a boyfriend with granite muscles and not an ounce of body fat made her pay slightly more attention to her own upkeep, lest people think Ned was only interested in her for her inheritance. Thinking about it made her laugh because she knew it couldn't be farther from the truth. She and Ned had too much in common. Nonetheless, Victoria had applied a little gloss to her lips and brushed her hair when she got home from work.

Three of Victoria's greyhounds stood close by, between the heat lamps, their full attention devoted to a platter of cheese and crackers.

"Not for you," she told them as she put her feet up on the ottoman and leaned back against her chair.

"I'm glad you could leave work early," Ned said. "There's something I want to talk to you about."

"Oh. What's that?" She took the first sip of her wine and gave Ned her full attention.

"You."

"What about me?"

"I don't know what happened recently, you know with your nose and your stitched side, since you can't or don't want to tell me—which is fine, I get it—but when I think about you putting yourself in danger...it makes me sick, Victoria. I can't help it. Is there any way you can...you know, not be involved with cases that risk your life?"

"Because you don't think a woman with two black eyes and a broken nose is attractive?" Victoria joked, smiling at him, though she fully understood that's not what he meant. He'd worried more about her job ever since she came home banged up a few weeks ago, the consequences of a shootout that occurred while delivering witnesses from one safe house in Boston to another in D.C. She didn't want Ned to worry, but it was also nice that he cared so much.

Her phone vibrated on the stone edge of the firepit. She hesitated before leaning forward and grabbing it. Murphy's name lit up on the screen. "It's my boss. I better take this." She went inside as she swiped the screen to answer the call. "Hi, Murphy."

"Hey," the FBI Special Agent in Charge answered. "Where are you?"

"In my kitchen. Why? What's up?" she asked, looking around her sparsely furnished home. She was still feeling a little light-hearted because she was home with Ned, though she sensed both her mood and her situation were about to change.

"A twenty-two-year-old woman is missing. Avery Jennings. She was on vacation in Mexico with friends. She tested positive for Covid-19 yesterday, the day before she was supposed to return, which meant she couldn't come back to the States. An employee said he was taking her for another test and possibly to a quarantine area. No one has heard from her since."

"She's only been out of communication for one day?" Victoria asked, thinking aloud.

"Yes. The resort can't find her on their property. She's not responding to any calls or texts, which isn't like her."

"Still, it's only been a day?"

"Yes. Only a day since anyone heard from her," Murphy said. "But there some suspicious circumstances involved. And Avery is Payton's niece."

"Our Payton?" Of course it was their Payton. Same last name. Payton Jennings was the head of the FBI's Financial Crimes Department. She often talked about her niece, Avery, and had recently visited her at the University of Virginia.

"What are the suspicious circumstances?" Victoria asked.

"I'll let Payton fill you in from the beginning, but understandably, she doesn't want to sit idle while more time passes. Anyway, I know the police chief there. We worked an international case together and kept in touch. He's going to have a team look for her, and he's invited us to assist in the investigation."

"Oh, okay."

"I've got you booked on a flight to Mexico tonight. You'll arrive in the morning. I'll alert the FBI field office in Mexico and the U.S. Embassy that you're coming."

"Do I need to take a Covid test to get in?" Victoria asked, unsure of the protocol for different countries because policies were constantly changing.

"No. You only need the negative test to get back home. Payton specifically asked me to send you. She's at her brother's house in Virginia right now. My assistant sent you that address, along with your flight information. Can you get over there as soon as possible so you can meet with the family before your flight?"

"Yes. I'll go now. Talk to you soon."

If something had happened to Avery, Victoria knew every minute would matter. The first forty-eight hours of a missing persons investigation were the most critical. With each passing hour, the chances of finding that person decreased.

Victoria checked her email for the Jennings' address, called an Uber, and looked up the weather in Mexico. She grabbed the bag she kept packed for short notice travel and exchanged a heavier-weight suit for a lightweight one. After opening her closet, she changed out of jeans into black pants with a silk t-shirt, an outfit from a design service that sent her a box of professional clothes every few months.

Back in the kitchen, Victoria got out the laminated sheets that listed instructions for watching her animals: their feeding schedules, health issues, medicines, and individual quirks. No sooner had she set them on the counter, she picked them up again. Ned knew what the dogs needed as well as she did by now.

When Victoria returned to the patio carrying her bag, Ned was still nursing his beer. He watched her walk toward him.

"Sorry about the super short notice, but I've got to go," she said, pulling her blonde hair back into a ponytail.

"What did Murphy tell you?" Ned asked.

"Payton's niece is missing in Mexico. She just disappeared from her resort. That's pretty much all I know. I'm not sure when I'll be back, though it shouldn't be more than a few days. Can you take care of the animals, or should I schedule one of the vet techs?"

"I can stay. I'm working three days at the clinic this week. I'll schedule someone to come by if I'm not home by dinner on those days."

"Thank you so much." Victoria really didn't know how she could continue her job without his help. She didn't trust just anyone to properly care for her animals. Leaning down, she planted a kiss on his lips.

"Hold on," Ned said, rising from his seat. "That's not how we say goodbye."

He pulled her into his arms. She felt his strength and something fiercely protective as he kissed her deeply. When they finally separated, he nuzzled her neck for a few more seconds and said, "That's more like it. I love you."

"I love you, too."

That was a very new thing for them—saying I love you. She enjoyed the feelings it gave her. Warm. Hopeful. A little bit lightheaded. All her life, she'd preferred animals to most people, so Ned establishing a firm place deep inside her heart was no small feat.

She smiled up at him. "Don't worry about me. I can take care of myself. Okay?"

"I know you can. And if you want, I won't tell you I'm worried, but I can't stop it from happening. Just send me updates when you can so I know you're okay."

"I will." She kissed him again.

"Because...I don't know what your dogs would do without you." His tone made clear he wasn't just talking about the dogs. "I hope you find Payton's niece."

Victoria said goodbye to each of her dogs, stroking necks and ears, before heading down her driveway to wait for her ride outside the tall iron gate.

When her Uber appeared, she called Payton. The call went straight to voicemail. She was probably making a slew of calls trying to find out what happened to Avery.

Victoria left Payton a message. "It's Victoria. I'm so sorry Avery is missing. Murphy gave me your brother's address. I'll be there in twenty minutes, and I'll head to Mexico later tonight. See you soon."

CHAPTER 4

A horn blared behind Tom Jennings as he swerved into the adjacent lane with mere inches to spare, racing to get home. He wasn't one of those annoying drivers who normally wove in between cars, switching lanes constantly to gain a few extra seconds. Today was different. He wished he'd stayed home and hadn't gone to his office. Faced with impossible decisions, he'd certainly been avoiding it lately. He'd lost investments, slowly at first and then in a cataclysmic avalanche-like fall. He'd finally mustered the courage to tell Jennifer. There was no avoiding that now. The problem wasn't going away. He'd planned to tell her tonight. But that plan changed with Avery's disappearance, which had quickly thrown his other problems into perspective. Hearing from their daughter, making sure she was safe, became priority one. Everything else paled in comparison. They needed to find their daughter, their only child, and get her back to Virginia.

"I just called the resort again and talked to the manager. I told them we still haven't heard from her," Tom said to his sister, speaking through the Tesla's Bluetooth. "They're checking all the rooms again. Supposedly, they're checking everywhere."

"Good," Payton said. "I'm praying she's there, that there's been a misunderstanding and she's just sleeping through all of this."

"But you and I both know that's not Avery," he said. "She's not that...clueless."

"I know. Anyway, the FBI is getting involved. They're sending someone to Mexico tonight. A friend of mine. Victoria Heslin."

"I can't believe this is happening." Tom stared through his windshield, barely registering the traffic. "Are you with Jennifer?"

"Yes. I got to your house about ten minutes ago."

Tom was more worried about Avery than anyone or anything else, but that didn't stop him from being concerned about how his wife was handling the situation. It was fair to say Jennifer micromanaged their lives down to the last details whenever she could. She didn't cope well when events strayed from her own carefully made plans and what most people would consider a perfect life. Her dream house and surrounding weed-free yard. A rewarding job with colleagues who were also friends. Vacations. New cars. And most of all, the child they always wanted. Avery. She turned out to be healthy, intelligent, and a pleasure to be around even through her teen years.

"Is she...how is she?" he asked.

"She's doing all right, considering." Payton lowered her voice, making Tom think his wife must be nearby. "She's anxious for you to get home."

Tom flicked his blinker on as he cut back into the adjacent lane and accelerated. "I'm almost there. I'll see you soon. Thank God you can help us figure this out. Really, thank you, Payton."

"Of course. You know I love Avery just as much as you and Jennifer. It's going to be all right, Tom. I just know it. It has to be. Drive safe and I'll see you soon."

Questions raced through Tom's mind as he maneuvered through the streets in a panicked daze. Later he wouldn't be able to recall making the drive home at all. Could Avery really be in danger? Or was a reasonable explanation lurking somewhere close, about to come to light and wipe out what was quickly turning into any parent's worst nightmare? The weight of guilt added to his mounting fear. If someone had taken Avery—the thought sent a dizzying wave of terror coursing through him—it was his fault. If not for him, she wouldn't have been there. Jennifer hadn't wanted her to go.

"Why can't they go to somewhere nice in Florida?" Jennifer had asked. "Then they wouldn't have to deal with Covid tests to get home. People are getting stuck in foreign countries because they're testing positive before they can leave. It's her last semester of college. I don't want her to miss any of it. And what if she got sick and needed medical help there? I really don't think she should go, Tom. I don't want her to go. I'm saying no."

Jennifer tended to focus on worst-case scenarios and overanalyze things. It often fell to Tom to tell her not to worry. Everything would be okay.

"She should go with her friends and have a great time," he'd said. What he didn't tell Jennifer was that there would be no vacations like that or any others in their future. Not for a long time. Not unless his business made a miraculous recovery.

Jennifer shook her head. "I don't want her to go."

But Tom persisted, running through a checklist of reasons Avery shouldn't miss out on the vacation. "Brie's father is paying for the entire trip. The girls are all vaccinated and boosted. They're young and healthy. She's worked hard. She's already got a great job. She deserves it. It will be fine."

Now it appeared he'd been wrong.

There had to be a misunderstanding. Avery would show up. She had to. Because these things did not happen.

But I'd also never imagined my business could face bankruptcy.

Tom let go of the steering wheel and pressed a hand over his chest, feeling the sharp thump of his heart. He was on an emotional roller coaster and the simple act of pulling air into his lungs seemed a challenge.

Thank goodness for his sister and her FBI connections. Payton would help them navigate the unimaginable.

CHAPTER 5

V ictoria's Uber driver turned into a neighborhood of large two and three-story homes. After a few streets, he pulled into the driveway of a white, brick house at the end of a cul-de-sac. Payton's Jeep Cherokee was parked out front.

As Victoria walked up the slight hill toward the house on a path made of gray paving stones, the home's front door opened. Payton came out carrying her phone against her ear. She wore a pencil skirt and silk blouse and small heels, as if she'd come directly from the office. Payton lowered her phone, and the worried look she gave Victoria told her Avery still hadn't been found.

Victoria and Payton were about the same age—early-thirties—and assigned to the FBI's D.C. office. They were in different divisions but had worked together on several occasions. Victoria had recently provided Payton with evidence of art gallery owners laundering money for the powerful Salazar Cartel. Credible people were willing to testify against Salazar. If all went well, which was never guaranteed, some of the most powerful cartel leaders would end up permanently behind bars. Payton was spearheading the financial side of the investigation, bringing in departments across the

FBI to prosecute Eduardo Salazar and his top men. Caught up in perhaps the most important case of her career, she was working relentless hours. And now her niece had disappeared.

"Thank you for coming," Payton said. "I can't tell you how much I appreciate this."

"Of course," Victoria answered, stopping at the bottom of the front steps.

Payton gripped the corner of her rimless glasses and adjusted them before tucking one side of her straight bobbed hair behind her ear. "I'm praying it's all some misunderstanding, but Avery would never just disappear like this. It's not like her at all. She's in trouble."

"She might be." That wasn't what Payton and her family wanted to hear, but it was the truth and embracing it would be the first step to getting Avery safely home.

"It would be bad enough if she was missing at home...but in another country. It makes me feel so helpless."

Like Victoria, Payton's experience with the FBI would have taught her the realities of the situation and how difficult it might be to get foreign authorities to cooperate and communicate with them on the investigation.

"Tell me more about Avery's trip," Victoria said. "Who was she with?"

"Two of her sorority sisters from the University of Virginia. It was only supposed to be a four-day trip. Her friends came home yesterday."

"They left her in Mexico?"

"Yes. They did," Payton said, expressing her anger by enunciating each word slowly. "I've met them. They're all nice, smart girls, but...." She huffed and then seemed to compose herself.

"Murphy mentioned the Mexican police are investigating. Have they done anything yet, that you know of?"

"They're at the resort now. Investigating, or so they say. I filed a report, so Avery is officially missing."

"What about her phone? Have you traced it?"

"The last location is at the resort," Payton said. "It hasn't moved since Sunday night. God...I hope she's still there. We have access to her phone records. Jennifer and I combed through them. Avery hadn't been communicating with anyone other than her friends in their group messages. No random strangers or anyone new that she just met." Payton turned toward the house. "Come inside, you need to meet Avery's parents. They can tell you more."

"What do they do for a living?" Victoria asked, since she didn't know what information might be relevant yet.

Payton's hair swung forward. She tucked it behind her ear again. "My brother, Tom, runs a small financial investment company. His wife, Jennifer, teaches high school math."

Victoria followed Payton into a bright kitchen. A pot of coffee brewed on the counter.

Tom and Jennifer Jennings stood together on one side of a granite-topped island. Victoria could feel their fear and desperation from across the room.

Tom had the look of a middle-aged man who probably didn't get to the gym as much as he'd like. An athletic build with some softness creeping in. He shared the same light complexion as his sister. He wore a quilted jacket, as if he'd just come into the house.

Jennifer's blue eyes were red and puffy. Her fair skin appeared pallid even with freckles across her nose and cheeks. She clutched a tissue in her hand and sniffed as Payton made the introductions.

After setting his mug on the countertop, Tom extended a hand toward Victoria. His grip started out firm, normal, then quickly softened, as if he didn't want to hurt her. Even in his distraught state, his gaze slid to Victoria's missing fingers. He must have known from Payton that Victoria lost them to frostbite after a plane crash. Almost everyone in the country knew, thanks to the media blast that followed the ordeal.

"We're going to Mexico tonight," Tom said, picking up his mug and wrapping his hands tightly around it again.

"I believe we're on the same flight," Victoria said. "I'm so sorry you're going through this. I'll do everything I can to work with the Mexican police and help figure out what happened."

"Thank you, thank you," Jennifer said, twisting and tearing the tissue between her hands. "And thank God Payton is with the FBI. We're well aware that we might be all alone in trying to find Avery if it weren't for Payton's connections."

There was some truth to Jennifer's statement. The U.S. authorities had no jurisdiction in Mexico. If not for Payton's career and Murphy's connection, the FBI might not have been invited to assist. Even so, an investigation would still rely heavily on their Mexican counterparts.

"Payton told us you found a missing girl last year in Charlotte. She said you've located several missing people. Is that right?" Jennifer asked, focusing on Victoria.

"Yes."

Jennifer's face scrunched and she started crying. "I'm sorry. I'm sorry," she said, her face flushing. "I know that isn't helping the situation. I just can't help it. I'm so afraid. Do you have children, Victoria?"

"No. I don't."

"Oh. I mean...I don't even know why I asked." Jennifer brought her trembling hands together. "It doesn't matter."

Victoria could see how hard this was for Jennifer, and unfortunately, it might get harder. "It's okay. Listen, let's do some groundwork before we head to the airport. Tell me about your daughter's trip."

Victoria looked from Jennifer to Tom, but Jennifer answered first.

"The whole trip was paid for by her friend's father. I told her not to go. I thought she might get stuck there if she tested positive; I knew there was a chance." Jennifer's breath hitched in her throat. "But I never thought she would disappear. I never imagined that happening."

Tom handed Victoria a framed eight-by-ten photograph of his daughter. "This is Avery's senior year college portrait. They do these early for the yearbook. She's graduating in May. She already has a job lined up in New York."

Avery had glossy, black hair. Thick dark lashes surrounded her brown eyes. Her skin had a tan undertone, the color of coffee with more milk than espresso, as if she had some Middle Eastern, Hispanic, or Indian heritage. Above her V-neck sweater hung a black corded necklace with a silver triangle pendant. She was on the slender side but appeared healthy. What stuck out the most was that she looked nothing like her blue-eyed, fair-haired parents. They could not have a biological daughter with brown eyes. Payton hadn't mentioned another parent. If one existed, that might be relevant. Victoria might need to speak with him or her. In any other circumstance, it would be outright rude to ask about Avery's parentage. But avoiding a potentially touchy subject wasn't an option now. Any secrets the Jennings were hiding would come out during the investigation. Especially if they concerned Avery.

"Is Avery your biological daughter?" Victoria asked.

"No," Jennifer said. "She's not. We couldn't have children of our own. We adopted her when she was only a few months old. Avery's mother is from Mexico. They've never met. And we don't have information on Avery's biological father. Why are you asking?"

"I need to learn everything I can. It might help find Avery."

Jennifer lifted another photo from the kitchen island and handed it to Victoria, this one an unframed five by seven. Same girl, different look. No makeup. Avery had pulled her hair back behind her head. Loose strands curled at her temples. The same black cord with the triangle pendant surrounded her neck. "This is what she looks like most of the time," Jennifer said.

Victoria took snapshots of Avery's photos. "When was the last time you spoke with Avery?"

"She called us last night, but neither of us were available to answer," Tom said, grimacing as he spoke.

Jennifer curled strands of her hair around a trembling finger. "Avery left me a message at six p.m. saying she tested positive for Covid. She said she was getting retested, but she might have to stay in Mexico and quarantine. That was the last we heard from her."

The last contact with their daughter came approximately twenty-four hours ago. Victoria felt a flicker of hope. Avery might be all right and call any minute with an explanation. A dead phone battery because she'd misplaced her charger; left it behind in the other room because she wasn't thinking clearly enough to check the outlets. Maybe she'd been sleeping soundly because she wasn't feeling well.

"Did Avery have any health issues?" Victoria asked.

Tom responded immediately. "No. No health issues whatsoever. Avery is as healthy as anyone can be. We've talked to the resort's manager and the local authorities. They're searching the resort and looking in all the rooms, supposedly, trying to locate her, but...I don't know...they haven't found her yet and they've gone as far as to suggest that Avery is somehow responsible."

"What makes you say that?" Victoria asked.

"Just the manager's general attitude. He implied her disappearance has something to do with drugs." Tom set his jaw and emphasized each of his next words. "Avery did not do drugs."

Victoria knew better than to take a father's word on their child's drug use. Too many parents believed their children incapable of wrongdoing.

"I heard the resort has quarantine rooms put aside for people who test positive. They checked all of those?" Victoria asked, though the answer seemed obvious.

Jennifer covered her mouth and chin with her hands. "Oh, I thought Payton told you..."

Victoria turned to Payton. "Told me what?"

"That's part of what makes the situation so...confusing," Payton answered. "The manager said the paper with Avery's test result is still sitting at the front desk. No one ever picked it up. The test is negative. She didn't have the positive result someone told her she had."

A chill prickled Victoria's skin as her flicker of hope extinguished. If someone had lied to Avery, tried to trick her, she was definitely in trouble. "Murphy mentioned suspicious circumstances. Is that what he was referring to?"

Payton nodded.

"They have no idea what happened to her." Jennifer let out a small gasp almost like a hiccup. "I know some girls...some young ladies Avery's age might act irresponsibly and leave the resort without telling anyone. You know, make up an excuse so they could do something they shouldn't be doing or go somewhere they shouldn't go. I know it happens, none of us are perfect. But Avery wouldn't do that. She wouldn't. She just wouldn't."

"We know," Payton said, rubbing her sister-in-law's shoulder. "We'll find her. I promise you."

Payton's words made Victoria cringe inside. Payton wasn't a field agent. She primarily dealt with white collar criminals, prosecutors, and tax codes. She didn't know the FBI didn't give family members promises like that. Promises they might not be able to keep.

CHAPTER 6

With less than an hour before they had to head to the airport for the flight to Mexico, Victoria sat down in front of her laptop on the Jennings' dining room table and clicked to clear her background image of snowy mountains.

"Which of Avery's friends saw her last?" she asked Payton.

"Brie Vanderhorn," Payton answered. "One of Avery's best friends at Virginia. Her father is the one who paid for the trip. It was a birthday present. I called Brie and talked to her just before you arrived. I have her number."

Victoria wanted to hear Brie's version of events and analyze the young woman's body language. She took Brie's number and set up a video chat.

"I'd like to speak with her alone, if you don't mind," Victoria said. She intended to speak to Brie alone, whether or not they minded, but she couldn't shake her instinct for politeness, a result of her upbringing. If she was to help find Avery, it was important she interviewed Brie without anyone else in the room. Teenagers and young adults often suffered from misguided concerns. They might be more worried about getting in trouble than getting to the truth. Maybe not Avery's friends. But Victoria didn't know that for sure and didn't have the luxury of time to find out.

"I'll make sure the other girl Avery was with, Haley, is available and let her know you'll be calling," Payton said after a slight hesitation. She left with her brother and her sister-in-law and closed the dining room door behind them.

Brie answered Victoria's call and appeared on screen. The college senior had styled her hair in a messy bun with wisps of hair coming down on either side and wore no makeup. Her brief time under the Mexican sun had given her a golden tan. On the wall behind her hung a poster of Ruth Bader Ginsburg with the letters R.I.P. The décor took Victoria back fifteen years, to her first year at Georgetown. Her roommate, now an attorney, had a poster with a younger version of the same Supreme Court justice.

"Hi, Brie. I'm Special Agent Victoria Heslin, with the FBI. It's just the two of us on this call. I'm going to do everything I can to help find Avery. I know you've given your account to many people already, but I need to hear it again. I'm recording this."

"Hi. I'll tell you whatever you want to know, as many times as you want to hear it," Brie said. "I just want to find Avery. Where should I start?"

"Do you have any idea where she is?" Victoria asked point blank.

"No." Brie placed her hand at the base of her throat. Confusion combined with annoyance, altering her expression. "Obviously not...or you wouldn't be looking for her."

"Then tell me about your last day with Avery."

"Sure." Brie seemed to recover quickly from Victoria's previous question. "So...Sunday...we woke up around ten, hung out for a while doing stuff on our phones, I guess, then we went to get some food around eleven. We sat on the beach for a few hours. All three of us." Brie crossed her arms, cradling her elbows and rocking forward. "I fell asleep, but I know Avery and Haley left at some point to go paddleboarding and came back. Then Avery went to our room to change clothes for an exercise class. I went to the registration desk to see if our Covid test results were there. After I got my test, I returned to our room, where I saw Avery leaving for Zumba. I hung out there...posted some pictures, spent some time catching up on things on my phone, for about an hour I'd say. Um, Haley came back to shower. That's when we got Avery's text."

"What text is that?"

"That she tested positive. Then she came to the room to get her things."

"And you saw her then? Was she alone?"

"No. A guy from the resort was with her. An employee. He waited partway inside the doorway while she packed."

"Had you seen him before?"

"No. And now the resort can't figure out who he was."

"What makes you say he worked there?"

"He was wearing one of the staff's uniforms. The blue shirts. At least, I thought he was. Or why else would I think he worked there? Now I'm not sure. Maybe I just thought he was an employee because he was telling her what to do. It's hard to remember all the details because Avery was freaking out and I was freaking out too, about Avery having to stay in Mexico. Alone."

Something flickered in Brie's eyes. She glanced away, then down at the floor. It was enough to convince Victoria that Avery's friend was hiding something.

"Is there anything else you want to tell me?"

"No...I mean, what else do you need to know? What would help?"

"Did the man say anything while he was waiting for Avery to pack?" Victoria asked.

"Yes. I talked to him. I asked him where he was going to take her. He said it would depend on which rooms were open, and if she tested positive again."

Brie placed her hands over her mouth, then moved her fingers to her temples. Either the questioning or the memories were stressing her out.

"Close your eyes, Brie."

"Why?"

"So you can relax and concentrate."

"Oh." Brie closed her eyes. "Okay."

"Picture yourself in your room at the resort. The man is there too, standing in the doorway. Describe what you see. The first things that come to mind about him."

"He was muscle bound. Not so much like a bodybuilder, more like...a boxer?"

"Good. How tall was he?"

"Maybe a little taller than average. Like my father. He's five ten. Or maybe he's six feet, I'm not sure."

"Okay. What about his face?"

"He wore a black baseball cap and a mask, the blue ones the resort staff always wore. So, I couldn't see much of his face. His eyebrows were thick. I think he was wearing a blue uniform shirt, like I said. And he definitely had one of those digital bracelet wristband things on. Oh...wait. All the guests wear the wristbands. So, that would mean he wasn't an employee...or did the employees wear the wristbands also?"

"I'm not sure. Keep going, you're doing great."

"Okay. Well, he leaned his arm on the door. That's how I saw the wristband. And he had a tattoo on the same arm. I already told Avery's parents and her aunt and the resort manager and everyone else about it. That's the first thing I told them. Green ink. About the length of a tall Starbucks cup and a little wider. A heart with a crown on it and then swords going through the heart. I'm sure of that. Don't you think that should be a huge clue? I mean, how hard could it be to find the person with that tattoo?"

"I don't know yet, but it's certainly helpful information. Would you say he was attractive or unattractive?" Victoria asked.

"Uh...I don't know."

Which usually meant he fell somewhere in between. A man of average height and looks, wearing a mask and a cap, could easily go unnoticed in a crowd. The tattoo might be the game changer. Although...it occurred to Victoria that someone committing a crime ought to be more careful than to flash a distinctive tattoo during the act. This man had not been careful. Perhaps that was because he had nothing to do with Avery's disappearance.

"What about his skin color?" Victoria asked.

"He was tan. Not super dark. Italian maybe. Or Mexican American."

"What did he sound like? Did he speak with an accent?"

"Um...maybe a slight accent. But I think English was his first language. He had a deep voice."

"What about his cap? Did it have any words or logos?"

"Um...I don't remember. I'm sorry."

"That's all right. What happened next?"

"Once Avery had her suitcase and backpack ready, he said we should stay in our rooms and wear masks in case we had Covid too, and it just hadn't shown up on the tests. Which seemed so unfair to Avery, and I told him that, but he said there wasn't anything he could do about it, said he was just doing his job. Oh. See? He said he was just doing his job, so there's another reason I believed he worked there. Then he and Avery left. That was the last time we saw her."

"Did you hear from her after that?"

"No. She was supposed to let us know as soon as she got the new test result back. Tell us where her quarantine room was...if she ended up in one. Haley and I were going to visit and bring her favorite foods from the buffet and make sure she had everything she needed. But she never called or texted. We tried again and again and left messages. She never responded."

"What do you think happened to her?"

"I don't know. I really don't." Brie lifted her hands with her palms facing up. "Believe me, I wish we'd never gone to Mexico for the stupid trip. It's been nothing but a nightmare."

That's when Brie let out a loud sob and burst into tears.

"Did you and Haley stay in your rooms like the man suggested?" Victoria asked.

Brie's hands covered her face, and she didn't look up, but she shook her head.

"Thank you, Brie," Victoria said. "I'll be in Mexico tomorrow morning and I'm sure I'll want to speak with you again. In the meantime, if you think of anything else, please call me immediately."

Victoria had interviewed enough traumatized people to know Brie was lying or holding something back. Something that might matter. Was she protecting Avery or herself? That remained to be determined. Victoria didn't have time to press further. And she might not need to, depending on what Haley had to say next.

Victoria jumped to the waiting video call with Haley. A slender girl with shoulder-length pale blonde hair, she sat cross-legged on her bed, surrounded by pillows of various sizes and textures and gripping a furry, pinkish-white one between her hands. Tucked into the frame of a large mirror behind her were photos of people, dogs, and horses. Above the mirror hung an orange and navy flag with UVA's symbol—two crossed swords under a V.

Haley started crying right after Victoria introduced herself. "I'm sorry we let them take her. We didn't know."

"Them?"

"I mean whoever took Avery. Him? I don't know." Still crying, Haley reached for a tissue and blew her nose. "Sorry."

"Did you see the person who escorted Avery to your room?" Victoria asked.

"No. Only Brie saw him. I was in the shower, but I heard his voice. I couldn't hear what they were saying. I was shampooing my hair and felt a little weird about being naked a few feet away in the bathroom, you know, since I didn't know who was out there."

"Did you notice anyone paying particular attention to Avery during the trip? Did she meet anyone new there?"

"No. Not really. Guys were checking us out, but none of them were like overboard stalking us or anything that seems off now. Avery kind of had a thing for Henri. One of the resort's staff. He worked at the place with the sailboats. They flirted a little. She thought he was cute. But she didn't hook up with him, or anyone else, if that's what you mean."

"Did Avery argue with anyone or disagree with anyone during your trip?"

"No...well actually...kind of. The Zumba bi—, I mean the Zumba witch."

"The Zumba witch?" Victoria asked.

"A lady at the resort. An old lady."

"And what happened with the old lady?"

Haley seemed to gain her composure back the more she talked. "It wasn't a big deal, really. Just so strange. Our first day there, I went to Zumba with Avery. We got there early and stood in the front so we could follow the instructor. This old lady, one of the resort's guests, her name is

Teresa, came a few minutes before the class started and said Avery was in her spot. She wanted Avery to move. It was ridiculous, totally ridiculous. I think my mouth was like hanging open, we could hardly believe it. We just laughed it off and moved to the side. That's the only thing I can think of. The lady was just a...well, you know. But I don't think she had anything to do with what happened."

"Did you hear from Avery after she left your room on Sunday?"

"No. We tried to reach her. We left messages. We never heard back."

"What did you think then?"

Haley looked down at the pillow in her hands and hesitated before answering. "Well, we talked about it a lot, you know, Brie and I. Trying to explain why Avery wasn't answering. Brie thought Avery might be mad because she tested positive and had to stay, and you know, we didn't."

"You thought Avery might have been ignoring your calls and texts?"

"Maybe...not really. I don't know. See, before we left for Mexico *and* during the trip, we talked about what would happen if just one of us tested positive. Azure Cove has a policy that covers staying there until the quarantine period is over. You don't have full access to the resort anymore, because even if you don't have symptoms, they don't want infected people going to the restaurants or the pool or the gym, so it's not like an extension of your vacation, but Avery said as long as she had Internet access and a yoga mat, she'd be fine. All three of us have had Covid already, different times, and quarantined at school. It's not fun, I missed out on a lot of things that I really wanted to do, but it goes by faster than you think. So even though Brie and I felt terrible about leaving her—which we really did—we'd already agreed to that plan." Haley ran her hand over her pink pillow, pulling out fur and tossing it onto the bed as she spoke. "Everyone thinks it's awful that we left her. I know they do. But honestly, it didn't seem like a huge deal then. We were just wishing they put her in a room with an ocean view, you know."

"So, you *didn't* think she was angry and just ignoring you?"

"I don't know. I'm sorry. We were worried later but...well, the first time I got Covid, I was super tired. I slept for two days and didn't have the energy to get out of bed. So, you know, I also figured she might be sleeping." Haley quit pulling out fur and hugged the pillow to her chest. "In the morning, Brie and I had to get up super early for our flight. We were rushing to get packed and get out of there. We almost missed our shuttle. The front desk staff wasn't around when we had to leave, or we would have asked them where Avery was. I know that sounds bad now...it does...but it wasn't like we didn't care."

"And now what do you think? Is it possible she's still ignoring you and everyone else because she's angry?"

Haley bit down on her bottom lip. "No. She wouldn't do that. Avery isn't like that. She wouldn't go this long without letting someone know she was okay."

"Is there anything important you aren't telling me, Haley? Because now would be the time."

Haley opened her mouth. Her bottom lip quivered. "No," she finally said. "There's nothing else. I don't know what happened to Avery. I wish we had gone with her. Stayed with her. I hope she's okay."

"Yes. So does everyone." Victoria glanced at the time in the top corner of her screen to make sure she wouldn't miss her flight. "Thank you, Haley. If you can think of anything else that would help us to find Avery, please tell me. I'm giving you my cell phone number. And one more thing, I need you and Brie to send me any pictures you took during your trip."

"I will. Please find her." Haley was crying again.

When the call ended and Victoria's screen went black, she had a moment to think about what she'd learned. Avery's friends seemed overwhelmed with guilt. Was it because they believed something had happened to her? Or were they feeling guilty for other reasons?

CHAPTER 7

"Can you show me Avery's room before I leave?" Victoria asked Payton.

"Sure. It's this way." Payton said, moving down an art-lined hallway. "Did Brie tell you about the tattoo?"

"Yes. That should help us."

"I had her draw a picture of it, and I did some research while you were talking to the girls. Hearts and crowns and swords aren't unusual in tattoos. But together, the way Brie described then, it sounds like she might have seen a tattoo for a gang based in San Francisco."

"Hm. Mexico is a long way from San Francisco."

"We should find out if anyone on the resort's staff is from Northern California."

"Definitely," Victoria said as she climbed carpeted stairs, following Payton to the second floor of the Jennings' house and Avery's room.

"She's been at college for the last three years," Payton said, removing her glasses and folding them. "Everything you see here, it's what she chose to leave behind. So, I don't know how helpful it will be."

"It won't hurt to have a look around," Victoria said.

The room was neat. Framed posters of art and famous paintings hung on the white walls. Above Avery's desk, she'd crammed a bulletin board with photos of herself and friends, mementos from plays and concerts, and words of encouragement written on post-it notes. More or less what Victoria expected for a supposedly well-adjusted young woman with good friends and a bright future. Nothing seemed out of the ordinary.

"Did she have her laptop with her?" Victoria asked.

"Yes. She took it with her on vacation and left with it when she packed her belongings and left with the...stranger, employee, whoever he is. What did you get from talking to her friends?"

"Not sure yet."

"Do you trust Brie? Because Avery's mother doesn't."

"I don't know," Victoria answered honestly, looking into Avery's nearly empty closet.

"She left Avery behind."

"So did Haley," Victoria said. "I don't know that either of them is in any way responsible for Avery's disappearance, but they probably know more than they're saying. If that's so, we're going to find out sooner or later. Sooner would be best. I'll keep pressing them."

"I will too." Payton ran her fingers down a graduation cord hanging over the door of Avery's closet and said, "I can't believe this is happening."

Victoria and Payton went back downstairs and into the kitchen, where Tom and Jennifer stood close together, their hands in a death grip. The doorbell rang, which seemed to startle both of them.

At the front of the house, the door creaked open. "Hello?" came a man's voice. The newcomer had let himself inside. His shoes tapped on the hardwood floors.

Special Agent Dante Rivera walked around the corner and stopped in the kitchen entryway. Although his black hoodie and fitted gray jeans were casual, his expression was all business. He was lean and muscular, partly because his happy place, when not working, was on the basketball court. He'd recently told Victoria his knees were betraying him, showing the first signs he couldn't play his beloved sport forever. She'd told him that at his age, mid-thirties, it might already be time to find an activity that was kinder on his joints.

Rivera lowered his head to acknowledge Victoria before he and Payton stared at each other, communicating silently from across the room. Avery's parents were probably too distraught to pick up on it, but it was obvious to Victoria that Rivera and Payton had recently become more than just co-workers and friends. Rivera was a seasoned agent with a lot of determination, plus a big heart. He got along with people. Treated everyone with respect. It was easy for him to make friends, and to catch a woman's interest. And although Victoria had spent little time with Payton outside of work, Victoria considered her a good colleague and friend, and was happy for both of them.

"This is Dante Rivera," Payton said, introducing him to her brother and sister-in-law. "But everyone calls him Rivera. He's a close friend from the D.C. office. He's going to help us, too."

"Hello," Rivera said to the Jennings. No *nice to meet you* or other polite formalities that would fall flat considering the circumstances. "I've got a seat on the flight to Mexico with the rest of you."

Remembering how Agent Rivera had searched relentlessly for her and the other passengers of Skyline Flight 745, Victoria was glad the Jennings had him in their corner now.

"I'm sorry I can't go with you yet," Payton told her family. "I'm presenting in court tomorrow. I've been prepping for weeks and if I don't show...well, I have to be there...but I'll join you as soon as I can."

"Yes, you have to be there," Victoria reassured her. Payton's presence during the proceedings was critical. There was too much at stake for too many, some of them innocent people who were risking their lives to testify against the cartel.

"We've got this," Rivera said. "We'll do everything that needs to be done and keep you updated. And maybe we'll hear from Avery any minute and she'll be on the next flight home."

Payton turned to her brother and her sister-in-law. "Victoria and Rivera are my friends, but they're also incredible at what they do. Don't worry, they'll find her."

CHAPTER 8

Tony Barerra was halfway down the royal-blue carpeted corridor when he heard the girl's ear-piercing scream echoing through the yacht from the upper deck primary suite.

"No! Don't! Please! Please don't!" she shrieked.

Scowling, Tony went into his cabin, slammed the door, and grabbed his wireless headphones, returning to the podcast he started earlier—*Taking Control of Your Own Destiny*. He pressed play and cranked up the volume, but not fast enough to avoid hearing another horror-filled shriek. He couldn't take much more of it. Her fear and agony annoyed the hell out of him. His instinct, as well as his trained response, was to crush any signs of weakness. But he couldn't make her shut up because Eric wanted her to scream. The louder and more terrified, the more they begged him to stop, the better.

How had it come to this—assigned to look after Eric, a twenty-five-year-old fool with too much money, a heroin habit, and the sickest of hobbies? Tony was only five years older, but life had taught him to take care of himself and anyone else who made the mistake of pissing him off. Protecting others became his job, a job he was good at and took pride in.

But right now, watching Eric's back until the boss said otherwise, made Tony feel more like an angry and reluctant babysitter than a bodyguard.

With each passing day, Tony's hatred for Eric intensified like the heat from a wildfire.

The girl screamed again. She'd had enough. More than enough. She'd probably rather be anywhere else than trapped on the yacht with Eric.

She and Tony had that in common.

CHAPTER 9

Victoria and Rivera exited the airplane together in Mexico on Tuesday morning and went through the customs screening process for international law enforcement. While waiting, Rivera checked in with the Jennings for any updates.

"They still haven't heard anything from Avery," he told Victoria. "They're going straight to the U.S. Embassy. They'll meet us at the resort later."

Once airport security cleared the agents, they temporarily parted ways to freshen up.

Wearing the same outfit from yesterday, Victoria ran a comb through her hair and brushed her teeth with bottled water in the restroom.

Rivera came out of the men's room looking clean and freshly shaven. He'd changed out of his jeans and hoodie into a charcoal suit with a white dress shirt. No tie. He removed his suit jacket as soon as they stepped outside the air-conditioned airport into the humidity. It was almost ten thirty a.m. when they flagged a taxi to the Azure Cove Resort. Forty hours since Avery went missing.

In the back of the cab, the agents sent messages from their phones. Victoria told her father she was in Mexico for work. She liked to keep him updated when she could. Then she let Ned know she had made it through another flight without panicking, and she had landed safely.

Ned replied, *Be careful.*

I will. We're primarily assisting in the investigation. We'll be doing background checks on the American guests and staff. Searching along with the Mexican police and other volunteers.

Who is the "we"?

She answered, *Dante Rivera and me.*

Three dots hovered in the message bar on her screen, signaling Ned's response was on its way. Then the dots disappeared, and she thought Ned might have gotten pulled away to another task. The dots returned a few seconds later, along with his message. *That's good. I know you look out for each other. I love you.*

She wrote back, *I love you, too.* She must have been smiling because she looked up to see Rivera staring at her curiously. Before she could explain, their driver turned off the main road at a large sign for Azure Cove. Rivera looked out his window and Victoria sat up straighter, focusing on every detail. One of them might matter later.

Palm trees, yuccas, zinnias, and other flowering shrubs lined the entrance road. A Hummer limousine passed by going in the opposite direction. It had the words Azure Cove on the side, along with the resort's logo, two palm trees surrounding a sunset. The vehicle was followed by a new model Range Rover.

"Fancy place," Rivera said. "I was expecting more of a spring-break dive. What college kids can afford this?"

"The trip was one of Brie's birthday presents. Her father paid for it. He's a lobbyist."

"What sort of lobbyist?" Rivera asked.

"Pharmaceuticals."

"Hmm. Did you vacation at places like this with your family when you were growing up?"

"We rarely took island vacations. Mostly hiking and places we could drive to. My mother liked to travel with our dogs."

Rivera chuckled. "Who does that remind me of?" He rubbed his chin and narrowed his eyes, pretending to think hard.

Victoria smiled back. Yes, she and her mother, Abigail Heslin, were alike in many ways, except that her mother was already married with two children by the time she was Victoria's age. Abigail's life played a key role in influencing Victoria's choices. Abigail's abduction and subsequent death—even more so. It motivated Victoria to join the FBI, first as a profiler, and then as a special agent. She trained hard and stayed in shape to keep herself and others safe because helplessness and worrying didn't bring people home...strength and action did.

Victoria stared out the window to her right as they rounded a bend. Between the thick bamboo shoots, she glimpsed splashes of color—pink blooms, terracotta roofs, and pale-yellow siding. Bushes almost completely obscured the buildings hidden behind them.

Four people stood together at the edge of the bamboo. They wore light blue polos shirts with the Azure Cove logo and were studying a piece of paper held between them. Possibly a search party for Avery.

Around the next corner, a giant, elaborate arch crossed from one side of the road to the other. The words *Welcome to Azure Cove* graced the top.

A news van parked along one side of the archway. Two men wearing security uniforms stood in its path, preventing it from entering.

The agents' vehicle went around the news van and through the archway. They came to a stop a bit farther down the road in front of the resort.

The driver helped unload their suitcases and Rivera tipped him before joining Victoria in the open foyer. A woman, also wearing a light blue polo shirt, offered them refreshments—iced waters with orange slices and mint garnishes. Rivera drained the small glass, set it down on the woman's tray, and thanked her.

They continued to the reception area, rolling their carry-on suitcases behind them on the marble floors. High overhead, large fans circulated a breeze through the open foyer. Victoria inhaled the ocean's scent and something sweet. Tropical hibiscus.

Behind the reception desk, a stenciled greeting stood out on the wall. *Azure Cove welcomes you into a world of exceptional luxury, unparalleled beauty, legendary service, and unforgettable experiences.* Below those words hung a sign: *Our guests' experience is our highest priority. – Alejandro Fuentes, General Manager.*

"Welcome to Azure Cove," a young man said from behind the front desk.

"Hello," Victoria answered. "We're with the FBI. Your manager is expecting us. Please let him know we're here."

As the young man left through a door behind the counter, Victoria set her empty water glass down and covered a yawn as she eyed a large coffee dispensing machine to one side of the desk. She needed the caffeine.

The reception clerk returned a few seconds later and said, "The manager will be right out." He shifted his weight from side to side behind the desk, occasionally looking up from a computer screen at them, particularly at Victoria.

They didn't have to wait long before a trim man in his forties emerged with a white-toothed smile. He smoothed his hand over his hair and said, "Welcome. I'm Alejandro Fuentes. I trust you had a safe trip. Please, come into my office. We can talk there in private."

They walked behind the counter, where Alejandro stood aside in the doorway and ushered them in. As the door closed behind them, the air changed from humid to cool. They followed Alejandro into a spacious office with two glass walls. He flicked on the lights and pulled the shades down over the windows. His large desk held a laptop and a large monitor, a container of hard candies, and a framed photograph of him with a pretty Latina woman and two pig-tailed girls in white dresses.

"I'm surprised the FBI came so quickly. The missing girl must be a celebrity," he said.

"The Mexican police invited us to help because Avery Jennings and a large percentage of your other guests are Americans," Victoria said. "And may I ask how you know our arrival was quick? Have guests gone missing from this resort before?"

Alejandro's smile disappeared. "No, no. Never. Not from here. Nothing like this has happened before. We pride ourselves on delivering the best experience for our guests, which, of course, includes their safety. I only meant that I thought it would take longer to get American police or FBI here. That's all."

Alejandro took a seat in a large chair behind his desk. The agents sat in two chairs opposite him.

"Just so you know, we're providing the police full access to Azure Cove," he said, his chair squeaking as he swiveled it a few inches from side to side. "The same goes for you. We've asked our guests to come forward if they have any information. The police are here now, searching for Ms. Jennings. Our security and staff are also combing the area. But it's good you're here as well. The resort welcomes your help. We want this...mystery cleared up and Ms. Jennings located as soon as possible."

"Someone told Avery she tested positive for Covid," Victoria said. "Was he a member of your staff?"

Alejandro clasped his hands under his chin. "I'm aware of what Avery's friend said. When I heard, I didn't think any of our staff would be responsible, but I checked to be sure. No one here has knowledge of that happening. Avery's negative Covid test results are still at the reception desk. None of our employees contacted her about her test results."

"You're sure about that?" Victoria asked. "If an employee lied about Avery's test, perhaps to abduct her, I wouldn't expect him to admit it now, would you?" Victoria leaned forward, observing the manager's response.

"No, I would not. But I don't think that's what happened. Not with one of our employees. If Avery or anyone else tested positive here, that's not how we would handle the situation. Yes, we offer Covid tests onsite as a convenience for guests who need them to fly home. And yes, we've set aside rooms for those who test positive and must extend their stay, but regardless of the test outcomes, we don't require our guests to stay."

"But you've checked the quarantine rooms you mentioned?" Rivera asked.

"Yes. She's not in any of those reserved rooms. She's not in any of the rooms at this resort." The manager's chair squeaked again as his gaze briefly dropped to a notepad on his desk. "We checked all the unoccupied rooms yesterday, and again this morning with the police, just to be sure."

"And the rooms occupied with guests?" Rivera asked.

"Our cleaning crews have been in and out of all the occupied rooms as part of their daily schedules. They all knew to search for signs of Avery."

"What about the buildings we saw on our way in, behind all the trees?" Victoria asked. "Have you checked those?"

"Those are the staff accommodations. And yes, the police checked them," Alejandro said. "The staff were cooperative and left their apartments open to be searched."

"Are any of your employees locals who don't live at the resort?" Rivera asked.

"Yes. Most of them. Like our guests, the resort's entertainment staff hail from all over the world. They do nine-month rotations before switching to one of the resort's other locations. The cleaning, maintenance, and kitchen staff are all local hires. I've already compiled a list of the names of the staff *and* the guests who were here the day Avery Jennings disappeared. I sent it to the FBI and the police. Did you get the information?"

"We did, thank you," Victoria answered. "Does the resort have security cameras outside the guest rooms?"

"Yes." Alejandro rubbed his hand over his chin and sighed. "I'm sorry to say not all the cameras are working. We've endured technical issues with the system since it was first installed. Contractors have been in and out fixing it. The company finally agreed to replace the entire system rather than keep patching up the current one, which was flawed from day one. They'll install the replacement system next week. They were supposed to come weeks ago but couldn't because their crew contracted Covid. Then they got behind. There's been one excuse after another. I have all the documentation to show that it's been an ongoing issue and has nothing to do with Avery's disappearance."

"What about the cameras outside Avery's room or nearest her room?" Victoria asked, already having a gut feeling about the answer.

"Unfortunately, no, those weren't operating properly." Alejandro stole a quick glance at his watch as he answered. "But our IT department is sending some footage from the front entrance."

"We'd like to see it when it's available," Rivera said.

"Certainly. I hope to have it by this afternoon when we meet with the police. Oh, someone from the FBI sent a sketch of the man Avery's friend saw," Alejandro said, placing a copy of the drawing in the center of his desk where the agents could see it.

Brie had excellent artistic skills and had drawn the rendition herself. A mask covered the man's nose and mouth, but under his thick eyebrows, his eyes looked so real they almost jumped off the page.

"Does he look familiar?" Victoria asked. "Can you think of anyone who fits this description?"

"No. As I said to you, and as I told the police, I don't believe any of the resort's staff were involved with telling her she tested positive." Alejandro repeated his conviction with a patient resolve, but there was an edge to his voice. It might have been irritation, or simply exhaustion. He'd been courteous so far, and Victoria believed he wanted to find Avery, but his behavior also suggested they'd taken enough of his time. Unfortunately for him, they weren't finished.

"Do you doubt the information obtained from Avery and her friends?" Victoria asked, keeping any hint of accusation out of her tone.

"I didn't say that," Alejandro answered, though that's exactly what he'd seemed to imply more than once since they'd entered his office. The agents waited to see if he would elaborate, but he remained silent.

"We were told your staff directory has photos," Victoria said.

"Yes. Headshots and a full body shot of each staff member. Employment at Azure Cove is considered a prime job. We have our pick of staff. We don't hire anyone with a criminal background. We don't need to. Our guests, on the other hand—perhaps the majority are Americans, as you said—we have no say over their backgrounds or criminal records." Alejandro scooted his chair closer to his desk and tapped his computer, waking up the screen. "Anyway, I can give you access to our staff database."

"First, can you tell us if you have any staff from the San Francisco area. The tattoo we're looking for might represent a gang from that area."

After a few minutes on his computer, Alejandro answered, "No. None of our current hires have a permanent address in San Francisco. No one out of Northern California is working here right now. And the resort wouldn't hire a gang member anyway."

"You might not have known you were hiring a former gang member," Rivera said. "That info doesn't go on anyone's résumé."

"No, I suppose it wouldn't," Alejandro responded.

"We'd like to look at those staff photos right here, right now," Rivera said. "The full body shots."

Alejandro seemed to be fulfilling Rivera's request as he leaned closer to his desk and moved his fingers across his keyboard. When his phone rang, he took the call and put it on speaker without interrupting his typing. "Yes, hello."

"It's Michael at the front desk. Um...Teresa is here, and she wants to speak with you."

Victoria caught the accentuated rise and fall of Alejandro's chest, as if he was summoning patience before he answered. "Please tell Teresa I'm helping other guests at the moment, and I'll be with her as soon as I can. Ask if there's anything you can do for her in the meantime."

"Yeah, okay. But..."

"What does she want?"

"She couldn't find an empty chair on the beach near the Horizon Hut. She said people are still putting towels on the chairs to save them even though they aren't sitting there, and she wants us to do a better job enforcing that rule starting immediately. She wants to speak to you about it in person."

Alejandro studied his computer screen as he spoke without missing a beat. "Please thank Teresa for bringing the matter to our attention. You can remind her that our guests' needs are always our top priority and tell her I'll be out shortly." Alejandro dropped his phone onto his desk and swiveled his monitor to face the agents. "Here it is. This should help you. I've filtered the current employees to show only males. There are over a hundred, including myself. You can scroll through them." He stepped away from his desk and let the agents move into the space. "If you don't mind, I'm going to excuse myself for a moment."

"Go ahead," Rivera said.

Alejandro left the agents alone in his office as Victoria called Brie, who answered on the third ring.

"Hi, Brie. This is Agent Heslin. I'm at the Azure Cove Resort in Mexico."

"Have you found Avery?" Brie asked immediately.

"Not yet. We need you to look at some pictures and tell us if you recognize the man you saw. Are you somewhere with an Internet connection?"

"Yeah, I'm in my room," Brie said.

"I'm going to send you a link for another video chat." Victoria ended the call and connected to Brie again through video.

Brie flipped her camera around. The Ruth Bader Ginsburg poster filled the screen before the camera lowered and Brie appeared. Yesterday, she wore no makeup and looked slightly disheveled. Today, she'd made such an effort with her hair and makeup that she was almost unrecognizable from the previous day. Victoria wondered if it had anything to do with reporters looking to interview Avery's friends.

"I'm with Special Agent Dante Rivera. He's also with the FBI," Victoria said. "We're going to click through the photos of the resort's staff. Let me know if you recognize the man you saw with Avery."

Victoria scrolled through the photos one by one. Rivera stood beside her.

The resort's apparent bias for hiring athletic-looking men might have complicated the elimination of suspects, but with a confident efficiency, Brie dismissed the employees one by one. Everyone's arms were visible in the full body shots. None had the tattoo Brie claimed to see.

Victoria held her breath when they got to the picture of a muscular man with green ink peeking out from under his blue shirt sleeve. But Brie said, "No. That's not him. I'm sure of it. Keep going."

Victoria kept scrolling and Brie continued to say, "Not him," until they had exhausted the options.

Alejandro returned to the room and moved to stand behind Victoria, close enough to see her phone.

"Brie, this is the resort's manager," Victoria said.

"Hello, Miss Vanderhorn. So glad to see you're feeling better." Alejandro's snide tone hinted at insincerity. Victoria was instantly curious to find out why.

Brie answered, "Thank you," and quickly directed her attention back to Victoria. "So, is that all the male employees? There aren't any others?"

"That's it for now," Victoria said. "One of our colleagues is compiling recent photographs of each of the guests. Once we have those, we'll ask you to repeat this process. Hopefully soon. We'll be in touch."

"What was that comment about?" Rivera asked the manager as soon as the call with Brie ended. "Was Brie not feeling well when she was here?"

Alejandro huffed and crossed his arm. "You spoke with Avery Jennings' travel companions already, didn't you?"

"We did," Victoria answered.

"Then they *forgot* to tell you Brie Vanderhorn caused quite a scene on her last night here."

"What are you talking about?" Rivera asked.

"She's not the most reliable witness," Alejandro said.

"Why?" Victoria asked. "What happened?"

"I respect our guests' privacy. I think it's best if you ask her yourself. Let me just say this. We want our guests to have a wonderful time and relax, but we also have reasonable expectations regarding their behaviors." Alejandro sat down behind his desk again. "Are we done for now? Or is there anything else I can do to help you?"

Victoria and Rivera exchanged a look, a slight upward movement of Rivera's chin, and a barely perceptible nod from Victoria in return. They'd worked together so often, that's all it took to communicate. They would probably have more questions for the manager later, but based on his comments, Victoria wanted to question Brie again.

"I think we're done here for now," Rivera said. "Avery's parents are meeting the police at the reception area at four p.m. We'll be there as well."

"So will I." The manager straightened and glanced toward his door.

"We just need the keys to our rooms, then we'll head out," Rivera said. "If you can put us on the same floor where Avery and her friends stayed, that would be helpful."

"I can arrange that. I'll take care of your rooms myself. Compliments of the resort, of course, for your help in resolving this matter."

A soft popping sound followed as Alejandro cracked his knuckles. His plastered-on smile reappeared, but beads of perspiration had accumulated on his upper lip. With the chilly temperature inside his office, that could only be a nervous sweat.

CHAPTER 10

"W hat did you think about Alejandro?" Victoria asked Rivera when they were alone again.

"He's competent and organized. He left us alone in his office, so he's got nothing to hide in there at least. But he was nervous about something," Rivera said.

"I thought so, too. But does it have anything to do with Avery?"

"He could be anticipating the media criticism that will hit soon. If it hasn't already. They'll be under the spotlight, and it won't be good for business. Nothing leads to a surge in cancellations better than the un-explained disappearance of a guest, especially an American one. If Avery isn't found, the Azure Cove Resort could become a household name. From a liability perspective, they need her to have left the resort on her own accord. Anything short of that—something happening to her here, someone abducting her from here—and they could be liable."

"Yes, he has a lot to worry about. And he seems like a decent guy," Victoria said, thinking of the framed photo of the two little girls on his desk. "But until we know him better, I'm not ready to take his word for anything."

"I agree."

Following a directional sign, the agents stepped onto one of the paved paths that wound through the resort. A fat lizard lazed in the sun atop a wall, another nearby in the grass. The path led them through beautiful, lush landscaping to an open area. Chaise lounges surrounded a large pool made to look like a lagoon with rock formations and a waterfall. Soft music played from hidden speakers, and the faint hum of occasional conversation carried through the air.

There were no children in sight. The resort was adult only. Twenty-one and over. Avery and her friends had just made the cut.

Beyond the pool, framed by palm trees, a secluded beach beckoned, the ocean sparkling beneath the blue horizon.

Azure Cove was gorgeous and peaceful.

But ugly things could happen in beautiful places.

With discretion, Victoria studied everyone. Rivera was undoubtedly doing the same. If someone was responsible for Avery's disappearance, that person might be watching now, witnessing the chaos he or she had caused, or attempting to stay one step ahead of the investigation. Although, more likely, if that person knew what was good for him or her, they would be long gone. Fortunately, not everyone knew what was good for them.

On the beach, comfortable chairs were grouped in twos and threes with giant straw umbrellas and side tables between them. Most of the seats were unoccupied, but each held one of the resort's blue beach towels, just as the woman who wanted to speak with Alejandro had claimed.

Three women in bikinis stood knee-deep in the ocean and farther out, a man floated inside an orange tube. The water was a beautiful dark turquoise except for where brown swaths of seaweed floated in the cove.

Two men wearing rubber boots and wide-brimmed hats used pitchforks to pull the tangled seaweed from the water and toss it onto the shore.

Behind them, a small tractor drove over the sand, harvesting the brown coils. The tendrils rolled in on the waves, making the task of completely clearing the cove seem an impossible one.

"How'd you like to have that job?" Rivera asked.

"Looks Sisyphean," Victoria answered, getting a blank face from Rivera. "You know, the guy from Greek mythology who had to push a giant rock to the top of a hill. Each time he got to the top it rolled down and he had to start again."

"Right," Rivera said before consulting a map of the resort. "We're that way." He guided them to a paved trail running parallel to the beach.

A resort guest wearing a floral sarong over her tiny bikini sauntered past, her sandals flip-flopping on the pavement, leaving the scent of coconut oil in her wake.

"There's building D," Rivera said, pointing to a rectangular two-story structure made of white stucco. Each room had a small balcony with an ocean view.

Rivera checked his phone as they climbed the stairs to the second floor. "We've got two hours before we meet with the Federales. Payton has a break in her court schedule coming up. I'll give her an update and see if we can get started on the background checks."

"I'm going to call Brie and find out what she didn't tell us earlier. And so...you and Payton are...dating?"

"Yes. We are. We officially reported it to HR last week."

"Oh, that's great. Really."

"I'm glad you think so."

"Yeah. Payton is awesome. I like her a lot. There's a lot to admire."

"She's grateful you're here, searching for Avery."

"Of course. I mean, even if she wasn't Payton's niece I'd be fully on board, but I know she and Payton are really close."

"They are. And you and Ned...you're pretty serious now?"

"Yes. I think things are really good with us."

The conversation was slightly awkward because of the agents' past romantic history, which came down to a lot of sexual tension and one night of passion. Fortunately, both had moved on and they could focus on finding Avery without personal issues clouding the investigation.

On the courtyard side of the building, the rooms opened to a shared outdoor corridor. The agents' rooms were next to each other. Victoria held her wristband chip against the door's sensor pad. A green light came on as it unlocked. Inside, the room was light, clean, and airy. Two tightly made queen-size beds had cream-colored upholstered headboards and white bedding. A sitting area contained two cushioned chairs and a television. A nook held a desk and a mini fridge. Vibrant shades of blue and turquoise popped on throw pillows, the duvet, and a vase. A patch of ocean was visible from the balcony.

The temperature inside the room was even cooler than the manager's office. Sixty-eight degrees, according to the digital controls. But that couldn't be right. It felt more like fifty-eight. Victoria pressed the up arrow on the panel. Nothing happened. She tried again before giving up. Even if the problem persisted, she wouldn't ask anyone at the resort to fix it. She wasn't on vacation, and she didn't expect to spend much time in the room.

After unpacking her toiletries in the gleaming marble bathroom, she settled into one of the plush chairs. Time to call Brie back and get some answers.

"Hello," Brie said. Heavy breathing came over the line, as if she was hustling to get somewhere.

"It's Agent Heslin again. I have a few more questions for you."

"Sure. I'm on my way to class. Do you have the guest photos ready...or...did you find Avery?" She suddenly sounded hopeful and excited.

"Neither. Not yet. After our conversation a little while ago, the resort's manager mentioned that something occurred the night Avery disappeared. He said you caused a scene. Please tell me what happened."

For several seconds, the only sounds were Brie's breathing and bits of conversation coming from somewhere in the background.

With her phone tucked between her chin and ear, and the FBI woman on the line, Brie silently groaned. If only she could have a do-over. She'd choose Florida or anywhere else for her birthday celebration. She had so many regrets about Mexico now. She longed to put the entire experience behind her and forget it had ever happened. But with Avery missing, that was impossible. Brie's stomach tightened as she tried to recall everything that happened on Sunday night, the last night of the vacation.

Clouds had slid across the moon, drenching the area beyond the dance floor with shadowy figures, angled arms, and swishing hair moving in a way that reminded Brie of voodoo dolls. "I need another rum punch," she told Haley.

"Okay. Get one." Haley answered without looking up, typing away with her thumbs on her phone. A second later, her message popped up in the group chat on Brie's screen.

Avery! Let us know what's going on. Did you get the retest results back yet? Where are you? We can bring you a Dirty Monkey to cheer you up. Not the same without you. Miss you so much!! XOXO

Haley stared intently at her screen for a few seconds before frowning. "Avery still isn't responding."

"What the heck? I'm calling her again." Brie let the call ring until it went to voicemail. "She didn't take my call either. Do you think she's mad at us? I mean, she must be."

With her almost-empty cocktail hovering inches from her lips, Haley scowled. "If she is, that's just BS. We talked about this. We knew this could happen. No one can be mad at anyone."

"I know. If she's mad, that's just wrong. Mrs. Jennings is going to be furious though. You know she didn't want Avery to come because of the whole Covid test thing, right? And I swear her mother has never liked me."

"Why wouldn't she like you? Everyone loves you, Brie."

"Maybe she thinks I'm a bad influence." Brie grinned. "Which reminds me..." She opened her purse and shook the last of her birthday pills onto her palm. She placed the mint green, diamond-shaped one on her tongue and swallowed. "Happy Birthday to me!"

Haley, who refused to take any pills that didn't come from a sealed bottle, pursed her lips in a look of disapproval. "Do you even know what that is, exactly?"

"No. But I've had it before. It's like Molly. I think."

Haley rolled her eyes skyward and set her empty glass on the bar. "I've made up my mind. I'm trying the Grasshopper drink next. Want one?"

Brie scanned the rows of premium liquors lined up in front of the mirror like an enticing work of art. "I'm sticking with the rum punch. It's so, so good."

That much Brie remembered.

Flashing zig zags of color interrupted her vision. The liquor bottles spun, and a cold sweat broke out on her skin. She gripped the edge of the bar and held on tight. What was going on? The bartender came toward her, his cheeks bulging in and out as if he was a fat fish taking great puffing breaths underwater.

"What can I get you, ladies?" he asked, looking like a walking, talking freak show.

Brie's heart was beating much too fast. It wasn't normal. Something bad was happening. Fear shot through her, making her heart race faster.

"What's wrong, Brie?" Haley asked in a grotesque, slow-motion way, her skin stretching, turning into giant sheets of pinkish taffy and pulling away from her face.

Brie leaned away from Haley. Her stool toppled over. She hit the ground hard, taking another stool down with her.

"What happened? Are you okay?" Haley's mouth opened, impossibly large, cavernous. Others joined her, leaning in, their skin slid over their faces like bubbling soup.

Someone screamed like a lunatic, "Go away! Get away from me!" It must have been Brie though it sounded nothing like her. She tried to recoil into a ball, but her legs were tangled with the stool's. She pressed her hands against her temples as hard as she could, trying to keep her own face together as voices buzzed above her like a swarm of mosquitoes. "What's wrong? What happened?"

Brie had an instant of rational thought and understood what was happening. "It's my birthday!" she shrieked. "Don't let me die!"

Then the night sky was bouncing along above her. A guy she didn't recognize carried her like she was a toddler. She remembered her skirt had hiked up to her waist, she'd worn a pink thong, and anyone could see it.

Voices were in and out.

"Brie, Brie, are you okay?" Haley's voice sounded different. Panicked.

Brie's skin was hot and sweaty. Tiny ants crawled up and down her arms and legs, underneath her skin. Whatever she'd taken, it wasn't Molly. More like terrible LSD or shrooms that didn't agree with her in any way.

Haley's voice came from somewhere nearby. "We're taking you to the health room. They have a doctor there. Or a nurse." Haley sounded terrified.

Brie remembered pounding. Someone pounding on a door. Her heart pounding like a mini jackhammer.

A nurse who seemed to hate her.

There was shaking and sweating. Chills and flashes of heat. Sticks in her arm. Pinches on her fingers. Icy cold things on her fiery skin. She squirmed and shouted things she only vaguely remembered and didn't want to recall.

The angry nurse kept telling her, "Hang in there. You're going to be okay."

Haley held her hand, echoing, "You're going to be okay."

That's mostly what Brie recollected from the worst and most terrifying night of her life before waking up inside their room. Haley shook her shoulder and forced a water bottle into her hand. It was still dark out. The overhead light was blinding. "Brie, come on," Haley said. "Get up. We have to go or we're going to miss our flight. You have to get up. Hurry."

"I guess that's why you weren't as concerned about Avery as you should have been. From now on, I need you to tell the truth no matter what," Victoria said.

"I...I didn't lie about anything. No one asked me."

"All right, well, unfortunately, this makes your statements less reliable. The information you gave us was our best lead. That's all been compromised."

"I'm sorry," Brie said. "I really am. But I was fine when Avery came back to the room to get her stuff. The guy who took her leaned his arm on the doorframe right in front of my face. His tattoo was right there."

Victoria knew drugs were behind most of the reported violence and homicides in Mexico. The problems used to be most prevalent away from the tourist areas. Not anymore. American and European tourists wanted more recreational drugs. The drug cartels were catering to their demands. Was it possible Avery and her friends had gotten mixed up with drug suppliers?

"Where did you buy the drugs?" Victoria asked.

"I didn't. Someone gave them to me."

"Someone at the resort?"

"No. Here. At school. For my birthday."

"Did you buy drugs from anyone while you were in Mexico?"

"No."

"Did Avery take the drugs, too?"

"No. Definitely not. She never did drugs. She wouldn't."

"Then she has that going for her. All right, Brie. I have to go. I'll be calling you again, I'm sure." Still frustrated and disappointed, Victoria ended the call.

She had a feeling there would be more surprises to come.

CHAPTER 11

A rustling sound came from the corridor. Thinking it was Rivera, and hoping he had some good news from Payton about Avery, Victoria opened the door of her room. There was no one in sight. In fact, the entire area surrounding the building was eerily quiet, but someone had parked a cleaning cart outside the next room. They'd also left the door propped open, so Victoria peeked in.

The man inside wore a uniform with the resort's logo—white pants and a white shirt that looked a bit more stiff and less comfortable than the blue polo. He didn't see Victoria, and he continued to scoop used towels from the shower floor.

"Excuse me," she said from the entry.

He quickly straightened and faced her. His name tag said Carlos.

"Hi. Sorry if I startled you. I'm with the FBI. I'm helping the police find a woman who went missing on Sunday." She removed her badge and showed it to him. "I'd like to ask you a few questions."

He shook his head. "No English."

"Okay. No hablo Español. Un momento." She left the room wishing she spoke Spanish rather than French and Italian and wondering if she'd gotten un momento correct.

She knocked on Rivera's door. "It's me."

Rivera answered holding his phone. One hand covered the speaker. "Give me one minute, I'm just updating Payton." He backed up, gesturing for Victoria to enter.

"No, that's okay. Just let me know when you're done." Victoria closed his door, wanting to give him time to update Payton, who was probably having a difficult time being stuck in D.C. rather than helping to find Avery at the resort.

Rivera's black hoodie sweatshirt hung over the railing in the corridor. Victoria scooped it up and brought it into her room, where she put it on. It was soft and lightweight, with just enough extra fabric to make her feel cozy inside the frigid room.

Less than a minute later, Rivera was at her door. "Payton assigned some-one to work on the background checks while we meet with the Federales," he said. "I need to grab some food first. You want to come?"

"Sure. I'm hungry." Victoria placed her hand over her heart, her fingers finding the zipper of his sweatshirt. "Mind if I wear this? My room is freezing. So was the manager's office. The dining area might be just as cool."

"I don't mind. Go for it. We can be casual here. And it hides your side-arm."

She lowered her voice and looked down the hall. "There's a man named Carlos cleaning the rooms. We should talk to him. In case he saw Avery before she disappeared. He speaks Spanish. And as you know...I don't."

The cleaning cart had moved further down the corridor. Carlos was inside a different room, tucking the sheets under the corner of a bed. His eyes widened when the agents entered the room together.

Rivera introduced himself and after a few minutes of back-and-forth conversation in Spanish, he turned to Victoria and said, "He wasn't working on Sunday. His supervisor and the police showed him Avery's picture. He'd never seen her before. He doesn't know how she disappeared. He's going to open her room for us now, but it's already been cleaned."

They followed Carlos to room 235, where he opened the door and stepped aside for them. The room was a carbon copy of Victoria's. She didn't doubt Carlos did an excellent job of cleaning and wiping all surfaces, or guests would have complained by now. But she grabbed a few tissues from a tissue box anyway and used them to grasp the closet handles. She looked inside the closet and the dresser. All empty. Rivera kneeled to look under the beds and the nightstands, and even between the mattresses. They didn't expect to find anything there, and they were right. Still, Victoria turned a slow circle in the middle of the room, scanning every inch of the space, trying to absorb any clue as to Avery's whereabouts.

Without saying a word, Carlos watched them from the open doorway.

Rivera thanked him again when they left.

Victoria waited until they were downstairs to share her thoughts. "I got the impression he wanted to tell me something. Maybe if there hadn't been the language barrier. Did you pick up on it at all?"

"He seemed cooperative, humble, appropriately concerned. I didn't pick up on any guilty vibes. But I trust your gut. Do you want to go back and talk to him again?"

"No. Not yet."

Victoria followed Rivera to the dining area, but her thoughts were still on Carlos. She trusted her instincts. Just like Brie had done, the man was holding something back.

CHAPTER 12

Victoria and Rivera climbed a long and curving flight of stairs to the main dining area. At the top, an attractive woman wearing the Azure Cove polo shirt with a white skirt took their temperatures before welcoming them inside. Several rooms surrounded a central area containing the all-inclusive meal options. Each room held dozens of tables with crisp white tablecloths and vases of flowers. Glass walls offered elevated views of the ocean, the cove, or the tropical foliage. One room extended outside to an open veranda.

Victoria strolled through the food stations in the central area, surveying the choices and the people working behind each set up. They all wore the resort's short-sleeved polo shirts under long white aprons. Even though Brie didn't identify any of the resort's employees as the man she'd previously seen, Victoria wanted to check for herself. She pretended to be deciding on her order at the stir-fry station to get a better look at the fit guy tossing ingredients in a wok. He had thick eyebrows, but no tattoo. She also lingered at the panini station, where a man with rippling biceps added layers of meat to a guest's sandwich. He also matched the general description Brie gave them. But no tattoo.

After selecting a shrimp and avocado salad, a chunk of French bread, and a plate with chocolate and fruit tarts, Victoria chose a table outside on the open veranda. White curtains hung from above, swaying in the breeze, framing a panoramic view of the ocean and any guests who walked past on a boardwalk path.

Rivera found Victoria. He set two entrees on the table. "I'll be right back," he said. "Gonna grab a few more things while I'm here."

A young woman came to the table and filled their water glasses. "Can I bring you anything else?" she asked.

"This is fine. Thank you," Victoria said. She felt a pang of conscience for relaxing even a bit while Avery was missing, when every minute could be the difference between coming home to her friends and family and her future...or not. But there wasn't much she and Rivera could do before getting an update from the police, and they needed to eat eventually.

She lifted a placard from the center of the table and scanned the QR code on the bottom. The resort's daily schedule of activities popped up on her phone. They offered sports clinics and exercise classes throughout the day, including the daily five p.m. Zumba class Avery took before disappearing.

Rivera returned carrying another plate. He pushed the other two aside to make room for the new one. "I could get used to this."

"And now you only have a few minutes to wolf it all down."

"No worries there." He pressed his fork into a piece of flaky white fish with mango salsa and took his first bite. "Oh, wow. This is good."

An older woman with a stern look walked toward them. She was somewhere between late sixties and mid-seventies, thin as a rail, and deeply tanned. Her gorgeous silvery-blonde hair was straight and smoothed back from a wide, unwrinkled forehead. Most of the guests wore casual clothes, but she wore a linen sheath dress with pink shoes, carried a matching Kate Spade purse over her arm, and large sunglasses on top of her head. She held a small triangular-shaped plate with fruit and cheese, her manicured pink nails appearing over one edge. Victoria expected her to walk right past them, but she didn't. She stopped beside their table, cleared her throat, and said, "I usually sit there."

Confused, Victoria sat up straighter and looked around at the other empty tables on the veranda. "Oh, I'm sorry. I thought we could sit at any open table."

The woman gave a slight shake of her head. "Yes, but this one has the best view. It's safer outside, you know, fewer germs floating around. That's why I came here, to the resort, to spend more time outside and avoid getting sick. But you wouldn't know that if you just arrived."

Victoria wasn't sure if the woman was joking. Her face remained almost expressionless, which made it harder to judge her intent.

"It's okay, dear," the woman said. "I'll sit elsewhere. You two just enjoy your meal." She walked to the next table and sat down, leaving Victoria even more confused about what had just happened.

Rivera grabbed his napkin and covered his mouth, but not before Victoria saw the upward curl of his lips indicating he'd found the encounter highly entertaining.

As soon as the woman sat down, a server appeared at her table and filled her water glass. "Good afternoon, Ms. Teresa."

"That's Teresa," Rivera whispered, his eyes beaming as he lowered his napkin. "It has to be the same one who called about the towels on the chairs when we were with Alejandro."

"I'll have a glass of the Fontaine Chardonnay from your premier list," Teresa said, loud enough for the agents to hear her. "And your mask is slipping, dear. I can see your nostrils. Some of us didn't come here to get sick and die."

"Sorry," the server said, pinching the top of her mask and pulling it above her nose. "I'll be right back with your wine."

"I'll be here. And when you return, please sit down with me, wearing your mask properly. I'd like to go over a few things with you. I have some advice to offer. Advice that will help you do your job better. Please correct me if I'm wrong, but I'm assuming you want to provide good service."

The server left, rolling her eyes after she turned her back on Teresa.

Teresa moved her plate to the side of her table. From her purse, she removed a floral-covered journal and placed it in front of her. She pulled out the silver pen attached to it, opened the journal to a page mostly full of writing, and jotted something down. Finished, she shut the journal, returned it to her purse, and slid her plate into its previous position. Each movement occurred with a practiced efficiency.

"We need to talk to her," Victoria whispered. "She's obviously paying attention to things. Hopefully, some things that might matter." Victoria put her mask on as she stood. "I'll be right back."

She walked to Teresa's table and stood across from her. "Hello, I'm Victoria Heslin, a special agent with the Federal Bureau of Investigation. I did just arrive a few hours ago. To help find Avery Jennings, the young woman who disappeared from the resort last Sunday."

"And I'm Teresa Middleton." Sitting with the straightest posture, Teresa folded her hands in her lap and gave Victoria her full attention.

"I can see you're observant," Victoria said, because flattery often encouraged people to be helpful. "I'd like to ask you some questions."

Teresa seemed to study Victoria from her head to her shoes, unapologetically, as if she had all the time in the world to consider her reply, and one side of her mouth crinkled, suggesting displeasure. Apparently finished with her inspection, her gaze was direct when she asked, "They let you join the FBI with your deformed hands?"

Temporarily at a loss for words, Victoria was grateful for her mask. Teresa reminded Victoria of her great aunt, who said whatever she pleased, no exceptions. A personality so established, she'd never change, and it was a waste of energy for anyone to try. Her aunt had the utmost confidence and believed her opinions were more than just that. In her mind, they were the indisputable truth. Most people didn't care for Victoria's aunt. They didn't realize her outrageous behavior stemmed from deep insecurities. Perhaps there were similar issues fueling Teresa's personality. Victoria wanted to give the woman the benefit of the doubt.

"I had ten fingers when I joined the bureau," Victoria answered. "I lost part of three to frostbite last year after being exposed to sub-zero temperatures. I'm happy to say the FBI didn't kick me out. I've learned to do everything I need to do in my work life and personal life with the fingers I have left."

"Oh. Well, that's certainly interesting, isn't it? Hmm. And it's really no difference to me about your fingers. You're the one who must make the most of it, I suppose. Sit down, please. I'm going to get a stitch in my neck from looking up at you like this. I'll answer your questions. Because you're quite right, dear. I do notice things. I've been going to resorts my entire life. Azure Cove is fairly new, and they still have plenty to learn if they wish to produce the unparalleled experience they claim to deliver. Basic principles that relate to top service. I know because I've been here for two months, staying in one of the luxury bungalows, of course."

"This seat isn't taken?" Victoria asked, gesturing to the seat in front of her. Teresa wore a giant diamond on her ring finger. Perhaps her significant other was on the way.

"I wouldn't have told you to sit down if it was, would I? I'm here alone. From Pennsylvania. My sister was going to join me, but...well, very last minute, she couldn't come. Please, sit down."

Victoria pulled out the chair and settled into it.

The server returned with Teresa's wine. "Is there anything else I can get you?" she asked. "Either of you?"

"That will be all for now," Teresa said. "But do make sure you come back and check our water glasses sooner rather than later."

The server dipped her chin and left them as Victoria thought even her aunt couldn't hold a candle to Teresa's personality.

"Did you see anything over the past few days that might relate to the disappearance of Avery Jennings?" Victoria asked.

"I may have." Teresa swirled her wine, took a sip, and put it down. "I've already told the manager they need better security measures. People come into the resort at night from the beach. I've seen them. People who don't belong."

"They aren't wearing wristbands?"

"Oh, they are. But they aren't guests of this resort. That's the mystery."

"Then...how do you know they aren't guests here?"

"I'm very observant. Believe me. I know things."

Despite Teresa's enormous confidence, a response like that would hardly stand up in court.

Without compromising the straight line of her back, Teresa leaned forward and crossed her arms on the edge of the table. "I'm aware they're looking for a man with a tattoo. I may have seen him."

"You may have?" A flash of excitement made Victoria sit up taller. She hadn't expected to hit the equivalent of a home run. "What makes you say that?"

"I remember the tattoo because I found it distasteful, more appropriate for a seedy bar than a resort touting itself as exclusive. It should have been covered."

"And...he was a guest?"

"No. No. One of the resort's employees. He wore the uniform shirt. Poorly, I would add. It didn't fit him properly. He needed a larger size. That's what made me take notice of him."

"And do you recall details of the tattoo?"

"A heart with a crown. Some other details. But those were the most prominent features."

The information left Victoria thrilled for an instant until further reflection tamped down her excitement. The police and the resort's security team had already questioned guests and staff. They'd probably mentioned the man and the tattoo. Word would travel quickly around the resort, with everyone hungry for information and anxious to learn if the resort housed a criminal in their midst. Teresa was traveling alone. She might be lonely and craving the attention that would surely come with sharing the information as if it was her own, though the detail about the improperly fitting uniform shirt sounded authentic.

"Have you spoken to the police yet?" Victoria asked.

"I have not, out of personal preference. I called the tip line. I trust whoever is working it has relayed my information to them, but perhaps I shouldn't have assumed."

"Where did you see him?" Victoria asked.

Teresa sighed. "I'm not sure exactly."

"Was he with anyone else?"

"I don't believe so."

"Did you see where he came from?"

"I did not."

"Did you see where he was going?"

Teresa arced a finger through the air in a gesture that was graceful and pompous and had nothing to do with what she'd said. "I don't have any other information for you. All I can tell you is that I saw the man with the tattoo and his ill-fitting shirt somewhere. If you sit with me while I eat my meal, perhaps more recollections will return to me by the time I'm finished."

From the next table, Rivera cleared his throat. He dabbed his napkin at his mouth, then stood up. "Excuse me, Victoria, we better go."

"That's my colleague Dante Rivera," Victoria told Teresa. "He's also with the FBI. We have to meet with the Federales now. But I'd like to speak with you as soon as we're finished. I'd like to help you remember more about the man with the tattoo."

Teresa clasped her hands and looked down at the plate in front of her, as if considering Victoria's proposal. "I can meet with you after my Zumba class. Six p.m. sharp at the Horizon Café. I'm there most nights. I sit at the center table, closest to the beach, for my post-workout, pre-dinner cocktail."

"Thank you," Victoria said. "I'll see you then."

"Don't be late. I'm on a schedule," Teresa said. "Oh, and lose the sweatshirt, dear. Perhaps it's part of your FBI-issued uniform, but I have to say, it isn't becoming."

Victoria repressed her smile as she joined Rivera.

"Hold on," he said, before making a detour back to the food area and grabbing a slice of bread. "Oh, wow. This is amazing. I don't know what's in it. White chocolate maybe?"

Once they were down the stairs, had passed a wine room, a few boutiques, and a spa, and were and out of earshot from anyone else, Rivera asked, "Did you learn anything helpful from Teresa?"

"She said she saw the man with the tattoo we've been searching for. But she doesn't know where she saw him or what he was doing. She didn't give me anything to go on. She certainly seems to believe she saw him, but I'm not so sure. I think she's lonely and maybe looking for attention."

"Are you going to talk to her again?" he asked, as they reached the path leading to the reception area.

"Absolutely. After we meet with the Federales. Now let's go find out what they know."

CHAPTER 13

S tanding in the shade of an enormous umbrella by a thatched-roof bar, Victoria downed an iced tea and Rivera a Coke. Their location provided an excellent vantage point over the center of the resort.

"When we're with the Federales, don't forget, they invited us to *assist*," she told Rivera. "Murphy wants us to acknowledge that."

"I won't do anything to get us cut out of the loop," he said. "It's you we have to worry about." One corner of his mouth hinted at a smile. He was joking, sort of. Victoria had broken protocol during investigations before, but only for the greater good. And Rivera had always been right there with her.

They left their drinks unfinished and stepped away from the counter when they spotted Avery's parents.

Tom acknowledged the agents with a slight raise of his hand.

Carrying a large black purse over her arm and squeezing the corded strap between her fingers, Jennifer focused on every guest as she passed them. She stared to her left at the woman reading by the pool next to a dozing companion, then to her right where a man slid his hand down a woman's back toward her bikini bottom. When she reached the agents, Jennifer craned her neck to take a longer look at the two young women helping each other apply sunscreen.

"Hi. Have you found anything or heard anything?" Tom asked the agents straightaway. "Any news?"

Rivera told Tom what the agents had done since they arrived, adding, "We have the guest list now. The FBI is doing background checks on the American guests, and we'll request information on foreigners from their respective countries. We're looking for criminal records, compromising Internet posts, anything that might propel them into person-of-interest status...in case someone abducted Avery."

"Someone *did* abduct her. What else could have happened?" Jennifer continued speaking without waiting for an answer to her question. "So you haven't spoken with the Federales yet?"

"No. This is our first opportunity." Rivera said. "Let's head over there now." Once they were on the path heading toward the reception area, he asked, "What happened at the U.S. Embassy?"

"They sent out a notification with Avery's description and picture," Tom said. "They wanted to help us file a police report, which we've already done. And they gave us resources for emotional trauma support. They said there's not much else they can do for us."

"Because you're already doing everything that you can at this point," Rivera said. "For a missing person investigation, you're way ahead of where we would usually be right now."

"That's what they told us," Jennifer said, her gaze on one of the resort employees wearing white shorts and a light blue polo. "Thanks to Payton, we've done everything we should do. Everything except actually finding our daughter."

"They gave us a list of private investigators," Tom said. "I guess we hire one if the police don't take this seriously or...I don't know...don't do what they should or don't have the time or resources. Do you think we should hire one?"

"Why are you asking them that question?" Jennifer said. "I told you we should. Why wouldn't we?"

"I know. I know," Tom said.

"It can't hurt," Victoria told them. "One more person working to find Avery. Someone who knows the area well. Maybe wait and you can decide after we meet with the police."

Victoria didn't know what to expect from the Mexican police. From what she'd heard, their officers were often undertrained and underpaid. The latter made it harder to resist the bribes that came their way, resulting in systemic corruption. But Murphy seemed to have confidence in the Chief of Police. Victoria hoped his crew wouldn't disappoint.

The FBI were almost always the outsiders coming into a crime investigation. They either joined the local authorities and shared responsibilities, or they took over. Here, as Americans, she and Rivera were more outsiders than ever. Victoria wondered how much information the Federales would willingly share.

At the reception area, two armed men in black uniforms stood with the resort's manager. They reminded Victoria of the FBI's SWAT teams. No one would mistake them for civilians. They were about the same height as each other and Rivera, a few inches over six feet. One had a mustache and strands of gray hair peeking out from under the side of his cap. A good sign if his maturity represented experience.

Rivera introduced himself first. He said a few words in Spanish before switching to English, establishing it as the primary language for the rest of the meeting. The man with the gray hairs introduced himself as Leo. The other, younger by about ten years, was Vince.

"Have you found any sign of her yet?" Tom Jennings asked, looking at Leo.

The more senior officer shook his head and frowned at three resort guests who had moved closer to the group and appeared intent on catching every word.

"Let's continue our conversation inside," Alejandro suggested.

They eased through the door behind the reception area and into a conference room, where they sat around an oval table. Alejandro took the head chair. A laptop sat open in front of him.

"Thank you for allowing us to assist in your investigation," Rivera told the Federales. "Any of the FBI's resources are available to you. Just let us know what you need."

"That is good to know. Allow me to bring you up to date on what we've been doing," Leo said in accented but perfect English, his voice deep and serious. "Our teams completed a thorough search of the resort—the rooms, suites, bungalows, and the staff accommodations. We haven't found Avery. We're fairly confident she isn't here, though we can't rule out the possibility."

The Jennings looked crestfallen as they listened. Jennifer's skin was as pale as any corpse.

"We've searched the surrounding resort and beach areas, using volunteers to cover more ground, and we'll keep that up," Vince added, his English even smoother and less accented than his colleague's. "We have a tracking dog coming tomorrow morning. That's the soonest we had one available."

"Meanwhile, is someone monitoring your phones at your house, in case someone calls you?" Leo asked Tom.

"We don't have a landline. Only our cell phones," Tom said. "And what do you mean by 'in case someone calls?' Are you talking about a ransom call?"

"Yes," Leo said. "It's possible. If that happens, they will tell you not to notify or involve the police or the feds. Do not listen to them. You tell us anyway. We can help you."

"Yes," Victoria said, emphasizing Leo's advice.

"Of course. Of course," Tom said, and Jennifer nodded in agreement beside him.

"We will do all we can to find her, to find out what happened to her, but if someone has her and wants money from you, the safest thing is usually to pay," Leo told them. "We can try to get the money back later, once your daughter is safe."

"We should get the cash together, right? Just in case," Jennifer said to her husband. "We could borrow from your business accounts, couldn't we?"

Rivera shot the Jennings a warning look, telling them to cut off that discussion immediately. Victoria caught it, but the Jennings did not.

"Um, we can get a line of credit on the house," Tom said, rubbing his forehead and staring at the office wall as he thought. "And we could borrow some from our retirement account. That should get us to a hundred thousand, maybe?"

"Huh? What if that's not enough?" Jennifer asked. "Can't you get—"

"We can help you with that later," Victoria said, cutting her off before anyone heard more information on how much cash the Jennings could access.

"They might only ask for a few thousand," Vince said.

Victoria didn't think so. Not after taking the risk of abducting someone from a resort like Azure Cove, where most of the guests had deep pockets. But she didn't voice her opinion. It wasn't the time or place.

"So...you think we might get a ransom call?" Jennifer asked, looking from Leo to Vince and back to Leo. "Is that what this situation looks like to you? I mean, did you hear or see something that makes you think that could happen?"

"I don't know what it looks like yet," Leo said. "It's possible."

"But we can't just wait," Tom said. "What can we be doing until then?"

"We won't be waiting, don't worry. We'll continue to do all we can to find her," Leo said. All eyes were on him as he cleared his throat. "We need to consider all possibilities. Can you think of any reason your daughter might have wanted to stay in Mexico rather than go home with her friends?"

"No," Tom blurted. "None."

Leo kept staring at Tom. Waiting. Victoria got the sense the Federales knew something that she did not.

Tom clenched his jaw. "I said no. Definitely not. She had to get back to school. It's her last semester. She has so many reasons to be back in Virginia right now and no reason to stay."

"I apologize if this is upsetting," Leo said. "But we need to know everything there is to know to help us find your daughter. And her friend gave us some conflicting information."

"What friend?" Jennifer snapped. "What are you talking about?"

Leo took out a notepad and flipped a few pages over before answering. "Haley. Her friend Haley."

Whatever the Federales were about to reveal, Haley hadn't mentioned anything about it to Payton, Victoria, or the Jennings. What had Haley held back from them?

"When did you talk to Haley?" Tom asked.

"I spoke to her yesterday," Vince answered. "From what she told me...it's possible Avery made up the story about testing positive for Covid. Adding to that possibility...no one else can confirm what happened."

Jennifer leaned forward and glared at Vince. "This is bullshit."

Tom held out a hand, either to quiet his wife or comfort her. Victoria wasn't sure which. "What about the man Brie saw? You heard her describe him. He's the one who took my daughter somewhere. He must have."

"We don't know who he is," Vince said.

Victoria held back on mentioning that Teresa claimed to see the man. She didn't want to get the Jennings' hopes up if Teresa was mistaken.

Tom's face reddened. "Just because you can't find him doesn't mean he doesn't exist. Why would Avery want to stay here? Give me one good reason."

"Haley said Avery found out who her birth mother was. She said that's one reason Avery wanted to come to Mexico on this trip. Her birth mother has family here."

"That's *not* what happened," Jennifer said, glaring at the police officers.

"No. No." Tom shook his head. "We've never hid her ancestry from her. Avery has always known her birth mother's identity. If she wanted to locate her biological family, we would have helped her. We would have come down with her. She knows that. She wouldn't keep us in the dark. She wouldn't make up a story and leave the resort by herself. There's just no way."

"Perhaps," Leo said, jumping in to support his colleague, who was taking the brunt of the Jennings' frustration. "Or perhaps not. If you want to find your daughter...we should explore that route and any others. Can you get in touch with her birth family?"

Tom and Jennifer looked at each other before Jennifer replied, "Yes. We can and we will. But we're not going to find her there. You have to keep looking."

"That's exactly what we are doing," Leo said before turning to the resort's manager. "Any good news from your IT department on the security video? Were they able to produce any useful footage? Were they able to produce any?"

"Yes. They were," Alejandro answered, tapping his laptop. "It's limited, but it's from a camera in front of the resort. Near the entrance. It shows everyone coming and going."

"Um, we shouldn't all watch it together," Victoria said, thinking there might be something the Jennings shouldn't see.

"Let's watch it now. Together," Leo said, looking at Avery's parents to confirm they wanted to watch. "Show us Sunday evening."

"I already downloaded the footage on my laptop." Alejandro scooted his chair in and began tapping on his keyboard. The others got up and gathered behind him as he opened an app, clicked on a dated folder, and pressed play. Images appeared on his screen. A view of the entrance road just beyond the front lobby. Few resort guests arrived late in the evening or left late at night, so there wasn't much to see. Alejandro sped it up, returning to regular speed each time a person or vehicle came into view. Several service vehicles and staff vehicles came and went, along with a few taxis. A group of guests left with their suitcases.

"Wait!" Jennifer sprung toward the screen. "That's Avery!"

In the video footage, a man and a woman walked away from the resort, traveling a few yards together before disappearing onto a trail. The couple was visible from the back and only for a few seconds. The woman had a trim, athletic shape, with dark hair and a scarf or shawl wrapped around her shoulders. Just before they went out of sight behind the bamboo forest, the woman reached for the man's hand.

"You're sure that's Avery?" Victoria asked.

"Yes. It's her. I don't recognize what she's wearing, but she could have bought something new or borrowed it from one of her friends."

"Do you think it's your daughter?" Leo asked Tom.

Tom looked at his wife, then leaned closer to Alejandro's laptop. "I think so."

"It's her. I'm sure of it." Jennifer hadn't taken her eyes off the images on the screen. "Who is she with? He's wearing the resort's uniform."

Alejandro rewound the video and played it again. "I think that's Henri. One of our entertainment staff employees. He's in charge of water sports."

"Haley mentioned Henri when I spoke with her," Victoria said. "That there might have been some mutual interest."

"We have to find him," Jennifer said. "He might know where she is. He might have her."

Leo turned to the manager. "Where do we find Henri?"

Alejandro's face tightened. Everyone backed up as he pushed his chair away from his desk and said, "I'll take you to him."

"We're coming with you," Jennifer said.

"I'm not sure that's such a good idea," Rivera said at exactly the same time Leo answered, "That's fine. You can come along."

CHAPTER 14

Forming a short procession, the manager led the way to the water sports area, followed by the Jennings and the Federales, with Victoria and Rivera taking up the rear. When they reached the pool, guests stopped chatting, looked up from books and magazines, and watched them pass.

"Did you find her yet?" a woman asked, peeking out from under a large colorful sun hat on one of the chaise lounges.

Alejandro stopped to answer her. "No. Not yet. Thank you for asking. Please do let us know if you have any information. You can call the front desk or come to my office."

Leo handed the guest a business card.

The group had to walk single file on a boardwalk with guests coming from the opposite direction. When the path widened, Leo began a conversation with Tom Jennings and Vince fell into step beside Victoria. He was a handsome man in his mid or late twenties.

"I apologize if our questions in there seemed heartless," he told her. "I assure you we're not."

"I understand," Victoria answered. "There can't be any secrets and we need to explore all possibilities, or we might waste time going off in the wrong direction."

"Exactly," he said. "Believe me, we want to find out what happened to Avery Jennings. We want to find her and bring her home to her family. Maybe this Henri is the person who will help us do that." They walked a few more strides before he asked, "Where do you live in America?"

"Virginia. Near Washington D.C."

"Ah, I've been there. You enjoy working for the FBI?'

"What we do…it's important to me." She wouldn't continue otherwise. Thanks to a trust from her grandfather, earning an income wasn't essential. But finding Avery and sparing other families from what Victoria had been through…that was critical.

"What does your husband think of your job?" Vince asked, breaking through Victoria's inner reflections.

"I don't have a husband. I have a boyfriend. And I think he's proud of me. But he worries," Victoria said, surprising herself by disclosing the information, but also realizing that she and Rivera might gain a better working relationship with the Federales if they got to know them and established some trust. "What about you?" she asked. "Does your wife or your family worry about you?"

"Not married," he said. "My mother worries more than enough."

Victoria smiled. "I get it. Have you worked a missing person case before?"

"Yes. I have."

"Alejandro mentioned that no one has ever gone missing from Azure Cove before. Have any women disappeared from nearby resorts?"

"Not from Azure Cove, but thousands of Mexican women have disappeared or gotten murdered over the last few years. Poor ones usually. One of them was my sister."

"Oh, I'm so sorry. Was it...recently?"

"Six years ago. She was sixteen when it happened. I was eighteen. My family never saw her again. It's a problem here, and we know it. But not usually for tourists. Especially not at resorts like Azure Cove." He opened one arm, addressing the opulence of the property.

"Is that why you joined the police force?" Victoria asked. "Because of your sister?"

"Yes. What we do. It's also important to me." He smiled slightly and appeared shy for a moment as he nearly quoted her.

Victoria understood how the thing he couldn't control, the thing that made him feel most helpless and frustrated, possibly the single worst event in his life, had driven him to his occupation. She and Vince had that in common.

"Two more locals went missing in the past three weeks," Vince said. "Two young women. We found one yesterday. Well...we didn't find her. A fishing trawler hauled her in with a catch. She was dead."

"Do you know how she died, or who is responsible?" Victoria asked.

"No. No one saw anything, and she obviously can't tell us. We don't know her exact cause of death, but we do know that she was tortured before she died. She had missing body parts. Someone had cut off her ear. It must have been hell for her."

"That's terrible," Victoria said, imagining what the poor woman had endured and thinking there were far too many evil sickos in the world. She hoped Avery hadn't encountered one of them.

The walkway came to an intersection with a path running parallel to the beach and a café with a sign that read *Surfside Snacks*. Jennifer broke away from the group and rushed toward three women who were waiting at the counter. One woman had black hair pulled back in a bun. Jennifer grabbed her by the shoulder and shouted, "Avery!"

The woman spun around, wide-eyed. A frosty pink concoction spilled over the sides of her martini glass and down her arm. "What the...?"

"Oh. I'm sorry. I thought...I thought you were my daughter," Jennifer said.

The woman scowled, said, "Yeah, well, I'm not," and pivoted back to the bar.

Jennifer returned to twisting the strap of her bag as she rejoined the others.

After witnessing the interaction, Victoria began to doubt Jennifer's ability to think clearly and accurately identify her daughter. Was Jennifer so desperate that she'd simply seen what she wanted to see in the video footage earlier? In any case, having the parents so closely involved with the ongoing investigation was a mistake. If Victoria was in charge, it would not be happening.

Farther down the path, they came to the water sports pavilion, a structure with a hexagon-shaped roof, open to the air on all sides. A row of brightly colored kayaks and paddleboards lay on the sand. Catamarans and Sunfish with striped sails waited on the beach by the water's edge.

Alejandro approached one of the employees there. "Hola, Miguel. We're looking for Henri."

Miguel, another fit and attractive staff member with a deep tan, stopped dipping life jackets into a trough of soapy water and looked up. "Uh, I'm not sure Henri is here. I think he's on break."

"Never mind. I see him," the manager said, focusing on a blond man holding the ropes of a Sunfish at the water's edge. "That's Henri," he told Leo. "But wait a minute. We seem to be attracting a lot of attention here.

If possible...perhaps just one person could walk down there and question him."

Leo turned to Vince and Victoria. "The two of you. Find out what he has to say. We'll wait over here."

Grateful for the offer and the extension of Leo's trust, Victoria walked with Vince toward the ocean, where Henri was busy pulling the sailboat farther from the water. He didn't see them approaching.

"Henri?" Victoria asked.

"Yes. What can I do for you?" The young man spoke with an endearing French accent. He turned, dropping the boat's rope into the sand, and flashed a charming smile. It quickly disappeared as his eyes went to Vince. "You're here about Avery Jennings, aren't you?"

"Yes," Victoria answered, making introductions.

"Is that...are those her parents?" Henri asked, glancing toward the pavilion. Even from a distance, Jennifer's glare was unmistakable and aimed squarely at him.

"Yes. They flew in today to look for her," Victoria said, deciding not to mention the security video yet and hoping Vince wouldn't either. "We wanted to talk to you because one of Avery's friends said you and she might have a thing."

Henri shook his head. "No. That's not...no. Not at all. There was no *thing* between us. I talked to her a few times, maybe. Took her on one of the Sunfish and tried to teach her how to sail. Signed her out with a paddleboard once or twice."

"There wasn't any involvement beyond paddleboarding?" Vince asked. "You didn't flirt with each other?"

Henri crossed his arms. "I flirt with everyone. The guests' needs are our highest priority," he said, in a way that conveyed the motto was the resort's rather than his own. "I'm supposed to make them feel special. But that's all.

I didn't spend more time with Avery than I did with any other guest who comes out to do water sports. We're not supposed to have—," he seemed to search for the right word and came up with, "—relationships with guests." Henri glanced away and looked down at his sand-covered feet with that last sentence.

"Were you with a woman on Sunday night?" Vince asked, possibly trying to trap Henri in a lie.

Henri moved his foot from side to side, digging it into the sand. "No...I didn't have to work Sunday night. I wasn't at the resort at the time people say Avery had disappeared."

"That's odd." Vince remained patient, staring at Henri, prolonging the mounting tension that was making Henri look increasingly more uncomfortable.

"Why is that odd?" Henri asked, scratching the side of his neck.

"We saw a security video of you leaving the resort on Sunday night with a woman who looked a lot like Avery," Vince said. "You were holding her hand. You led her into the bushes."

"Oh." Henri dropped his hand from his neck and twisted the top button of his polo shirt.

"Why are you lying to us?" Vince's voice rose as he reached for Henri's arm.

Henri jumped back at the same time Victoria became aware of Jennifer Jennings running toward them, shouting, "Where is she? Where is my daughter?"

Her husband chased after her, yelling, "Jennifer, stop!"

Jennifer fell against Henri, either intentionally or due to a last second stumble, and grabbed his shirtsleeve. "Where is Avery? What did you do with her?"

"Whoa, Jennifer, please let go of him," Victoria said, prying Jennifer away from the startled employee.

Tom had reached them. He took hold of his wife's shoulders and pulled her back as Vince gripped Henri's arm and pulled him in a different direction, saying, "You're coming with us. You have some things to clear up if you want us to believe you."

A young couple carrying a kayak between them had stopped to stare at the escalating scene. On the other side of the sailboats, a man held up his phone and appeared to film the encounter. Exactly the type of attention the authorities, and especially the manager, had hoped to avoid.

Back at the pavilion, a woman's shouts rose above the others. "Hey! What's going on?" In a graceful show of athleticism, she leaped from the top step of the pavilion into the sand and ran across the beach toward them. She wore skin-tight red shorts and a colorful sleeveless top that left her midriff bare. A single braid trailed from the back of her head. She stopped in front of Vince with her hands on her hips. "Henri didn't do anything!"

"Please, step away," Victoria told her, reading the nametag pinned to the woman's top, which said Nicole.

"But he didn't do anything," Nicole said. "He was with me on Sunday night. We left the resort together and were with each other until the morning. In my room."

"And someone can confirm this?" Victoria asked, studying Nicole. There was no denying she looked like a match for the woman in the video.

"Yes. Definitely. The people on either side of my room can vouch for us. I'll give you their names. I promise, Henri has nothing to do with Avery's disappearance."

"Why didn't you tell us who you were with?" Vince asked, releasing the young man's arm.

"Uh, because we're not supposed to, you know..." Henri glanced back at the manager, who was watching from the pavilion, rubbing a hand through his hair.

"Did you know Avery?" Jennifer asked Nicole. "She's my daughter. Did you know her?"

"Yes." Nicole took a deep breath and turned to face Avery's parents. "I knew Avery. She came to my Zumba class every day. We talked for a bit. She told me she lived...I mean...she lives in Virginia. She's a really nice person. I'm so sorry that she's missing. Yesterday and this morning, I helped search for her. I really hope you find her."

"Did you notice anyone paying particular attention to Avery during her vacation?" Victoria asked Nicole.

"No. I didn't notice anything unusual, or I would have said something to the police for sure. And I didn't recognize the person they say was last with her. But I don't think you're looking for anyone who works here. The staff are the nicest, hardest working people you'll meet. All of them."

"I'm sure they are," Victoria said.

"Actually, Avery had a little problem with Teresa before one of my classes," Nicole said.

"I heard she was in Teresa's spot in class, is that what you're referring to?" Victoria asked.

"Yes," Nicole answered. "I'm surprised you knew that. But it's not unusual. Teresa seems to have issues with everyone. I don't even know why I brought it up. I was just now remembering Avery looking a little shocked at the time. I guess that's all it was."

"We never know what might turn out to be useful information," Victoria said. "If you remember anything else that might be helpful, please let one of us know immediately." She handed her own business cards to Nicole and Henri. "Thank you," she said, before walking back to the pavilion behind the Jennings.

"I should take one of your cards," Vince said, falling into step alongside Victoria. "So we can communicate."

Victoria handed him one, and he was sliding the card into his pocket when ahead of them, Jennifer broke away from her husband and marched straight to Miguel, the young employee who was still busy washing the life jackets.

"Please, have you seen my daughter?" Jennifer stopped in front of Miguel and held up a picture of Avery.

Holding a dripping jacket in each hand, Miguel gave her his full attention. "No. I'm really sorry. I don't know what happened to your daughter."

"What about a man with a tattoo of a crown and heart on his arm? He was wearing one of the blue polo shirts." Desperation rang out in Jennifer's voice as she moved closer. "He had a black cap. Thick eyebrows. Muscular like a boxer or someone who works out a lot."

Miguel took a step back and stumbled over the edge of the pavilion, falling into the sand. Even though he was lying on his backside looking a little stunned, Jennifer persisted, now showing him a copy of the photo Brie had drawn. "Do you know who this man is? Do you know anyone who fits that description?"

Miguel spent several seconds staring at the drawing. "No. I don't. I don't know who that is," he finally answered, getting to his feet and brushing sand off his legs.

"Show me your arm," Jennifer demanded.

"Hey, hey," Rivera said gently, trying to draw Jennifer's attention away. She remained intensely focused on Miguel.

Looking unsettled by the entire encounter, Miguel hesitated before rolling up his sleeve.

Jennifer grabbed his wrist and rotated it, scanning his arm. There were no markings on his skin. "What about your other arm?"

Miguel peeled his shirt over his head and turned a slow circle with his arms raised. "I don't have any tattoos,"

Victoria appreciated the patience Miguel demonstrated, which came at the expense of his own dignity.

"I'm sorry," Tom told Miguel. "We're just...our daughter is missing."

"I know. It's okay," Miguel said. "I hope she's all right. I hope you find her."

"Thank you, Miguel," Alejandro said, stepping between him and the Jennings. "I understand how upset you both are," he told them. "But you can't...you can't go around assaulting guests and staff."

Clasping Jennifer's arm, Victoria led her away from the pavilion.

Leo said something to Tom, who looked almost as shaken as his wife, though he was still holding it together. Back on the path, he took over for Victoria, wrapping his arms around Jennifer. "She needs some rest. She hasn't slept in almost 48 hours. We'll be in our room," he said, looking from the agents to the Federales to the manager. "Please...let us know as soon as you hear anything or find anything. Please."

Victoria understood their torment. Her heart ached for the Jennings as they trudged away on the boardwalk. Yet she would never have allowed them to be present while interviewing potential suspects. For so many reasons, it was not a good idea.

"You've talked to all the guests and the staff. Perhaps you should be looking somewhere else now," Alejandro said to Leo.

"This is our investigation," Leo answered. "We decide where to look and when."

"I know. I just meant…never mind. I apologize. It's been a difficult few days. Avery's disappearance has consumed my every waking moment." Alejandro clasped one hand over the other and cracked his knuckles. "Continue to do whatever you need to do. Please. And Azure Cove will help every way we can."

"I want to let you all know that I'm meeting with one of the guests at six," Victoria said. "Someone who says she saw the man with the tattoo."

Alejandro widened his eyes. "Who?"

"Teresa."

"Oh. Good luck," Alejandro answered. "You'll get an earful about what we need to improve on here. And I'm not joking when I tell you that if she said don't be late, don't be a minute late. Although…don't expect her to operate by the same set of rules and don't take it personally if she doesn't show just to prove how important she is…in her own mind."

CHAPTER 15

Wired from a steady flow of caffeine, Payton leaned close to her laptop screen. One knee bobbed up and down beneath her newish dining room table which, to her chagrin, had been used primarily for work and not once yet for entertaining. Her current case was her biggest and most important since she'd been promoted within the FBI's financial crimes department, and she was determined to see it through to a successful finish. Though she'd never met anyone from the Salazar Cartel face to face, the more familiar she became with their business practices, the more they frightened her. The FBI and the DA's office needed to nail this case down tight. For weeks, nothing was more important to her than seeing the cartel leaders get sent to prison...that is until Avery disappeared. Payton's personal family tragedy had certainly put her work life in perspective. Her niece's situation consumed her thoughts, relegating the cartel case to second position.

Unfortunately for Payton, the Salazar Cartel's attorneys had unlimited manpower and resources. Keeping up with them challenged the FBI's already overworked team. To make things worse, the judge presiding over the case had pushed the initial hearing forward a day and instructed Payton and the prosecuting attorneys to prepare their findings in a different format.

Rather than traveling to Mexico to be with her family, searching for her niece, Payton had spent the day reworking spreadsheets and decks with her exhausted team. At least she'd managed to carve out an hour of time to go through photos of the resort's guests with Brie. If only that effort had delivered better results rather than leading nowhere. Brie had recognized none of the guests as the man who presumably took Avery.

Payton's personal phone buzzed, causing the dining room table to vibrate. Her brother's name lit up her phone screen. Payton grabbed the device. In her haste, it slipped through her fingers and tumbled to the floor. She kneeled to scoop it up and was still on one knee when she answered with, "Have you found her?"

"No. Not yet."

"I'm so sorry I can't be there with you. But I will soon." She didn't like the way her words came out; the way they implied Avery's missing status might continue indefinitely. That was the last thing she wanted and could barely stand to even consider the possibility. "How is Jennifer holding up?"

"This is tough on her. She practically assaulted one of the resort's employees earlier today. It wasn't pretty. I'm in another room right now, but I think she's finally resting." Tom sighed and Payton could picture him scrunching up his face and running his hand through his thick hair, something he'd done when frustrated ever since they were kids. Though his current emotional state went far beyond frustration now. As far as Payton knew, he'd never faced a situation like this before.

"Are Victoria and Rivera with you?" Payton asked. Ever since she and Rivera started dating, she'd looked forward to eventually introducing him to her family. This wasn't how she had ever imagined it happening, but she was grateful he was in Mexico, helping to find Avery.

"They were earlier. Listen, Payton, I might need to borrow some money from you. For Avery."

"Why?" Her mind raced through possibilities. "Did you get a ransom call?"

"No. We still don't know what happened. But in case...the thing is...my business is...I'm having some financial problems right now. Jennifer doesn't know. And I won't tell her until this is over. Until we find Avery."

"Oh, I understand." The news of her brother's financial difficulties surprised Payton. They had running jokes about his "easy" money and his lucrative business compared to her government salary.

"The police said if that's what we're dealing with, it's best for Avery's sake to pay. It hasn't happened, but I have to make sure we're prepared if it does."

"Of course I can help," Payton said. "How much...well, I guess you don't know that. I have savings and I can borrow from my retirement fund, use the home equity line. Don't worry. We'll have money if they ask. Just make sure that if someone contacts you, you let the agents and the Mexican police know immediately."

"I know. I will."

"Okay. We'll find her, Tom. I know we will."

"She's been missing for over two days, Payton. I...I don't know what to do."

"Let the police and FBI do their jobs. Tell them anything you can think of that might help. Make sure they don't overlook anything, no matter how small. That's all we can do right now. Just...hang in there, Tom."

If only there was something more that would bring Avery safely home immediately. Payton wouldn't hesitate to do whatever it took.

CHAPTER 16

A zure Cove's most luxurious accommodations were on the opposite side of the resort from the agents' rooms and farthest from the stage area where the nightly entertainment and dance parties occurred. Their seclusion came with peace and quiet. Each had a balcony and a small rooftop pool overlooking the ocean.

Victoria was a few yards short of the bungalow where Avery's parents were staying when Rivera asked, "When we were on our way to find Henri earlier today, was Vince hitting on you?"

"No," she was quick to answer. "He was just being friendly. Professional networking maybe. He seems like a nice guy. Might have gotten a little aggressive with Henri when we were questioning him, but nothing unreasonable. He's worked missing persons cases before. Lots of them. But when I asked him how those cases ended up, he didn't give me a lot of hope. His own sister went missing, never to be seen again. The odds seem to be against any woman who disappears here."

"Let's do our best to help him improve on his stats," Rivera said before resuming his walk to the Jennings' bungalow. He stepped up to the door and knocked. "Looked like he was hitting on you, though."

Before Victoria could disagree, Jennifer met them at the door and raised her brows, looking from one agent to the other. "Any news?"

"No. We came to check in with you," Rivera said, and Jennifer's face fell with his response.

She led them into the spacious white bungalow with large windows overlooking the ocean. Thick white throw rugs warmed the marble floors. A large vase filled with exotic flowers graced the coffee table. The resort appeared to have spared nothing in selecting the exquisite décor.

"It's beautiful in here," Victoria said.

"It might be, but we're in no mood to appreciate it," Jennifer responded. "The resort put us in here and comped it. A perk of having your only child disappear at Azure Cove." She let out a sharp laugh that gave Victoria more reason to worry about how she was holding up.

Tom came out of a bedroom holding his phone. "Hey. I've got Payton on the line. She wants to hear what you two have to say." He put his phone on speaker and set it down on the coffee table. The agents said hello as they gathered closer.

"What do you think after meeting with the Federales?" Payton asked. "Are they doing everything they should do?"

"They're very organized," Victoria answered. "They've done a lot already." She didn't mention that it had been a terrible mistake to allow Tom and Jennifer to be so involved with an active investigation.

"They haven't staked out their territory or any of that crap," Rivera added. "They've welcomed our help. And as far as we can tell, the resort's management is also communicating openly with us. They had issues with their security cameras, and I got confirmation from Azure Cove's parent company and IT group that what the manager told us about the camera system was true. The entire system was malfunctioning prior to Avery's disappearance."

"Still, that doesn't mean they aren't hiding something," Payton said.

"True, but they don't act like they are. In fact, I'm surprised they don't have attorneys here blocking the exchange of information or preventing anyone from speaking with us," Rivera said.

"Yet we still haven't found the guy who might have taken her," Payton said.

"We've got the tracking dog coming tomorrow morning," Victoria said, making sure she sounded positive.

Payton sighed. "Good. Good. Well, on my end, two of our interns compiled photos of all the resort's guests. I went through them one by one with Brie."

Jennifer's body tensed and she gripped her husband's arm.

"She didn't recognize any of them," Payton finished.

"She's sure?" Jennifer asked.

"Yes. She seemed positive. We went through the images twice."

"So if he's not a guest, and he doesn't work here, who is he?" Jennifer asked as she rolled the bottom hem of her shirt into a tiny tube of fabric. "Just a random stranger who came out of nowhere and told my daughter she had to quarantine? It doesn't make sense. I just don't understand why no one saw her when she left with him. It's like she disappeared into thin air. How is that possible? With this place being so private, so exclusive, shouldn't that make it easier to notice something suspicious? Like a girl being carried off against her will?"

"We don't even know that's what happened," Tom sank onto the couch and dropped his head into his hands. "We don't know."

"Avery wouldn't leave the resort without telling someone. There's no way she would do that. I know she wouldn't." Jennifer shook her head, not bothering to wipe her tears away.

Everyone was quiet for a few seconds, giving Victoria time to own the frustration she felt, to harness its energy and let it drive her. It was still early in the investigation, but those early hours mattered the most. They didn't just want to find Avery. They needed to find her alive and well.

Jennifer broke the silence, her eyes blazing through her tears. "I can't do this. I can't. I have to know where she is. We have to find her."

"I know," Victoria said, lowering her voice and taking Jennifer's hand. "I know what you're going through."

On a fall day over ten years ago, Victoria slung her backpack over one shoulder, said goodbye to her friends in the dining hall, and headed to class. Though the leaves were a blazing mixture of red, orange, and yellow, the weather was unseasonably warm, and she'd tied her sweatshirt around her waist. Her biggest concern was her upcoming physics exam. She hated physics. She'd selected it to fulfill her science requirement anyway, embracing the concept that one should face their weaknesses head on and turn them into strengths. Great idea in theory. In reality—not so pleasant. But Victoria wasn't a quitter, and she was determined to tough it out. After an entire weekend spent studying in groups and alone, she was ready to prove she had mastered the painful material.

A ringing came from inside the front pocket of her backpack. She kept walking as she swung her bag around and pulled out her phone. "Hey, Dad. Perfect timing. I've got a seven-minute walk to physics. I've got an exam. Wish me luck."

"You have to come home, Tori," he said. No hello. No, how is your day going?

"Huh?" Victoria frowned. "When?"

"Right now."

Her first reaction included disbelief and defiance. "I can't. I told you, I've got an exam in a few minutes and a paper due on Friday. I'm right in the middle of so many things." She managed a quick smile as she waved to a friend from her foreign affairs class and headed up the hill behind the dormitories. "What's going on?"

"Just trust me now and I'll tell you more soon. I sent a car. The driver should be there in twenty minutes. He'll call you with the code phrase. Your brother and I are on our way home from the lake house. I need you home where we can protect you. Don't worry about your schoolwork. Once you're safe, I'll call the University and let them know the situation."

He'd told her just enough to frighten her. An icy chill ran through her body as she kept trekking up the hill toward the physics building. "What situation? What happened?"

"Your mother is missing."

Victoria imagined her mother went hiking in the woods, something she did with their dogs nearly every day, and hadn't returned home as expected. Maybe she'd sprained an ankle, broken her leg. "Where is she? I mean, where was she?"

"We don't know." Her father let out a heavy sigh.

"Dad, what aren't you telling me?"

"Tori, your mother was abducted. I received a ransom call. I didn't want to scare you, but I also need you to take this seriously and apparently you have to know what happened to cooperate. Once we're together, we'll try to piece together all the information we have. But please, head to the front of campus right now and wait in an open area with other people around. Be alert. Don't get in the car with anyone unless they give you the codes."

Victoria stopped walking. His words didn't immediately register. When they did, she had even more questions. "Do you know who has her?"

"No."

"Are you going to pay them? Will that get her back?"

"Yes. I will pay them whatever they want. Tori, listen to me, I need you to go to the front of campus and wait for the car."

"But my exam," she said, though she had no intention of taking the test now. As if she could focus on magnetic flux after the news he'd delivered.

"You'll have to make it up. You need to be somewhere you're protected as soon as possible."

"I can't...I have to go to my room and get my computer and some things I need."

"I'll stay on the phone with you while you do that. Do not stop to talk to anyone. Get your things quickly and get back outside to wait for the call from your driver. Follow the procedure."

"Okay. I'm going." Victoria switched direction and hurried to her room. "Can you tell me what you know?"

"There isn't much. Your brother and I went to the lake house with the dogs last night. Your mother had a meeting. She was supposed to join us this morning. I never heard from her, and today I received a ransom call. The FBI is already working to find her."

"How? What will they do?"

"Let's all pray they'll do whatever it takes."

Inside her dorm room, while asking more questions her father couldn't answer, Victoria grabbed a suitcase and threw in some clothes, then stuffed books and notebooks into her backpack. She left a note for her roommate on their shared memo board saying she had to leave school for a family emergency. She was looking around the room, trying to decide what else she might need to do before she left, when a message came from the driver.

Uncle Jack is waiting for you.

"The car is here," she told her father.

"Good. Go straight there. Let me know once you're in the car."

Before responding, she mentally reviewed the procedures created for her family in the event of an emergency exactly such as this.

She typed: *Who else is with you?*

He responded: *Jasper. It's his birthday.*

How old is he?

He'll be nine at three this afternoon.

Okay.

He sent the car's plate number and his location.

She forwarded the information to her father, who confirmed it. Then she hurried to meet the driver at the front of campus. A man with movie-star good looks waited for her by the back door of a black limousine. He wore jeans, a dark coat, and sunglasses. She'd never seen him before, but knew his skills went beyond driving. He could protect her if necessary. Normally, the chauffeured limousine's presence would embarrass her. But right then, she was too worried about her mother to care what anyone else thought about her.

She checked the license plate before getting inside. When the driver pulled into traffic, Victoria called her father again. "I'm in the car and headed home. Have you heard anything?"

"No. Not yet. My other line is ringing. It's a private investigator. I have to go. I'll see you soon. Be careful. Do what the driver says. I love you, Tori."

"I love you, too. They'll find mom. They have to. It's going to be okay."

Victoria tried calling her mother several times, hoping there had been some terrible misunderstanding. Maybe the ransom call was someone's sick idea of a joke, and her mother was fine. Victoria imagined her mother answering with, "Tori, why on earth did you call me so many times? You know there isn't always service in the mountains. I'm fine." But the phone only rang and rang before going to voicemail.

The ride from Georgetown to Victoria's home took three hours, but it felt much longer. She called her father every twenty minutes or so to ask if he'd heard anything. The answer was always no.

"What are they doing to find her?" Victoria asked.

"Everything they can, Tori."

Victoria's anxiety grew. She could no longer breathe normally. She rolled her window down and gulped in the cool air.

"Are you okay?" the driver asked. "I'm not supposed to stop unless it's an emergency."

"I'm fine. Thank you," Victoria answered from the backseat, twisting her hands and feeling so helpless she might throw up.

"Who took her mother? Where was she? Was the FBI going to find her?" The waiting and not knowing was killing her.

CHAPTER 17

Tony didn't know her name, but she'd been pretty when she first came on board. Not anymore. Blotches mottled her skin. Red veins riddled her sunken eyes. Once Eric got going on her, she'd been more than willing to take all the heroin she could get to dull her pain. The drug delivered on that count, but unfortunately for her, it did nothing to fight infection. Raw stumps festered where her toes should have been. Puss oozed from the ugly scab that used to be her ear.

With a grunt of disgust, Tony heaved the girl's body over the side railing. She hit the ocean with a giant splash and disappeared beneath the roiling sea. He didn't have to finish the job Eric had started. It was easier to dump her overboard and let the sharks do the work.

For days, the girl had begged and cried to get off the yacht. Well, she'd just gotten her wish. Tony wanted off, too. More than anything. But not like that.

Most of the time, the yacht barely felt as if it was moving. It had multiple sun decks, eight guest cabins, a separate living area for the crew, and an entertainment area where Eric melded with the couch and his video game console, wearing his headset, and randomly shouting in either victory or defeat. The semi-custom yacht also provided plentiful compartments for hiding things they didn't want found.

Despite the luxury and practicality of the accommodations, Tony couldn't shake the awful feeling of being stuck in the middle of the ocean with four other guys, because that was exactly the situation. Staying below deck made him claustrophobic. Above, seeing nothing but ocean in every direction freaked him out even more. He weighed two-hundred-fifty-three pounds—solid muscle—and he couldn't swim. If he somehow ended up in the water, he'd sink like a giant boulder. Like the girl he'd just thrown over. The thought made him laugh until he remembered what it felt like to drown. Humiliating. He was just a kid at a local YMCA. The family who took him along as their guest never even asked if he could swim. And it never occurred to Tony that he, of all people, physically strong and capable for as long as he could remember, couldn't do something simple that just about everyone else could do. How hard could swimming be?

Lots of kids from his school belonged to the YMCA. Many were there that day because it was a hot one. Following his friend, Tony cannonballed off the side of the pool into the deep end, discovering to his shock and horror, that not everyone can naturally swim.

He'd flailed his arms and kicked his feet but just kept sinking. His friend was splashing around right next to him, close enough for Tony to hear his laughter, but not close enough to grab him. Finally, when Tony's brain and lungs were fit to burst, he managed to get his mouth above the water long enough to gurgle out a scream for help.

A lifeguard pulled him out of the water and dragged him over the concrete edge of the pool, ending Tony's terror and cementing his shame. Everyone surrounded him—so many people, classmates and strangers—staring down as he choked and gasped for breath. Sputtering on the side of the pool, he'd lost the only thing he really had going for him back then. His sense of invincibility.

"What happened to Tony?" a kid from school asked. "Can't he swim?"

"He couldn't. Tony was drowning," someone else said. "He almost died."

Tony had never been so embarrassed and angry in his life and vowed he never would be again. He'd wanted nothing to do with pools, ponds, lakes, and especially not oceans. Yet here he was, relegated to the yacht. The only thing between him and sure death was the propensity of the yacht's glossy white, outer shell to stay afloat. He was stuck for who knew how long, safeguarding the boss's idiot son, and cleaning up his messes; the girl he'd just tossed overboard being one of them. Tony wiped his hands against his pants, then gripped the railing and let out a slow sigh. Someday, Eric would do something so stupid, no one could fix it, no matter how many hired guns or attorneys his father paid. As long as that didn't happen on Tony's watch, he didn't care. If Eric died, there would be one less fool in the world.

Over thirty yards away, a sleek yacht glided past in the open water. A beautiful woman in a red bikini and a gray-haired man with a paunch and man boobs waved to him from lounge chairs. Perhaps they wondered if Tony was a celebrity. Despite his hatred of being out in the ocean, he waved back with a sense of pride. For all they knew, the larger, more expensive yacht belonged to Tony. It didn't of course. It belonged to Eric's father, something Tony pointed out to everyone on board occasionally, lest Eric forget.

Just thinking about Eric ignited Tony's anger.

A noise came from behind him. Wearing aviator glasses, a shirtless Eric stood there staring at him.

For an instant, Tony felt caught, as if Eric could read his thoughts. Tony's whole body tensed, every muscle ready for action.

Eric wiped the side of his nose with the hand not holding his beer. He'd been snorting again. Heroin made him even more stupid, but also slowed him down and kept him quiet. He'd stop complaining and probably sleep for a few hours.

"She gone?" Eric asked.

"Yeah," Tony answered. "She's gone."

"Damn. I'm gonna miss her. But you know what they say. In with the new and out with the old, right?" Eric grinned, flashing impossibly white teeth and deepening his dimples. Chicks loved those dimples. They played into the whole idea of Eric the charmer. Someone who could show them a good time. How wrong they were.

"Listen to me, Eric. Don't touch the girl." Tony knew his tone had crossed a line into insubordination. But Eric was too drugged to notice.

Eric pinched his nose between his fingers. "But maybe after we do that thing. Once it's done, yeah?"

Tony shook his head. His hands were already balled into fists. "Don't touch her, Eric."

CHAPTER 18

Teresa Middleton, Azure Cove's most demanding extended-stay guest, settled against the caned-back chair. She wore a cardigan and had a blanket draped over her slender legs as she gazed out the glass walls of her sitting room at an unobstructed view of the ocean. Rolling her Caran d'Ache pen forward and back on the marble desktop, she contemplated the important matter at hand.

Young people these days...it was a wonder they survived to become adults at all. They took risks and made terrible decisions. They popped pills and had sex with near strangers, people they only just met and knew literally nothing about. With that knowledge in mind, Teresa fully expected the young lady who disappeared to reappear by now in a haze of embarrassment and apologies. But she hadn't.

No one could find Miss Avery Jennings, and no one claimed to know what happened. But someone knew. That person had kept his secret hidden so far. But Teresa understood all too well that secrets were only safe until the moment someone uncovered them, and if the authorities or anyone else dug deep enough, they would find what they were looking for.

She'd been thinking about Miss Jennings all day, long before the encounter with the American FBI agent on the veranda. Teresa had seen Avery's picture posted on the television screens next to the resort's daily schedule.

Teresa set her pen down and gripped her diamond, shifting it side to side as she often did while thinking.

What a tragedy it would be if Avery were never found. She was young and had her whole life ahead of her.

What sort of response would ensue if I disappeared?

Because the older you got, the less you mattered to the rest of the world, though Teresa didn't feel old or less significant than when she was younger. If anything, her sense of appreciation for herself had intensified.

An image appeared in her mind. Two girls, the spitting image of each other, in matching gingham dresses. Teresa and her twin sister, Cordelia. Her best friend and the only person who ever understood her.

What was the point of living so long just to be alone in the end? Not to mention the middle and the beginning...really the entirety of her life.

To make a difference? Yes—that was the point. Making a difference. Trying to help people take a little pride in their work and to be their best selves. They didn't always appreciate her advice, but that had never stopped her from trying. When she was gone and her remaining fortune went to dozens of charities, they'd want to thank her then, though it would be too late. But helping to find Avery...that could really matter right now.

As far as Teresa knew, no one recognized the person suspected of leaving with Avery. No one else had even seen him. But Teresa had. She paid attention to details, and details mattered. If only she could access them from her memory now. Where had she seen him? And what was it about him that bugged her? Because something did. Something more than the unattractive tattoo and his too-small shirt. She needed to remember and let the FBI woman know.

Teresa's mind wasn't what it used to be, despite Sudoko and crossword puzzles and the absolute healthiest diet one could maintain, but she was still sharper than most. Yet this specific, important memory eluded her.

Her alarm rang at 5:35 p.m. Time to head to the exercise pavilion and claim her front row spot. Consistency was important. Finding the best spot and owning it: center left by the water cooler in the yoga room, the corner breakfast table on the veranda, the quiet, shaded area of the beach beside the spa. Establishing her space required effort. With the guests coming and going, she had to start over so many times. She remembered her only interaction with Avery and it made her a little uncomfortable. Perhaps she'd caused more of a fuss than she should have.

Eventually she'd have to leave the resort and go back to Pennsylvania to clear up unpleasant matters and all of it will have been for naught. That's what her life had come down to—establishing her space and procrastinating about unpleasant matters.

Maybe the class would jog her memory. And wasn't it the truth that she often came upon the thing she needed to find only once she stopped searching?

Teresa pushed her orange and white headband over her hair and checked the mirror. She turned her head left, then right.

You might be lonely, but you can still be fabulous. Don't you worry...the truth will soon come to you.

CHAPTER 19

Tony dug his feet into the warm sand, grateful to be off the yacht, though his body hadn't completely adjusted. It still felt as if he was in the ocean, as if the ground swayed under him. Carrying his shoes, he strolled down the beach under the glare of the late afternoon sun, with a gun tucked against his back and a knife strapped to his lower leg. Always prepared.

The wristband his cousin gave him pinched his skin. The chip wasn't activated. He couldn't go into any of the rooms, but he could hang out around the bars and take all the drinks and food he wanted. Later, when the resort switched from relaxation to party mode, he'd blend into the crowd.

When he reached the blue flags marking the edge of Azure Cove's long stretch of beach, the swagger in Tony's step had returned.

Up ahead, his cousin trudged through the sand, carrying a paddleboard under each arm. Tony stopped to watch him, wondering when Miguel had learned to swim and sail so well that the resort considered him a water sports expert. Before or after Tony perfected the use of the AK-47?

Miguel's expression changed when he spotted Tony. No welcoming smile.

Something must have happened. Tony stopped in his tracks and didn't go any further down the beach. He reclined on a chair under the shade of a palm tree to wait for his cousin. The water sports pavilion appeared to be hopping. A hot blonde handed oars to a couple wearing long-sleeved swim shirts that reminded Tony of wetsuits. A blond dude chatted up some middle-aged women with flabby thighs.

A man drove past on a tractor, carrying seaweed off the beach. He pretended not to see Tony and Tony pretended not to see him, but he did note the man's silver watch with the blue face.

A break came in the flow of guests asking questions and signing out equipment at the water sports pavilion. The blonde chick sat down and chugged from a water bottle. Miguel finished hosing sand off the paddle-boards. Finally, he walked over to Tony, but didn't sit like Tony expected. In a low voice, he said, "Two American Feds are asking about someone who looks like you."

"Like me? What about me?"

"They're asking about someone who looks like a bodybuilder or a boxer. Italian or Mexican American. The guy they're looking for has a tattoo on his arm. A heart and crown."

Tony scrunched up his face. "That's not me. I don't have a tattoo like that, bro." He extended his bare arms to make the point.

"I'm missing one of my uniform shirts," Miguel said.

Tony shrugged. "And?"

Miguel glanced back at the water sports pavilion. "Did you come back to the resort on Sunday?"

"Nah. I was working."

Tony could tell his cousin was confused. He hadn't figured anything out, but he was suspicious and seemed to be searching for answers. Tony maintained his poker face.

"You said you're working in security?" Miguel asked.

"That's right. Private security."

"Sounds good. Well, I've got to get back to work," Miguel said. "You should get rid of that wristband because someone might notice. I don't want any trouble. I only have a few more weeks here, then they send me Turks and Caicos. Supposed to be really nice. Most beautiful water in the world. Maybe we can catch up there, okay?"

"Yeah, okay. Sorry, bro. But I didn't do anything." Family was family. They had each other's backs. Tony didn't want to mess up Miguel's job or the straight and narrow thing he had going for him.

"Yeah, I know you didn't." Miguel nudged Tony in the shoulder, then leaned closer and gave him a quick hug. He let go and said, "It was great to see you, Tony."

"You, too," Tony said. But Miguel was already walking away. He didn't look back.

The blond dude stared at them from the sports pavilion. Tony had the urge to smash the guy's face in, cut off his feathery blond hair and sever his neck. But not now. Not if people were already asking questions and searching for the girl. Tony needed to get back on the yacht. Shame, he was hoping to stay at Miguel's place again tonight and he might be in the area for a few more weeks.

Feeling angry and disappointed, Tony trudged back along the edge of the beach closest to the resort. He didn't expect a rogue wave to suck him under or anything like that, but the farther he could stay from the water, even if only for now, the better. He was nearing the blue flags when someone shouted, "Hey! You! Where are you going?"

The demands came from a woman wearing a tight pink outfit and an orange headband that reminded him of the shiny exercise clothes women wore decades ago. She was as old as his great grandmother, and as thin as his great grandmother was fat. Smooth skin pulled tight across her forehead and tiny veins rippled beneath it. Sharp collar bones jutted out below her neck.

Glaring, she waggled a bony finger in his direction. Something about her tone rubbed him the wrong way, pushed him to the brink of his frustration. She believed she had power over him. It wasn't physical, so it had to be about wealth. Her confidence probably came from a lifetime of bossing others around. People like her and Eric developed a false sense of comfort they didn't deserve.

There was no one else around. A thick hedge of flowering bushes shielded them from view. It would be so easy to wrap his hands around her scrawny neck and twist it. With minimal effort, he could crack her brittle bones, bringing an odd sense of satisfaction, like when he used to pop the bubble wrap that came in his boss's packages. Snapping her neck would put her in her place for good.

"You! Come over here," she said.

"Yes, ma'am." Still smiling, he stepped further into the shadow of the trees to meet her.

"I recognize you! I saw you after my Zumba class on Sunday," she said. "And that wasn't the first time. I just remembered where I saw you before. Saturday night, just right over there." She pointed to the beach. "With Avery Jennings and her friends."

The old lady was observant. But Tony didn't let that rattle him. He didn't miss a beat. "I think you have me mistaken for someone else, ma'am."

"Don't be smart with me. I know what I saw. Roll up your sleeves."

Feeling smug, Tony rolled his sleeves up, held out his arms, and flipped them over, just like he'd done for Miguel.

The old lady placed her hands on her skeletal hips and scowled at him. "I don't know what game you're playing, young man, but I'm not mistaken. I know what I saw. I'm meeting with an FBI agent in a few minutes. You better come with me and explain yourself."

He almost laughed aloud when she pivoted and walked away, expecting him to follow her.

Tony did just that.

CHAPTER 20

A t two minutes past six p.m., Victoria arrived at the Horizon Hut, one of the resort's casual outdoor restaurants. She located the beach-side patio's center table. A small placard atop the glass marked it reserved. She pulled out one of the chairs and settled in to appreciate the view.

Looking toward the ocean, palm trees tilted inward from each side of the beach, framing a beautiful, unobstructed view. Over the sparkling water, the sun was just dropping on the horizon, creating swaths of pink, orange, and lavender across the sky.

Victoria understood why Teresa preferred the spot. How nice it would be if Ned was there, seated across the table. Perhaps soon they could book a relaxing, long weekend getaway at a resort. Though it wouldn't shock her if they did and something wild happened. Through no fault of their own, their recent "vacations" had turned into spectacular disasters. First, a flight to London that crashed in the arctic. Then a trip to Boston for a wedding, which should have been fabulously romantic until Ned's best friend, the groom, didn't show. But maybe a resort vacation would finally allow them a peaceful trip.

A man wearing Azure Cove's blue polo shirt and khaki shorts approached the table, pulling Victoria's attention away from the gorgeous view.

"I'm sorry," he said, pointing to the placard. "This is a reserved table. If you wouldn't mind moving over to one of these empty ones..."

"I'm meeting Teresa here."

"Oh. Oh, good." The server's shoulders seemed to relax with his relief. "In that case, what can I get you?"

Victoria scanned the menu, which contained light-fare items and dozens of cocktails. It was eight minutes past six o'clock when she ordered a plate of fresh fruit and a fish taco with mango salsa. "I was a few minutes late," she told the server. "Teresa didn't show up and leave already, did she?"

"No. I haven't seen her yet. She usually gets here sometime between six and six-twenty. After that we usually stop holding the table for her. She doesn't always come."

"Thank you," Victoria said.

Out of curiosity, and to assess Teresa's credibility, Victoria did a quick Internet search for *Teresa Middleton, Pennsylvania.*

The most recent article containing Teresa's name was an obituary from two months ago.

Victoria looked up from her phone and scanned the cafe for Teresa before returning to the information.

Cordelia Middleton of Manhattan had died two months ago from a sudden heart attack at age eighty-seven. The obituary noted Cordelia's father had been the founder of a prestigious New York law firm and a successful real estate investor. Cordelia's late husband had been a partner at that same firm. Cordelia was a widow with no children, survived by her twin sister, Teresa Middleton, and no other immediate family members.

No spouse, late spouse, partner, nor children were listed next to Teresa's name.

If Teresa and Cordelia were twins, that meant Teresa was also eighty-seven-years old. Victoria found that almost impossible to believe. Teresa looked much younger.

Victoria continued to search and found little else on Teresa. In person, she left an indelible impression with her outrageous personality, but online, she'd barely left an imprint.

Victoria's food arrived only minutes later. She ate while watching the activity on the beach. Individuals and couples strolled along the sand. The seaweed crew remained busy, still raking and scooping. Unfortunately for them, there didn't appear to be any less seaweed in the cove.

At 6:24 p.m., when Victoria finished her food, there was still no sign of Teresa.

Victoria checked her emails. Back in the D.C. office, Sam, an intelligence analyst as well as one of Victoria's friends, had completed the background checks on the American guests and sent a summary report. Out of the guests who were present the day Avery went missing, three individuals had DUI charges, one woman had an embezzlement charge, one person had been accused of insider trading, and the courts had convicted a male guest of sexual assault.

Victoria was still scanning the list when Rivera called and asked, "Did Teresa pan out with any information?"

"She didn't show. I don't think she's going to. But Sam sent the results of the guests' background checks."

"I was just looking through those. The man convicted of sexual assault is still here. He's in bungalow seven. I'm going to head over there soon to talk to him, if you want to come along."

"Go ahead. I'm going to try to catch up with Teresa. If I can't locate her, I'll meet you at bungalow seven." Victoria pushed her chair back and left the table. She passed the server on the way. "Excuse me, you said Teresa doesn't always show up for her after-dinner drink?" Victoria asked.

"Right. Sometimes we hold that table for her and it remains empty. Then other guests wonder why we told them it was reserved. But she comes more often than not."

"Okay. Thank you. If she shows up, please tell her I was here and I'm looking for her."

Teresa seemed to be a stickler for etiquette, but Alejandro had warned Victoria that Teresa didn't operate by the same rules she expected others to follow.

Victoria went to the front desk to find out where Teresa was staying. After showing her credentials, the woman working the desk gave her the information. Bungalow ten. Conveniently close to the Jennings and the man Rivera planned to question.

Victoria walked to bungalow ten, knocked on Teresa's door, and waited. There was no response.

Disappointed, Victoria wrote a message on the back of her business card asking Teresa to call as soon as possible, then slid the card under the door. There was still time to catch up with Rivera.

The man with the sexual assault charge from bungalow seven was trim and tan in a white linen shirt and salmon-colored dress shorts.

"Dan Young?" Rivera asked.

The man stepped outside, and a woman's pleasant voice came from behind him, asking, "Who is it, Dan? Did you order something else?"

"It's nothing. I'll be right back, hon." He closed the door fully behind him and said, "I was wondering when someone was going to ask to see me." He slid his hands into his pockets as they showed him their badges. He didn't look angry, just resigned to the fact that they were going to question him.

"You know why we're here?" Victoria asked.

"Of course. The missing woman. And I've got a criminal record, so it's not the first time it made me...someone the authorities wanted to talk to, even though it happened over fifteen years ago, and if I'd had a better lawyer the charge would have been contested and dropped. Instead...my cross to bear."

"Then tell us where you were on Sunday afternoon and evening, when Avery Jennings disappeared," Rivera said.

"I've been with my girlfriend since I arrived. She can vouch for it, though I'd prefer you didn't ask her. She doesn't know about the charge. She doesn't need to. It was a lifetime ago. But I know you need to confirm what I say and I can make that easy for you. We had a couple's massage at five p.m. on Sunday. Then we came back here. The resort delivered a bottle of champagne. I signed for it and left a tip, so it's on my account. We had a late dinner, then some dancing. My girlfriend takes photos constantly, so there are those with the timestamps, as well as other tips and charges on my account throughout the night. On Monday morning, we went on a snorkeling expedition. The staff can confirm we were both there. I can write all this down for you if that helps you move on."

"Thank you. We appreciate your cooperation," Rivera said.

"I guess you have no idea where she is then, and you're just grasping for anything, huh?" he said. "The poor woman."

Victoria wished there wasn't so much truth in his words. And they needed to do something to change that.

CHAPTER 21

Tony entered the yacht's kitchen. Eric and the crew called it the galley, but Tony wasn't a sailor, and didn't want to be one now. He took simple pleasure in ignoring them and sticking with the word kitchen. They'd finally stopped correcting him.

The deckhand Tony liked, Marinero Uno, which meant sailor one, stacked clean plates in the cabinets. He was only eighteen. Not even old enough to order a drink in a bar without a fake ID. His sturdy frame made him look older and his hair made him look wild. It stuck straight up in the wind and stayed that way for hours. He was probably a second or third cousin of Eric's. He worked hard, did what he was told, and kept his mouth shut. Tony appreciated that.

"You bring the girl a plate?" Tony asked.

"Yes. I left it inside her cabin," Uno answered, making eye contact when he spoke. Something about the way he did that made Tony trust the kid.

Tony looked around. A mirror and razor blade rested on the table. He didn't touch the stuff. He'd seen what it did to people. So had Eric, but that didn't stop him. The longer they stayed on the yacht, the more Eric used. An extended vacation in a rehab joint could fix the addiction, at least. Unlike Eric's stupidity, which was there to stay.

"Was Eric just here?" Tony asked.

"He left about ten minutes ago. Said he was going to sleep."

"Word of advice—stay away from him if you can," Tony said. "Don't let him pull you into his habits."

"Yeah. I know."

"And one more thing...on this boat, you see nothing, you hear nothing, and you say nothing. Got it?"

Uno nodded. "Eric who? Right?"

"Glad you understand. Because I'll find out if you don't." No need to remind the kid what he'd do. He'd seen enough already.

"Can I get you some food?" Uno asked.

Uno was a decent cook. He made simple meals with pasta, steak, and chicken, nothing strange or exotic that Tony needed to be wary of, and all of it tasted pretty good.

"Nah. Not hungry," Tony answered. "But I came looking for something. You got a bottle of olive oil?"

Uno pulled a dark green bottle from a shelf and handed it to Tony.

Uno asked no questions as Tony left with the bottle, reaffirming Tony's opinion of him.

Inside his cabin, Tony took off his long-sleeved shirt, poured the greenish-yellow liquid onto a washcloth, and rubbed it in small circles over his arm.

When Tony left his cabin, clean and shaven, Eric was in the hallway, outside the door of the room where they were keeping the girl.

A ball of fury ignited inside Tony as he scanned Eric's hands and clothing for blood. If only Eric wasn't the boss's son; Tony was itching to knock him down a few notches to where he belonged.

"What are you doing?" Tony asked

"Nothing."

Even in the low light of the yacht's hallway, Eric's pupils had constricted to small black dots in the center of his eyes, but his hands and clothes weren't bloody, and Tony hadn't heard any screams.

"Did you go in there?" Tony asked.

"Only for a minute. I brought her dinner."

Eric's lie caused another jolt of anger. "No, you didn't. Uno did."

"Okay. So what? I heard her shouting. I went in and told her to shut up or I'd cut out her tongue. I didn't touch her, man. I was just talking to her. I'm bored as hell here. I've had enough of this. I'm going crazy."

"She shouldn't even know you exist, except you had to go in there. Damn it, Eric. Can you think before you do things for once? Why can't you listen to what I tell you?" Tony's voice rose along with his frustration.

"Hey!' Eric glared at Tony. "Watch how you talk to me. You're not in charge here."

"My job is to keep you safe," Tony reminded him.

"Who is she going to tell?" Eric snorted. "Besides, we aren't really going to let her go, are we?"

"That matter hasn't been decided yet. It depends on how this plays out."

"Yeah, well, she heard the other girl screaming. Wanted to know what we were doing to her and where she is now."

"*We* weren't doing things to her. That was all you, so let's get that straight." Tony clenched his teeth and did all he could to keep from pummeling Eric. "What did you tell her?"

"Nothing. I offered her something to help pass the time while we wait." Eric took a small baggie from his pocket and shook it. "And then I got out of there because she said you told her she has Covid. Does she?"

"How the hell do I know? If I told you she did, would you stay away from her?"

"Yeah. That virus can do some weird stuff, man. If you don't know, then why did you tell her that?"

"To give us time. If people think she's in quarantine, she isn't really missing yet."

"That what you think?" Eric sneered. "She's already on television."

That was news to Tony, but he wouldn't allow Eric to catch his surprise.

"I'll show you." Eric poked his thumbs around on his phone before handing the device to Tony. "See for yourself."

Missing in Mexico, said the headline below the girl's photograph.

They were already looking for her. That wasn't good, though Tony wouldn't admit it aloud. He needed everyone on the yacht to believe he was one step ahead of everyone else.

"Don't watch or listen to any of it," Tony said. "The police try to psych people out with the stuff they put out there."

"Does anyone know you took her?" Eric asked.

"Would we be standing here having this conversation if they did, Eric? No one who knows is going to say a word about it unless they want their balls sliced off while watching their family members bleed to death in front of them." As soon as the words were out of his mouth, Tony cringed. Yes, they did those things. He had personally orchestrated and carried out variations of those things. But it was business, nothing more, and Tony found every minute distasteful. He wanted to be Eric's opposite in every way, except for his wealth. Smart, while Eric was stupid. Resourceful, where Eric was useless. But it was too late. Eric was already nodding and grinning as if they finally had something in common and were one and the same.

CHAPTER 22

After dinner, guests congregated at the center of the resort, where they held the nightly performances. The staff had set comfortable chairs in neat rows from the stage all the way back to the lagoon pool. Victoria and Rivera selected seats near the pool, far from the stage, where they could see everyone in front of them. They knew Avery and her friends had attended all the nighttime entertainment events. Perhaps Victoria and Rivera would find something by doing the same.

Servers carrying trays laden with brightly colored cocktails moved between the chairs, delivering drinks and taking new orders. Rivera asked for a beer and Victoria ordered a frozen, nonalcoholic coffee concoction.

On the stage, a beautiful woman dressed in a white angel costume, complete with large gossamer wings, played the violin to contemporary songs, entertaining the guests prior to the main show.

The crowd grew, ordering more drinks. The perfect rows of chairs became clusters as guests moved them around to suit their needs. Conversations and laughter grew louder.

Victoria shifted her weight in her chair and sipped her drink, alert to everyone and everything happening around her. She kept an eye out for

Teresa but didn't see her. The resort had seemed almost deserted during the day. But now everyone had come out of their rooms or returned from daytime excursions and gathered together. There were a lot more people than Victoria previously imagined.

Suddenly, which is always how it happened, she'd had enough. The long day of interacting with others had depleted Victoria's energy. Like any introverted personality, she wanted nothing more than to politely excuse herself and return to the quiet of her room to recharge. But this was work, not a social event, and being in the center of the resort might be exactly where she needed to be. The place where they would find the missing piece that would lead them to each successive clue until they located Avery.

After the violinist finished her playset and took a bow, Alejandro took the stage. He welcomed everyone to Azure Cove, and introduced the night's main event, a dance and acrobatic troupe from London. He wished the guests a wonderful stay. He said nothing about Avery Jennings.

Despite her coffee and a fascinating Cirque de Soleil style performance with bizarre feats of strength and flexibility and a strange, dark vibe, Victoria couldn't stop yawning. She got up and circled the area several times to study the crowd.

When the show was over, Rivera offered to stay up for the dance party that followed.

Victoria accepted his offer and would owe him one for staying, though he didn't seem to view it as a hardship.

———

Inside Victoria's room on the second floor of building D, the air conditioner continued to blast cold air, causing goosebumps to prickle the skin on her legs. She fiddled with the controls but still couldn't turn it off. If she'd known what to expect, she would have stuffed her warmest flannel pajamas into her small suitcase. Instead, she wore Rivera's hoodie over her sleeping shorts and T-shirt.

Aside from the soft hum of the air conditioning, quiet prevailed. When she slid open her balcony window to let in warmer air, the faint rhythm of dance music traveled in on the breeze.

Her phone rang. For a second, though it was very late, she thought it could be Teresa getting back to her.

It was Ned. And that made her smile inside. This would be the first time she'd heard his voice since she left Virginia yesterday, and she missed him. Being with him never drained her energy. His companionship provided comfort and happiness. Ned was patient, kind, and reliable. He loved her animals as much as she did. And his sex appeal didn't hurt.

"How are things at home?" she asked. The way she said it, unintentionally, made it sound like they shared a place. Which wasn't so off. He was there most days of the week, though he stayed in a guest room whenever Victoria was out of town. The thought occurred to her, and not for the first time—why not move in together and enjoy each other's company more often? But she had yet to mention the idea to him.

"Everything here is good. The dogs have had their snacks and settled in for the night. How is it going there?"

"Well, I don't know if all the Azure Cove Resort locations look like this one, but it's gorgeous. It's new, so everything is clean and...it just makes you want to hang out and do absolutely nothing. If they allowed dogs, I'd love to walk them on the beach. But they don't. Still, maybe we could go somewhere like this for a few days."

"That sounds great."

"Let's really do it. Look at your schedule at the clinic and see when would be a good time. We'll get someone to watch the animals for a few days."

"I will check my schedule. So, I'm guessing you haven't found your friend's niece, or that would have been the first thing you told me, right?"

"Yes. It's not going so well, though that could change at any moment. God, I hope it does. It's been a whirlwind day and we don't have a whole lot to show for it. We ruled out a few suspects but come up with no new ones. Meanwhile, our best lead, a man her friend described, is a dead end so far. We can't find him either."

"Avery's story was just on the news. They didn't say much about the investigation, just that it's ongoing."

"Oh, hold on. I should check it out." Victoria grabbed her iPad and went on the Internet, searching for a news clip about Avery and selecting one of the many options.

A newscaster with platinum hair started off in a cheery voice and adjusted her tone a few words into the announcement, as if she'd just realized the nature of the story. "This is Sally Walters with a breaking story we're following. A University of Virginia senior disappeared the night before her scheduled trip home from Mexico. Mexican authorities are searching for her right now. Friends of Avery Jennings told us the FBI sent agents down to Mexico to help the police there with the ongoing investigation. Meanwhile, we've got Matt Fox live on the UVA campus."

The screen changed to the University of Virginia where students had gathered on a quad. The camera focused on one attractive coed in a winter parka.

"Everyone likes Avery," the student said. "We're just all really worried and we're praying that they find her and she's okay."

Matt turned to face the camera. "This is Matt Fox with WNBC, and you heard it from right here on Virginia's campus. They're all concerned for their classmate. They all want their missing Wahoo back."

"Wahoo?" Victoria asked Ned.

"That's what they call themselves. The Wahoos. Sometimes just Hoos for short."

"So, Avery is a missing Hoo. Would be super cute if the whole situation wasn't so sad."

The scene returned to the woman in the studio. "Azure Cove is an exclusive resort. What do you think this means for travelers who were considering booking a trip there, Matt?"

"Well, Sally, it doesn't bode well for the resort at all," Matt said. "Depending on what happened to Avery Jennings."

Yet outside Victoria's room, the drinks were flowing. The music thumping. Avery had made international news. Everyone at the resort had to know she was missing, even guests who had just arrived. Though they might be concerned, the situation hadn't seemed to deter anyone from enjoying their vacation. The complimentary cocktails might have suppressed their fears. Or maybe they simply didn't believe anything bad could happen to them. Which implied Avery was somehow at least partly responsible for her disappearance. And in general, they were right. Rarely was a victim's selection completely random.

So, if someone had abducted Avery, what was it that made them choose her?

CHAPTER 23

A few minutes after her alarm went off, Victoria threw on shorts and a tank top, pulled her hair back into a ponytail, and stuck a cap on her head. With the sun still rising, she jogged down the stairs and stretched her legs near the pool while waiting on Rivera. They planned to explore the area around the resort and running allowed them to cover more ground.

The resort hopped with activity last night. Now, all evidence of that was gone. The property was remarkably quiet and clean. Not a stray glass or cocktail napkin or cigarette butt in sight. Azure Cove's staff either worked long into the night or arrived well before the crack of dawn.

Victoria leaned over to tighten the laces of her running shoes and had the sense she wasn't alone. Someone was watching her. She straightened and caught a flash of movement. A man slipped from view, disappearing around the towel dispensary shed. She'd glimpsed enough to recognize the man was Carlos, the housekeeper, or someone who looked very much like him who also wore a housekeeping staff uniform.

"Wait, un momento," she called, hurrying in the direction he'd gone. She wasn't sure if she was speaking Spanish, but surely he'd understood.

On the other side of the towel dispensary, she slammed into Rivera.

"Hey," he said, stepping back and looking around. "What's the hurry?"

"I thought I saw Carlos. He was watching me. Or he wants to tell me something." She scanned the area, but there was no trace of him.

"I didn't see him. Do you want to go after him?"

She exhaled loudly. "No. Forget it. I'm not sure the manager will be okay with us cornering him again." She focused on Rivera for a second and noticed his bloodshot eyes. How long did you stay out last night?"

"The official party shut down at one a.m. when they stop serving drinks. I hung around until about two thirty to talk with guests who were here when Avery disappeared."

"Did you learn anything we should follow up on?" Victoria asked, still craning her neck to spot Carlos.

"Unfortunately, no."

"Well, thanks for staying up. If we don't find Avery today, I'll do the dance party thing tonight."

"Only you would say that as if it's a chore," Rivera said with a laugh.

"You know me, Rivera. Parties aren't my thing. Sure you don't need to go back to sleep for an hour?"

"No. I'm good. Let's run on the beach, see what else is near the resort, in case the search parties missed something."

Victoria cast a glance over her shoulder as they headed to the beach.

At the water's edge, two men in boots slogged through the thick brown seaweed carrying pitchforks. Apparently, their shifts started before the crack of dawn. Victoria waved to them. One didn't see her. He moved with his head down, and his shoulders stooped into his task. The other waved back. He wore a silver watch with a blue face. She thought it might be a nice knockoff, then realized it must have been a decent waterproof piece because the man reached his hand into the water, submerging his entire wrist and the watch.

"Hold on," Victoria said to Rivera. "I want to check something out." She walked to where she'd seen the tractor take the seaweed. Two white-washed stucco walls rose from the ground, mostly camouflaged by mangrove trees and flowering plants climbing up swirling vines. As she got closer, a flock of birds erupted from the bushes, loudly flapping and squawking.

In an underground space between the white walls, a pickup truck with a cargo bed full of seaweed faced away from the ocean. The cleaning crew dumped seaweed from the tractor into the truck's cargo bed through a carefully concealed and fenced hole above ground.

Victoria walked around the truck, searching for anything that stood out. Lowering herself to her knees, she peered underneath.

"I did the same thing yesterday," Rivera said. "But another set of eyes can't hurt."

She saw nothing.

From the underground garage space, the agents followed a nearby path that led directly to the health center. Further to the right was a spa, where two women spoke softly in Spanish and the scents of eucalyptus and jasmine wafted through the air. Continuing along the path led them back to the water sports pavilion and the beach.

They stood on the path for a moment, taking in their surroundings. Victoria thought a revolutionary idea might be seconds away from making itself known.

It wasn't.

Victoria pulled the rim of her hat down and tucked her chin as they jogged into the rising sun. She settled into a rhythm of stride and breath beside Rivera. They ran close to the water on the firmest sand, occasionally jumping away from the larger waves that rolled ashore.

Ahead of them, a long pier jutted out from the sand and over the water. Waves crashed underneath the weathered planks, churning up seaweed that had stuck underneath the shallowed area.

Someone had nailed a flyer onto a pillar.

Missing. Avery Jennings. If you've seen her, please call police immediately.

The agents stopped to look at the black-and-white picture: Avery with a relaxed smile and a few strands of hair falling around her face. The necklace with the silver pendant surrounded her neck. The image looked familiar. It was one of the many photos Avery and her friends took at Azure Cove. Victoria had seen it several times by studying the recent pictures the young ladies had posted on their social media sites and from the images Brie and Haley had forwarded.

They headed into thicker sand to get around the pier, noticing another flyer on the opposite side of the structure. Victoria wondered who had posted them. The resort? Volunteers?

A break in the long stretch of upscale resorts and gorgeous beachfront homes came when they reached a Marina. Anchored between the docks were dozens of boats, ranging from small fishing boats to gleaming yachts. They reminded Victoria of her father's house at Lake Lucinda, where he kept a sailboat and a speed boat. The last time she visited, a mysterious woman had drowned in the lake. The investigation had proven to be darker and more complicated than she'd first imagined, and for weeks it had rocked her family's world. Rivera had driven up to help them sort through the difficult situation. Once again, she'd been grateful for his assistance.

"Hola! Refresco!" a man called, interrupting Victoria's thoughts. He stood behind the open-air counter of a small store in the center of the marina. Picture signs on the front wall advertised water bottles, sodas, and snacks.

The man had old, wrinkled skin and was small of stature. He also wore a shiny, silver watch that caught the sun as he waved to them. Victoria couldn't help but notice it, now that the other one had caught her attention. It must be a status symbol in the area.

Refresco!" the man called out again.

"Gracias. La próxima vez," Rivera answered the man before turning to Victoria. "Want to turn around here?"

"Yes, let's do that." She was eager to meet up with the dog handler. Maybe the dog would have better luck than the police and FBI.

CHAPTER 24

Victoria and Rivera waited for the Jennings near the lagoon pool, in sight of the walking trail that led from the bungalows to the reception area. Victoria spotted blue towels on the otherwise empty chaise lounges, and Teresa sprang to mind. If Teresa didn't return her call soon, Victoria planned to return to bungalow ten after the dog search to speak with her. In the meantime, just in case, since the woman was nearing ninety, Victoria had left a message with the manager asking for someone to make sure Teresa was okay.

"I wonder how Avery's parents are doing," Rivera said. "I'm not sure it's a great idea for them to come along on this search. Do you?"

Tom and Jennifer walked around the corner before Victoria could give Rivera her opinion. And she wasn't sure what she thought about the issue. Jennifer had lost her composure yesterday, which only detracted from the investigation. But if Victoria were in the same situation now, with a missing family member, she wouldn't let anyone prevent her from joining the search.

"Good morning," Rivera said to the Jennings.

"Morning," Jennifer answered, without stopping or slowing her march to the reception area. "Is the dog here?"

"We're about to find out," Victoria said, following her.

"Do you know how this works?" Tom asked. "Have you worked with search dogs before?"

"We have," Rivera answered. "And I'll let Victoria explain the process. She's definitely the dog person here."

Every time Rivera had visited Victoria's house or the lake house, his allergies had flared, manifesting into a runny nose, bloodshot eyes, and plenty of sneezing. Victoria, on the other hand, had always owned dogs. She enjoyed explaining the power of a dog's nose.

"Tracking dogs are extremely effective at finding people," she said. "A dog's nose has millions more olfactory receptors than our own. And the part of their brain devoted to smell is fifty times bigger than ours." Victoria waited for a sign that either Jennifer or Tom was interested before continuing. Tom was looking at her, and Jennifer gave her a quick glance over her shoulder, so Victoria went on. "Every living creature produces a distinctive odor dependent on factors like their emotions and health issues. The human body also sheds tens of thousands of microscopic particles every minute. Those particles decay and emit that individual's scent. A trained search dog can detect a few targeted particles within a trillion others."

In front of the resort, the same two police officers, Leo and Vince, stood next to a beautiful, curvy woman with spiky hair. She wore a tank top with cargo pants and a wide leather belt. Next to her sat a black and tan bloodhound with long floppy ears and loose jowls. The dog gave the occasional thump of her tail and gazed up with deep-set hazel eyes.

"Hi. I'm Michelle, and this is my dog, Josefina," the woman said.

Victoria resisted her natural impulse to kneel and speak to the animal. Josefina had an important job to do, and Victoria wouldn't distract her from it by making a fuss.

"Victoria was just telling us how scent dogs work," Jennifer said. "But my daughter has already been gone for over two days. Is that too long? Is it too late to track her?"

"Josefina can follow a scent for miles, even one that's almost two weeks old. Even if other odors have contaminated it. She's nothing short of amazing."

Jennifer looked down at the dog as if she was their only hope. "Please find her. Please find my daughter."

"That's why we're here, ma'am," Michelle said, her voice kind and reassuring. "I promise you, this is far from our first search. I'm good at what I do, and Josefina is the best. She has an incredible tracking record, and she wants nothing more than to succeed. Together, we're going to do everything we can to figure out where your daughter went."

Michelle's confidence seemed to bring Jennifer some comfort. Her tight grimace loosened long enough for her to nod.

The more cases Victoria worked, the more appreciative she was of people like Michelle, who seemed truly kind and dedicated to helping others. Being a fellow dog person also biased Victoria's opinion of the handler toward the positive.

"It might be better if you stay here," Rivera suggested to the Jennings.

Jennifer untangled her fingers from her purse straps and plunked a hand on her hip. "We're coming with you. We have to be there if they find her. She'll need us."

"You can come along," Leo said.

No one said otherwise, and the matter seemed to be decided.

"All I ask is that everyone stay back and give Josefina space. Don't crowd her," Michelle said. "Now, who has Avery's personal items?"

"I do." Jennifer removed a zip locked plastic bag from her large purse and handed it to Michelle. "I brought her pillowcase and a sock."

"Good." Michelle clutched the plastic bag but didn't open it. "Let's start where Avery was last seen."

With Leo leading the way, the group was the same as yesterday, except with Michelle substituted for the resort manager.

"Are you also from Washington D.C.?" Victoria heard Vince ask Rivera. That was good. Rivera couldn't suggest Vince was hitting on her if he put forth equal effort to get to know Rivera.

When they came to building D, Leo climbed the stairs to the second floor with Michelle and Josefina, stopping in the corridor outside Avery's former room. The others watched from the path below. Michelle gave her dog commands. Josefina grew more eager to work, her tail wagging wildly. Michelle opened the bag and placed Avery's items in front of the dog's nose.

"Busca!" Michelle exclaimed, making it sound like the most exciting word in the world.

"That means search," Rivera said.

Fully attentive, Josefina sniffed the items, then waddled into the room. Less than a minute later, she came out with her nose to the ground. She trotted down the stairs and onto a paved walking trail. The police kept pace a few yards behind the handler. The agents and the Jennings fell into step behind them.

A couple dressed in tennis whites and carrying rackets moved aside and watched the procession. Josefina seemed oblivious to everything except her job. She alternated between sniffing the pavement and the bushes lining the path until she came to the health center. From there, she trotted off the trail and behind the building, where she sniffed furiously in a circular area.

The dog's behavior suggested Avery had gone to the health center after all, though the people working there claimed not to have seen her.

The bloodhound didn't linger at the health center. She lifted her head, sniffed the air, and was off again. No longer following a paved path, she tramped through the bushes and tall grasses, an area mostly obscured from the walkways. She headed straight to the underground parking area concealing the seaweed truck.

One of the same men Victoria had seen that morning was shoving seaweed toward the back of the cargo bed when Josefina trotted past his legs. Michelle said something to him in Spanish. He left the area, giving the dog and handler more room.

Josefina trotted a full circle around the truck. She stopped beside it and cocked her head.

"Oh, no. Is she in there?" Jennifer asked. Her face paled as she gripped her husband's arm and stared into the truck bed. Witnessing her pain and distress, Victoria wished the Jennings hadn't come along for their own sakes.

"We combed this area," Leo said. "She's not here."

"She's not here *now* or Josefina would have signaled," Michelle said. "But Avery was here earlier."

Victoria could not think of a reason Avery or any other guest would choose to enter the underground seaweed depository. As the unsettling information sunk in, Josefina seemed to make a decision. She exited the truck area and trotted along the beach.

"She still has Avery's scent," Michelle said, looking just as focused as her dog.

Josefina couldn't know her work was more than just a game. She appeared to enjoy herself, trotting confidently along the top of the beach where the resorts met the sand, stopping to sniff the vegetation in some places more than others.

The group followed, leaving some distance between themselves and Michelle.

Near the pier, Josefina left the trail she'd been following and headed toward the water, sniffing excitedly. After a few encouraging commands from Michelle, the bloodhound stopped, swung her head up, and returned to the top edge of the beach. She maintained her focus, sniffing the dunes and plants, all the way to the marina. It was much warmer than it had been earlier. Victoria's shirt was damp with perspiration when they arrived. Sand had seeped in around her ankles, filling her shoes.

At the marina, Josefina trotted down a long, wooden dock. She stopped at a bucket of fish and plunged her nose inside.

Michelle spoke in a sharp voice and got Josefina moving again. She hung a right off the main dock and trotted to an empty boat slip. At the edge of the slip, the bloodhound lowered to her haunches, looked up at her handler, and whined.

"Good girl, good girl," Michelle said. She scratched her dog's neck and gave her a treat, and then a plastic toy. While Josefina stuck her hind end in the air and made the toy squeak like a dying animal, Michelle turned to Avery's parents. "I'm so sorry. The trail stops here. Avery must have gotten into a boat. Or..." Michelle looked down at the dark water lapping the sides of the empty boat slip. Beyond, the vast ocean spread as far as Victoria could see to the horizon.

Jennifer moaned. The gut-wrenching anguish captured in her expression sent a shiver down Victoria's spine.

CHAPTER 25

A warm breeze blew across the docks as Michelle and Josefina left the marina for their next assignment. The others remained there, close to where Avery's scent trail ended.

Jennifer wrapped her arms around her middle, hugging herself. Her eyes held a vacant stare. "What do we do now?"

"Can you get a diver here?" Rivera asked the police.

"I'll have to make some calls," Leo answered.

Victoria scanned the marina, settling on the storefront she'd seen earlier that morning. The man with the balding head was still behind the counter. From his vantage point, he had a clear view of the dock where Avery's scent had ended.

Leo placed a hand over his sunglasses to further shield his eyes and followed Victoria's gaze. "We'll talk to him. Stay here," he told the others before he and Vince strode toward the man working the storefront. As the police approached the counter, the man appeared frozen in place. After a brief exchange, where he stole occasional glances toward the rest of the group, the Federales followed the marina worker through a door behind the counter.

Still on the dock, Jennifer clasped her hands below her chin and closed her eyes. "Oh, God, please let us find her. Please let her be okay."

Tom Jennings kept his hands stuffed in his pockets, attempting to mask his terror with a stony expression. "Can we call the Coast Guard? Would they get involved?" Tom asked. "How do we handle this now?"

"Let's see if there are any witnesses," Rivera said. "Maybe someone saw her get on a boat."

"And if she didn't get on a boat?" Jennifer asked, staring at the water with a tortured expression.

If they can't get a diver here soon, I'll borrow some scuba gear and get down there," Victoria said. It pained her to say this because obviously if Avery were under the water, it was a recovery effort, not a rescue mission.

Within a few minutes, the police came back outside. Leo looked their way, holding up a hand and one finger before he and Vince headed toward a dock to their left.

"Why does he want us to wait here?" Jennifer asked.

"I'm not sure," Rivera said, echoing Victoria's thoughts.

The Federales stopped to talk to a young man in shorts and a baggy T-shirt who was sitting on a metal folding chair under an umbrella, manning the gas pumps. Their conversation was brief and when the Federales returned, Victoria couldn't tell if they'd learned anything useful. Their expressions gave nothing away until they were face to face and Vince said, "I'm sorry."

"Sorry? Why? What did they tell you?" Jennifer asked.

"Did they see her? Either of them?" Tom asked before the Federales could answer his wife.

Leo shook his head. "Neither saw nor heard anything unusual. They don't have information that can help us."

"What about the boat slip?" Victoria asked. "Did you find out if it's rented to anyone?"

"Yeah. I asked. It's not one of their rented spaces," Leo answered. "Anyone can dock there."

"Did you ask if they have surveillance video?" Rivera asked.

"They don't," Leo answered.

Victoria found that hard to believe. Every marina had security cameras to monitor the expensive watercraft kept there.

"They don't have video," Leo repeated. "The man at the store has been here every day since Avery disappeared. He didn't see anything unusual."

"He can't have been the only one working all day and all night," Jennifer said.

"He was. He didn't see anything," Leo repeated. "He'll call us if that changes."

"If that changes? That makes no sense! How could it suddenly change?" Tom cried. "Did he see something or not?"

"Give me a chance to speak with him," Rivera said.

"No." Leo's voice was firm. "You're here to interview the American guests at the resort. Not to interrogate Mexican citizens." He lowered his sunglasses as he faced the agents, narrowing his eyes in a way that was meant to intimidate. "Don't forget this is our investigation."

"Interrogate?" Rivera asked, his mouth hanging open. "Why are you being territorial now? What happened? Just let me ask him a few questions."

"I said, no," Leo repeated as his phone rang. He glanced at the screen, then gave Rivera one last stare before walking away from the group with his phone to his ear.

"Is it possible your daughter left with someone she met at the resort? Like a boyfriend?" Vince asked the Jennings. There was something almost apologetic in the way he posed the questions.

Jennifer's face flushed red. "Why are you asking that now? She would never. Not alone. Someone lied to her about her Covid test and then kidnapped her! How is that not obvious to you?"

Tom Jennings added to his wife's conviction, his voice rising with each word. "Avery wouldn't leave the resort on her own. She knows better. And she wouldn't get on a boat with a stranger."

"Did you check with her biological mother yet?" Vince asked.

"We did," Tom answered. "Her mother has never heard from her. Not recently. Not ever. Which is what we told you."

"Vince! Come on! We have to go." Leo beckoned to Vince from the end of the dock.

"Sorry. Um, we'll be in contact about next steps," Vince said.

"What next steps?" Jennifer cried. "What are the next steps?"

"Uh, that's what we need to figure out," Vince said. "We'll be in touch as soon as we know more."

"Wait," Victoria called after him.

"We'll be in touch," Leo said, lifting one hand without turning around.

"That's it? That's all?" Sobs shook Jennifer's shoulders. She collapsed her head against her husband's chest.

Tom shook his head as he held his wife. "What the hell just happened?"

CHAPTER 26

An unnerving grinding noise broke the silence. It came from the marina store. The man working there dragged a heavy metal door against the pavement and closed off the storefront. On the other dock, the chair by the gas pumps was empty and the man who had been working there was nowhere to be seen.

"Does it feel like the police just gave up on the search?" Tom asked, summing up Victoria's thoughts exactly.

"Yes," she answered him honestly. "Something happened. But I don't know what."

"Let's head back to the resort and regroup there," Rivera said. "I'm going to call Murphy...our boss, to tell him what happened, see if he can talk to the Chief of Police, and we should check in with the U.S. embassy again."

With the sun on their backs, Victoria and Rivera hurried back to Azure Cove. Jennifer and Tom Jennings trudged behind them, looking more emotionally drained and defeated than before.

Rivera left a message for Murphy, asking for his advice. They didn't want to burn bridges with the Mexican police, but something needed to change with their attitude, and fast. Rivera didn't need to remind Murphy that if they were to find Avery alive, every minute mattered, but he did anyway.

They walked back to Azure Cove near the water's edge and were approaching the pier. The white flyers with Avery's picture stood out against the dark pillars. Victoria wondered how the Jennings would react to seeing them. Then something caught her eye. A flash of unnatural color amongst the ugly brown mass of seaweed below the structure. Something solid, tangled in the rocking tendrils. Victoria's breath caught in her throat. She hoped she was mistaken, that her eyes were playing tricks on her. She strained to make sense of what she was seeing without calling attention to it.

Long dark hair. Pale long limbs.

It was a woman.

With a flick of her wrist, Victoria signaled for Rivera to keep moving down the beach with the Jennings. The signal came too late. Jennifer stopped walking and stared at the agents.

"Come on, let's keep going," Rivera said, his voice gentle but firm.

Jennifer looked beyond Victoria and gasped as she spotted the figure churning in the waves. She rushed to get closer. "What's that? Is that...is that a body? Oh, my God. Is it Avery?" Jennifer stopped again and buried her face in her hands, wailing, "I can't look. I can't."

Tom ran past his wife, stumbling in the sand.

"Tom! Stop!" Victoria shouted.

Still wearing his shoes and clothes and ignoring the agents' shouts to wait, Tom charged under the pier and waded through the shallow water. His breath came in loud, ragged gasps. He was almost to the body when Rivera outran him and pulled him back.

"Don't," Rivera said. "It could be a crime scene. We can't touch her."

"But it might be Avery," Tom said, craning his neck in Rivera's grip to get a better look.

"Is it her?" Jennifer shouted. "Is it Avery?"

"I can see her and...I don't think it is. It's not Avery," Tom said.

Victoria experienced an instant of silent relief. A wave of guilt quickly followed, replaced by anger. It wasn't the person they'd set out to find, but it was someone else's daughter, sister, or friend. Someone too young to die.

Dripping wet, Tom moved away from the pier and fell to his knees in the sand. He dropped his head into his hands as Jennifer rushed to his side. She buried her head in her husband's shoulder and they sobbed.

Leaving the parents to recover, the agents stared at the body from a few yards away.

Long black hair mixed with tendrils of seaweed. Bloat had ballooned the corpse and its skin had started to blister. It hadn't been in the ocean more than a few days.

"Aren't you going to pull her out?" Tom asked.

"We don't have jurisdiction to gather evidence or enter the crime scene without permission," Victoria said. "I'm going to call Vince directly."

Her call connected in seconds. "Victoria?" He answered, lowering his voice to almost a whisper. "I'm sorry about what happened."

"Yeah, we need to talk about that," she said. "But that's not why I'm calling now. We were walking back to Azure Cove, and we found a woman's body under the pier. She's been dead for a few days now. I called you directly, but I can call a general emergency service number if you prefer."

"No, no, don't do that. We'll be back. Just wait there."

"All right. We're about a quarter of a mile from the marina, heading east. At the pier."

Victoria ended the call. "Vince said they're coming," she told the others.

"We'll wait for them. You two should go back to the resort," Rivera said.

Tom looked uncertain but one glance down at his wife and he seemed to realize it was best for them to leave.

A sunburn on Jennifer's nose made the rest of her fair skin seem extra pale. Where earlier she'd been wired, now she seemed weak.

"Call me if you hear anything," Tom said before leading his shell-shocked wife away.

Victoria dumped the sand from her shoes before putting them back on. Rivera remained shirtless. His olive skin glistened with sweat. They sat on the edge of the pier, above the corpse, and waited for the Federales. Beneath the boards, the body rocked gently against the pilings, blanketed in seaweed.

"What if this girl's death relates to Avery's disappearance?" Victoria said, praying it would not.

"I don't know," Rivera said, standing up. "I'm going back to the marina to speak with that guy at the store. If the police come, don't mention that to them."

He headed back toward the marina, leaving Victoria alone with the corpse.

Rivera returned before the Federales arrived. He carried two water bottles and handed one to Victoria.

"I spoke with the man behind the counter at the marina," he said. "He claims he doesn't know anything about Avery or the boat slip, just as they'd said. It's possible, but I don't know if I believe him. I could see security cameras on the top of the building."

"We have to get the footage," she said as Leo and Vince came toward them from the nearest resort.

"What about a forensic team?" Victoria asked them.

"There isn't much evidence when they've been in the water, but they'll process the body in the morgue," Leo answered. "How did you find this woman?"

"I just happened to spot her as we were passing. I remembered Josefina getting excited and coming toward the pier. Maybe the body was there, buried in the seaweed earlier."

Leo studied Victoria for a few more seconds before saying, "You can go now."

But Vince wasn't ready to dismiss them. "How old did she look?" he asked, clearly rattled, his eyes darting between the agents and the pier.

"I think she was an older teen. I'm certain she hasn't been in the water very long," Victoria said, wanting to make clear they hadn't found Vince's sister. Although...if the dead woman was older than she appeared, and someone had kept her alive for the past few years and only dumped her body recently...

"I said, you can go now," Leo repeated.

The agents moved back a few yards but looked on as the police carried the corpse from the water and laid it on an evidence collection sheet. Vince looked shaken, but not devastated, suggesting the body was not his sister.

The deceased woman's hands were tied together, making clear her death was no accident. She wore only panties and a bra. The bottom of one leg was gone. Cracked tibia and fibula bones protruded from a jagged cut. An injury like that would have come from an animal with large, sharp teeth.

"This could be the other local woman who recently went missing," Vince said. "I recognize those friendship bracelets on her wrist. Her friends showed me a picture of them."

The colorful bracelets were barely visible under the coils of yellow rope.

Leo lifted one corner of the sheet and wrapped it around the corpse.

"Wait," Victoria said, crouching down to study the dead girl's remaining foot. "What's this?"

All five toes were missing. There were no jagged tears or teeth marks in the remaining flesh. A sharp, smooth instrument had made those cuts.

CHAPTER 27

Back at Azure Cove, as the agents refilled their water bottles from a dispenser of iced-cucumber water at the Horizon Hut, Victoria couldn't stop thinking about the corpse they'd just found under the pier. Someone had cut off parts of her body, just like the other local woman who had disappeared. The Federales had the corpse now. It would be up to them to conduct an autopsy to determine the cause of her death. They would let Rivera and Victoria know if they found any connection to Avery's disappearance, wouldn't they? After the Federales' behavior at the marina, Victoria wasn't so sure anymore.

Rivera downed his water and went for a refill. When he returned, Victoria said, "Let's focus on what we learned from the tracking dog. According to Josefina, whom I trust—"

"Because she's a dog and dogs can do no wrong in your book."

"That's pretty much true. According to Josefina, Avery was inside the seaweed truck compartment at some point. Maybe someone hid her there, waiting for an opportunity to get her off the property."

"If they took Avery away inside the truck, Josefina wouldn't have followed her scent down the beach close to the resorts the way she did."

"You're right. So maybe someone hid Avery in the seaweed, waited until dark, and then carried her down the beach. But...how could that happen without someone seeing her? Even at night, people would notice someone carrying a woman against her will. Even if they believed she was drunk when they saw her, once word of the disappearance spread, they would have interpreted what they saw differently. And yet no one has mentioned seeing anything like that. What are we missing? How did someone get her down the beach without looking suspicious?"

"He could have pressed a gun into her back. But more likely, she was...not walking. She was either unconscious or...." Victoria didn't finish the sentence. Until they had proof Avery was dead, they needed to act on the belief she was still alive and needed help.

"I've got an idea," Victoria set her empty glass on a tray and started walking on the boardwalk.

"Where is your idea leading us?"

"To the water sports pavilion. It's close to the seaweed truck."

At the pavilion, Victoria first eyed the Sunfish sails. Then the kayaks caught her attention. Each was taller and wider than a person Avery's size.

Henri was sitting behind a small desk, signing equipment out to a couple. He stood when he saw the agents coming but waited until the couple grabbed their oars and headed down to the water before he said, "Hi. Are you still...what can I help you with?"

"Hi, Henri," Victoria said. "Do you have storage bags for the kayaks or the paddleboards? Or maybe bags for storing the sails?"

"No. We don't have those. This stuff just gets locked up inside the pavilion at night. Once it gets here, it pretty much stays. Why? Do you need one for something?"

"No," Victoria said, disappointed that her idea had led nowhere. "If you don't have them, no point in asking if you're missing one. Any chance you're missing a spare sail?"

Henri's eyes lit up. He spun around, looking for something...or someone, but then returned his focus to the agents. "Actually...Miguel...he works here, he's the guy Avery's mother pushed into the sand, then she made him strip—"

That's not exactly how Victoria remembered it happening, but she didn't interrupt.

"—Miguel has his own paddleboard equipment," Henri continued. "He owns a nice racing board. Someone stole his bag. I think Saturday night or Sunday morning. Not the equipment, but just the bag. It's a nice one. Has wheels on one end. He was asking everyone about it...thinking someone borrowed it because, you know...none of us would steal it. That's just not something you do when you live together, you know?"

"Thanks for the info," Rivera said.

The agents left the pavilion and got back on the path that would take them to the reception area. "Let's find Miguel," Victoria said. "I want to know if that bag ever showed up again, and who took it."

On the marble floors of the reception area, a group of employees in light blue polo shirts gathered around the manager. Neither he nor any of the staff were smiling as the agents approached.

"What happened?" Victoria asked, thinking perhaps the Jennings had told the manager about the newly discovered dead body near the resort.

"Teresa is missing," the manager said. "She made a reservation for a private excursion. When the diver came to pick her up, she wasn't here. I received your message this morning to check on her. I went to her bungalow myself. Her room doesn't appear to have been slept in last night."

"Have you called the police?" Victoria asked.

"I called Leo directly, in case there's a connection to Avery Jennings. The police came, but they had to leave quite suddenly. Apparently, you called them."

"We did," Rivera said.

That explained why the police left the marina so abruptly, but it still didn't explain their game-changing behavior prior to getting Alejandro's call.

"I've organized another search party," the manager said. "Just like we did for Avery. All volunteers are welcome. We're looking for two people now. And since Teresa is also American, perhaps you should contact her family."

She has no family, Victoria thought. Which meant that if Teresa remained missing, it was unlikely anyone would travel to Mexico and search for her.

"We'll do that," Rivera said. "We'll also need access to her room, before anyone else goes in there.:

"Do you think the disappearances are related?" a female employee asked.

"We don't know yet," Rivera answered.

It was unusual for a perpetrator to target a twenty-two-year-old and an eighty-seven-year-old, yet Victoria believed that's exactly what had happened.

160

The inside of Teresa's bungalow was nearly identical to the Jennings' accommodations, and just as beautiful. There were two separate bedrooms. The first one Victoria entered showed no signs someone occupied the room. Inside the closet, she found four unopened boxes on the floor. Handwritten in a penmanship that was more calligraphy than print, the mailing address was Azure Cove. The return address was for Cordelia Middleton in New York.

"These belonged to Teresa's twin sister," Victoria said. "They were supposed to travel together. Cordelia passed away right before the trip. She must have mailed her things here ahead of time."

"Teresa doesn't strike me as a grieving sister. More like the ultimate diva living it up here like she owns the place."

"I know. But all behavior has meaning. Maybe Teresa worries about what everyone else is doing so she doesn't have to deal with her own grief and loneliness. As far as I could tell from the Internet, Cordelia was Teresa's twin sister, and also her only family member."

The agents moved to the second bedroom. It was just as neat and clean, the bed perfectly made, but several things suggested someone was staying there. A hardcover novel and reading glasses sat on the bedside table. A bright orange cardigan was draped over the back of a chair. Slippers rested on the floor beside the bed.

Victoria opened the closet. Expensive resort-wear clothing in bright colors, both hanging and folded, filled the space. Four matching boxes sat side by side on the top shelf. Victoria took one down and opened it, expecting to find a hat. An exquisite silvery-blonde wig styled into a shoulder length bob nestled inside the box. Victoria had a feeling Teresa wouldn't want anyone to see her wigs. Even though Teresa was missing, Victoria wished they didn't have to search through her personal belongings.

On the other side of the room, Teresa's pink journal sat on the desk. Victoria opened it to the title page. *Azure Cove Vacation, March 15th*. Each page had a date underlined at the top, but it wasn't a diary. Nor was it an appointment or schedule book. Almost every page contained lists of things that, in Teresa's opinion, others needed to do. The first page had the header, *Massage Room Infractions*, followed by a list of things that annoyed Teresa during her Swedish massage.

Eucalyptus too strong. Sheet had wrinkles. Someone having a conversation outside the massage room woke me up and ruined the entire experience.

Victoria flipped through more pages. There was a list for every single day. Hundreds, possibly thousands of notes. Concerns involved the beach, the grounds, the dining areas, the spa, the pool, the exercise instructors, and the boutiques.

The air conditioning issue in my room persists. Three visits from maintenance and it's still too cold.

Attendees at seven a.m. yoga class hung their mats over the glass railing. No one sprayed them down. No one came to wash them before the next class. This protocol must change.

The French couple from room 365 rode exercise bikes inside the gym without wearing masks.

All "problems" of the rich and privileged. That was one way to look at it. Or did Teresa's journal entries represent how a grief-stricken woman distracted herself from personal pain? Were her lists of infractions giving her otherwise lonely life a purpose?

Victoria skimmed through pages. On Sunday, the day Avery disappeared, Teresa had written the following:

Managers must check to ensure staff uniforms fit properly. Should also mandate that staff with tattoos keep them covered. Small tattoos on ankles could be allowed, if deemed appropriate.

Victoria turned the pages to the most recent entry, written yesterday. The first item said, *Towels placed on fifteen different chairs to reserve them. Fifteen! All in the shade. That's three more than yesterday morning. This must stop!*

Waitress Rebecca wore her mask below her nostrils. I mentioned it to her. All staff need a reminder or constant reminders.

The last item on the list said, *Figure out where you saw the man with Avery and tell the FBI lady. The bonfire???*

Teresa had underlined the last sentence.

Victoria went to the resort's app on her phone and checked the weekly activity schedule. Every Saturday night, the resort hosted a Luau style bonfire on the beach.

Returning to Teresa's journal, Victoria flipped the pages backward, stopping at the previous Saturday's date. Teresa had compiled a list of observations related to the bonfire. Top of the list and underlined: *People who don't belong at Azure Cove are coming in from the beach and making themselves at home!*

Perhaps Teresa had left enough clues to help them find the person of interest. If only the information would also help them locate Teresa. Azure Cove's staff was searching every guest room, office, and outbuilding for her, just as they'd done for Avery. Almost all the staff knew *who* Teresa was but none of them knew *where* she was.

CHAPTER 28

T hree days had passed since Avery's disappearance.

The agents were still waiting to hear back from their boss on how to proceed regarding the police's sudden lack of cooperation. In the meantime, Victoria sat down at the desk in her room to make use of the information from Teresa's journal, specifically the bonfire reference.

Wearing Rivera's sweatshirt again, Victoria combed through the photos Avery's friends took during their trip. She'd seen them several times now—over two hundred images, taken consistently throughout the days. Most were selfies or posed shots of the young women in various places around the resort. Haley had taken dozens of photos of the artfully prepared entrees, desserts, and elaborate tropical cocktails. There were also sunsets, palm trees, and beach shots. It didn't appear the young women had taken a single photo at the bonfire.

Victoria typed a message to Brie and Haley. *Did any of you go to the bonfire/Luau party on Saturday night?*

After pressing send, Victoria massaged her temples, pressing her fingers firmly against her skull.

Haley responded first. *Yes. All of us.*

Victoria wrote, *I don't see any bonfire pictures. Did you take any?*

Haley answered, *I did, but I deleted them. They were bad. Too dark. They're still in my deleted album. Should I send them?*

Victoria swallowed her frustration. *Yes. Send them now. Both of you, please send ANY AND ALL pictures you took, including any you deleted.*

The photos began arriving almost immediately. Haley had taken several photo bursts a few yards away from a tall circle of fire. The ocean in the background was pitch black, darker than the night sky. Faces were hard to distinguish. Victoria transferred each shot into her computer where she enlarged and enhanced the images until Avery and her friends became recognizable. Their poses were more of the same. Full on big smiles, but also pouty, pursed-lip poses, one leg forward, one hip jutting to the side. Victoria enhanced the brightness of each image and adjusted the colors until finally, something caught her attention.

In the foreground, Avery and Brie had an arm wrapped around each other's waists. Behind them and to the right, wearing a bright orange shawl with a matching orange and white headband, Teresa stood with her thin legs slightly apart and her hands on her narrow hips. She was scowling. But not at the girls. Her focus was on someone or something behind them.

Victoria edited and enhanced the next pictures in the sequence. They held the same image, except Avery's eyes were closed in one, and Brie's eyes were closed in the next. A second burst of photos followed. Haley had moved to the right, capturing her friends from a different angle. All that remained of Teresa was a speck of orange shoe in the sand, but the object of her disdain was apparent. A man. Victoria zoomed in on his features. He was fit and muscular, in a way that could make a person think he was a boxer. His arm wasn't visible, so there was no way to check for the tattoo. But as far as she could see, in every respect except for one, he matched the man Brie claimed to have seen. He had the thick eyebrows she described, but a patch of one brow was missing. That was strange. If he was the guy, why hadn't Brie mentioned the unusual eyebrow?

Victoria saved the enhanced image of the man and sent it to Brie.

A knock startled her.

She pushed her chair away from the desk. In the entry, where she'd removed her shoes, she padded across grits of sand she could feel through her socks. When she opened the door, Carlos stood in the corridor with a cleaning cart behind him.

"Clean?" he asked.

"No, gracias," she answered, shaking her head, surprised he was asking about cleaning her room so late in the evening. But perhaps he'd been helping to search for Avery and Teresa and that had taken precedence over his cleaning schedule. She grabbed the Do Not Disturb sign from the inside of the door and hung it on the outside. "Not necessary. However..." On the off-chance Carlos knew a trick to adjust the room's thermostat, she gestured for him to enter. She pointed to the temperature control, then wrapped her arms around her body and shivered.

Carlos shook his head. Victoria wasn't sure if that was his standard response so he didn't get pulled into the guests' issues, of which there were probably many, or if it meant the thermostat could not be adjusted.

"Gracias, it's okay. Never mind. Denada," she said. Now that she had him in her room, she searched his face for any clue of what he might know, which was more important than the room temperature.

He lowered his chin, still staring at her.

Victoria placed her hand on her chest. "What? Is there something you want to tell me? Do you know something about Avery?"

Carlos surprised her by smiling and shaking his head before he turned and walked out of her room.

"Uno momento." Perplexed, Victoria went into the hallway to get Rivera so he could have a proper conversation with Carlos.

"No. No necessary." Carlos waved his hand. It looked like he was apologizing. He grabbed the handles of his cart and slowly pushed it down the corridor.

Victoria's phone beeped. She took her eyes off Carlos' retreating back to read the message. A reply from Brie.

That's him!!!! That's the guy who came to our room and took Avery!!

CHAPTER 29

Victoria rushed along the path toward the center of the resort, passing guests who strolled casually. The chairs were filling up around the stage, where two men sang and played guitar to warm up the crowd for the main show.

"Hi," she said when she reached the front desk. "I need to speak with Alejandro. Is he still in his office?"

"Yes. He hardly ever leaves this place. Especially now with all that's happening. Hold on just a minute, please." The desk clerk went out through the back door and returned seconds later. "He's talking to the resort's legal team. He asked for a few more minutes."

"I'll wait."

Two missing persons from the resort constituted a legal and publicity nightmare for Azure Cove. Victoria worried the resort's attorneys were about to sweep in and interfere with the investigation by telling the manager not to speak with the police or FBI without counsel.

Ten minutes later, the land line on the desk rang. The clerk answered and told Victoria she should go back to the manager's office.

Victoria found Alejandro behind his desk, his eyes moving between a paper in front of him and his computer screen. As she entered the room, he looked up, giving her his full attention. He looked exhausted, with dark circles around his eyes, like the world was hitting him with more problems that he could handle at once. Victoria again noticed the family photo on his desk and wondered how long since he'd been home to see them.

Alejandro sat back in his chair and swiveled to face her, shaking his head. "I can't believe what my job had come to. That was our legal team, crafting the message I'm supposed to share with the public. Tell me you have good news."

"I don't know that I'd call it that yet. Depends."

"Is this about Avery Jennings or Teresa Middleton?" he asked.

"Avery. I found an image of the man we were looking for. He was in a photo her friend took on the beach at the bonfire last Saturday. There are minor differences from the sketch Brie Vanderhorn drew, but she just confirmed that this is him."

Victoria showed Alejandro the photo.

He stared at the image. "I don't recognize him."

"Neither does the FBI's facial recognition software," she said. "I ran it through before I came. But it's not perfect. It doesn't always deliver for us unless someone is looking directly at the camera."

"So, now what?"

"I sent the photo to the Mexican police. I'd like you to share it with the staff and guests. And print some copies we can circulate."

"I'm just..." Alejandro turned to look at his desk, as if searching for permission. He sighed. "I'll shoot an email to our staff and put his picture on our app where the guests can see it." He glanced at his Apple watch. "I'll do it first thing tomorrow. I have to introduce tonight's show now."

"Trust me on this. Every minute matters," Victoria said. "I need you to do it now."

Later that night, Victoria returned to the entertainment area, where she went from chair to chair, asking if anyone recognized the man. No one did. Or at least they said they didn't. If anyone had useful information, they weren't talking.

Aside from the constant hum of the air conditioning, Victoria's room was silent at three a.m. That was the best time to commit a crime. Most people were deep in slumber. Not Victoria. Unable to sleep because her mind was racing, she went to her balcony and slid the doors open. Outside, she listened to the gentle whoosh of the ocean waves.

Landscape lighting illuminated the paths and accented the trees and buildings, though a few stretches of complete darkness remained. Places to hurt someone. Places to hide someone.

Their person of interest was out there somewhere. Was he afraid that they were closing in? Or smug about getting away with it what he'd done?

Victoria realized she was clenching her teeth. She let go her grip on the balcony railing and went back inside.

Every detail of the suspect's image was seared into her memory.

CHAPTER 30

At an outdoor dining table overlooking the cove, Victoria took a sip of her coffee. A nearby table had yet to be cleared of leftover breakfast food. A bird swooped in under the veranda, snagged a round of bread, and flew off again. Another did the same. Their antics were putting a dent in her solemn mood. Animals had a way of doing that without even trying.

Sitting across from her, Rivera edged his fork into a custom-made omelet and separated a large piece. "You heard from Vince?"

"No. I left another message for him this morning. I guess they're busy. Two missing persons and a dead body to deal with, and that's only what we know about their workload, but they could use our help more than ever. They have to keep us in the loop."

"Well, they aren't."

Rivera's phone vibrated face up on the table. Murphy's name appeared on the screen.

Rivera set his fork down and answered the call. After listening for several seconds, he lifted his brows and frowned. "I'm with Victoria now. I'll put you on speaker."

Empty tables surrounded them. There was no one around, but Victoria kept her voice down. "Hello, boss."

"Hello, Victoria," Murphy said. "What did you do?"

Murphy's tone, the way he emphasized each word, told her whatever she supposedly did wasn't a good thing. "I don't know what you're talking about."

"The Chief of Police called. He doesn't want your help anymore."

"He doesn't want my help?" Victoria asked. "He said I did something?"

"Not just you. Both of you have gotten yourselves uninvited from assisting with the investigation."

"That's ridiculous," Victoria said. "They need us."

"Did he tell you why?" Rivera asked.

"No." Murphy answered. "He only left me a message. Said he didn't have time to go into the details. I haven't been able to get hold of him yet."

"Like we told you, something happened yesterday with the police at the marina, but it wasn't anything we did," Victoria said. "They've been ghosting us since then."

"Or they're over their heads with the discovery of the drowning victim," Murphy said. "I know they could use our help, but apparently, they don't want it now."

"Wait...drowning victim? Did the Chief of Police tell you she drowned?" Victoria asked. "Because it was more than that. Her toes were cut off. And she just disappeared last week. It's likely there's a connection to Avery."

"There might be. And you may have found the body, but unfortunately, the investigation is not our territory. I don't know what's going on, but you can't charge ahead and assert yourselves. You have to be careful down there, walk on eggshells with the police, or we'll be cut out completely. Do what you need to do but keep a low profile for God's sake. If nothing turns up, as difficult as it may be...with Payton and all...you should come home. I'll let Payton know it's my call."

A man called Murphy's name in the background. Murphy shouted, "Hold on!" though muffled, as if he had covered his phone. When he addressed the agents again a second later, his voice was clear. "I have to go, but I'm going to leave you with this: as long as you remain there, do whatever you can to find Avery Jennings, but don't do anything to jeopardize our relationship with the police chief. It's an important one."

Murphy cut off the call, leaving Rivera and Victoria to stare at each other.

"This is BS," Rivera said. He pushed his plate aside, apparently having lost his appetite. "I'll go see Tom and Jennifer and find out if the Federales are still communicating with them."

"Call and tell me what you find out." Victoria took her napkin from her lap and placed it on the table. "I'm going to head back to the marina and look around. The tracking dog led us there. It's the best place to search for leads."

"Watch yourself," Rivera whispered as they both stood from the table. "Be careful and don't forget we've got limited authority here and now apparently we're not welcome." He met her eyes, waiting for her to acknowledge his words.

"I know," she told him. She also knew he wanted to find Avery and Teresa as much as she did.

Victoria slid her thumb down the side of her pocketknife and released the blade. She sliced the tag off the Azure Cove cap she'd purchased in one of the resort's boutiques, then snapped the knife closed. She tucked it into the running pack she wore around her waist. Besides her knife, the pack held her essentials—her gun, badge, phone, and some cash.

Jogging on the beach in shorts and a tank top, she looked like any other fit tourist out for a run. That was the plan. She kept her hands in loose fists as she ran, concealing her missing fingers. If no one knew she was an FBI agent, no one could complain if she accidentally or otherwise overstepped her bounds asking questions at the marina.

When she got there, she slowed to a walk. On one dock, a man was loading boxes from a wheeled pushcart onto a boat.

"Excuse me," Victoria said to him.

He turned around and shamelessly checked her out.

"Hi. Is this your boat?" she asked.

"Yes," the man answered as he lifted a cooler from the cart. "Why are you asking?"

A curvy woman lying on the top deck propped herself onto her elbows and stared down at Victoria from behind large sunglasses.

"I was wondering if you could help me," Victoria said. "I'm trying to find a guy I met a few days ago at my resort. Last Sunday, in the evening, he docked his boat in that slip over there." She did her best to look embarrassed about her request as she pointed to the empty boat slip where Avery's scent trail had ended.

The man broke into a smile, and he chuckled. "I'll look."

She handed him her phone, which served her story better than handing out printed flyers. Shielding the screen from the sun's glare, he stared at the picture, crinkled his brow, then handed the device back to Victoria. "I've never seen him."

"Um, he had a tattoo of a heart with a crown on it."

"Don't remember that either."

"You can show me." The sunbathing woman sat up but made no effort to come down to the dock.

Victoria stepped onto the boat, went up the ladder, and held out the photo. "Not a super image, but it's what I've got."

The woman pushed her sunglasses up to her forehead. "You could do so much better. Did he steal from you?"

"No, it's not that." Again, Victoria feigned embarrassment. "Have you seen him around here?"

"He doesn't look familiar to me. I would have remembered him with that scar."

"Okay. Thanks for taking a look," Victoria said.

"Good luck," the man said as Victoria got off his boat. "Check with the guy who works at the marina's shop. He sees everyone."

"I will. Thanks," Victoria told him, already heading toward the store. The space behind the counter was empty. She was only a few yards away when someone came out through the back area. He leaned on the counter, watching her approach. It wasn't the bald employee from yesterday. This man was younger.

Victoria stopped in front of the counter and scanned the items for sale. Sunglasses, hats, and belts. Snacks, beverages, beer, and ice. Sunscreen. Bait and tackle.

"Uno agua, por favor," she said.

He moved to one end of the counter and opened an upright refrigerated chest.

"Quiet around here," Victoria said, carefully removing Mexican pesos from the outer pocket of her stuffed pack and exchanging them for the cool plastic bottle.

"Si," he said.

She showed him the picture. "Have you seen this man?"

He leaned close to the screen and appeared to study the image. After a long moment, he shook his head. "No."

He seemed to understand her, so she continued with her story. "I met him a few days ago. I'd really like to see him again. He has something of mine. I know he owns a boat or drives a boat. That's all I know." She gave the man behind the counter a sheepish smile. "Is there anyone else around that I could ask?"

He held up a finger. "Hold on, someone coming. Can help."

Victoria scanned the marina. Other than the couple she'd already spoken to, she didn't see anyone else. "Someone is coming who might know the person in my photo?" she asked.

"Fifteen minutes," the man said, nodding vigorously. "Fifteen minutes. You wait?"

"Sure." She could wait. The man and the boat slip were their best leads. Someone had to have seen him. All it would take was a name to find him. And then Victoria would do whatever it took to get to Avery.

Victoria unzipped her pack and slid her phone back inside. She was no stranger to boats, thanks to her father's interests. She wasn't passionate about sailing, but it could be fun with the right people and in the right conditions. Walking down the docks, she checked out the larger boats for anyone else she could question while monitoring the road leading to the marina's parking lot so she wouldn't miss whoever was coming.

Five minutes passed.

Then ten.

Fifteen.

She'd walked up and down each of the docks and was about to return to the store when a shiny speed boat roared into the marina, traveling faster than it should and leaving a large wake. The driver, a man with longish dark hair, cut the engine, letting the boat glide into an empty boat slip. Victoria walked toward the slip. She looked over her shoulder, but still didn't see anyone coming from the road.

When she turned back to the water, the boat's driver had lifted an arm to wave to her.

Except...he wasn't waving. He was leveling a gun.

In the seconds that followed, there was disbelief, an immediate tightening of her muscles, and a rocketing surge of adrenaline. Victoria sprang forward, diving to the ground. Before she hit the dock, a bullet struck between her neck and shoulder. Too keyed up to register the pain, she rolled onto her back, staying low against the wooden boards, fumbling to get her own weapon.

Her fingers wouldn't respond.

She couldn't move.

Her mind clouded.

Then blackness.

CHAPTER 31

Tony was fuming and couldn't calm down. He never napped during the day. He barely slept at all. But out of sheer boredom, too much sun and fresh air, he had dozed off. Couldn't have been thirty minutes he'd been out, but that was all it had taken for Eric to go AWOL. Growing angrier and more concerned by the second, Tony paced the deck, shouting, "Where is he? Where did Eric go?"

"I don't know," the captain answered. "He didn't tell me he was leaving."

Tony glowered at Marineros Uno and Dos as they came out onto the deck. "Do either of you know where he went?"

"He said he'd be right back," Uno answered, looking sorry for knowing anything about the matter.

"If he's not back in ten minutes, take us to the marina," Tony told the captain.

Tony paced the upper deck some more. He was looking out at the water when a speedboat made a straight-line approach to *The Untouchable*. As it got closer, Tony spotted Eric standing behind the wheel, his hair blowing in the wind.

"Where did you go?" Tony shouted as soon as Eric was close enough to hear him.

Eric grinned from ear to ear, practically bouncing on his toes. "One of those losers at the marina just came through in a big way."

"What are you talking about?" Tony squeezed his hands into fists.

"I answered your phone while you were asleep. A guy at the marina says some chick is asking about you. Showing your picture around. Says she met you at a resort the other night and you've got something of hers."

Tony didn't know what that was about. With a wave of paranoia, he scanned the ocean again, making sure no one was coming for them. As usual, the only thing around was the endless water. Everything seemed to be okay, and his anger ebbed. Then he dropped his gaze to the bottom of the speedboat and saw her. A blonde woman sprawled across the front seats, either drugged or dead. She wore running clothes and a cap with *Azure Cove* stitched across the front. She had long, toned limbs and a lean, healthy body.

"Who is she?" he asked, clenching his jaw as his fury returned.

Eric's eyes gleamed and his head bobbed like a lunatic. "That's the woman who was asking about you. She's not real young, but she's hot. But that's not the half of it." Eric laughed. "You're not going to believe this"

Tony gritted his teeth as he lowered himself into the speedboat. What he couldn't believe was how he had to put up with an imbecile and his disgusting fetishes.

"So, the guy says—," Eric laughed again, "—he says she's got a chicken claw hand with missing fingers." Eric rocked on his toes. "You know I had to see that for myself. I mean, come on, I had to. And she does! And it's not just one hand! It's both!" Eric was practically salivating. "I thought she might be someone I'd already had some fun with, you know, and what the hell was she doing still walking around? But I didn't do it to her. I'd remember if I had."

Tony leaned over the woman he'd never seen before. He pressed his fingers against her neck. She was alive and breathing, with a slow but steady pulse, and he wasn't sure if that was good or bad yet. She wore no makeup and had smooth, flawless skin. Tony stuck his finger in her mouth and spread her lips. She had perfect, white teeth. Everything about her told him that someone would miss this lady. He didn't need that heat, not with everything else they had to hide.

Eric got out of the boat, still laughing. "She'll wake up, eventually. Lock her in one of the empty cabins. I'll visit her later. I'm going to savor this one."

Eric's offhand demand made Tony lose his cool. "I'm not your servant, Eric. I work for your father."

Eric turned. He was still smiling, but his eyes were cold. "No, Tony. That's where you're mistaken. On this yacht, you report to me. Maybe you need to be reminded of that, eh?"

As Eric sauntered off, Tony smashed a fist against the hull of the boat, imagining it was Eric's face. What had that idiot done? Who was the lady with the claw hands knocked out on the boat? He scooped her up in his arms and stood behind the driver's seat, staring into the ocean. He could dump her overboard right there and relish the satisfaction of defying Eric. He could, but he wouldn't. Tony was better than that. Smarter. He had to find out who she was first.

The woman's chest rose and fell with each soft breath as he carried her into a cabin, one of two whose doors locked from the outside. After tossing her on the bed, he tied her hands together. He didn't need her waking up and trying to scratch his eyes out or smash everything she could get her hands on like the last girl when she realized the yacht wasn't quite the party scene she expected.

Once he'd secured her wrists, he pulled her belt from her waist. It was heavier than he would have thought. Still roiling with hatred for Eric, Tony took it with him when he left, locking the cabin door from the hallway.

Inside Tony's own cabin, he unzipped the mystery woman's pack. There was a Glock inside. That was unexpected, and he wasn't sure what to make of it. Along with the gun, he found a pocketknife, an iPhone, and a thin, plastic, rectangular case, the kind that typically held credit cards. After setting the gun and phone aside on his bed, Tony turned the plastic case over and flipped it open. An identification badge for the Federal Bureau of Investigation stared back at him.

Tony's anger surged. He grabbed the woman's phone and shut it off. Hollering, "Uno!" Tony stormed into the corridor. The deck hand was already hurrying down the ladder when Tony got there.

"Tell the captain to kill off all sonar, radar, satellite for the ship." Tony said, thrusting the blonde woman's phone at him. "Then take this back to the marina, drive inland at least ten miles, and throw it out the window somewhere. A town. A field. I don't care. Just get it far away from us."

Uno took the phone. Tony followed him up the ladder. "Get your prints off it before you toss it. Wipe it clean. And remember... you know nothing. Not today. Not next month. And not next year. Nothing."

"I know," Uno said as they continued up a level, where Eric was lounging on a couch playing video games.

Tony flipped the badge open and shoved it under Eric's nose.

"Hey. Get that out of my face," Eric yelled, leaning around Tony to see the television screen.

Tony didn't move. As angry as he was, he appreciated the opportunity to point out Eric's stupidity. "Look how much you screwed up, Eric."

Eric threw the joystick down and stood up. "What's your problem now, Tony?"

"That woman you took is with the FBI."

"Oh." Eric frowned. "Look, who cares?"

"Who cares? The FBI cares. They'll go crazy trying to find her. They'll be everywhere trying to track her down."

Eric shrugged. "They won't look here. No one knows she's here. No one will ever know."

"You sure about that, Eric? Did anyone see you take her?" Anger rose with each syllable as Tony tried to think about the best course of action.

"Just the marina guy who called me. And the guy who puts gas in the boats. No one who matters. No one who would dare say a word about it. Both wore shiny, new watches. Looks like you were busy handing out presents."

"Just in case of something like this. That's why I hand out gifts and money, Eric."

"Yeah, well, it's a pussy way of doing business. We should make them pay us for the privilege of not getting crushed. We don't have to give presents." Eric snorted as he stuffed his hands into his pockets. "We'll get rid of her. Same thing as with the other girls. But not yet. It can wait a few days until I'm done with her."

"No, it can't. We don't have time to wait. She needs to disappear now."

CHAPTER 32

Victoria dreamed about a thumping noise. A rhythmic knock that continued until it pulled her from sleep. A few more thumps and the sound stopped, leaving her mostly awake, though she hadn't yet opened her eyes. Feeling woozy and hungover, she went to rub her forehead...and couldn't. Something secured her hands together behind her back.

Her eyes flew open.

Where am I?

She blinked. Bright circles of recessed light shone in the ceiling. Glossy teak walls and custom-built cabinetry. Gray silk sheets. A velvet duvet. Everything was shiny and sleek and sleazy at the same time. A hotel? Long rectangles of glass along the top of one wall framed the dark night. Portholes. She was on a boat and from what she could see, no ordinary one.

With a terrified gasp, she remembered the speedboat and the man who shot her. She tried to touch her chest, already forgetting she couldn't move her hands. She dropped her chin toward the pain emanating from her shoulder area. A few specks of blood dotted her tank top, nothing more. He must have used a tranquilizer gun.

How long since that man had shot her? She couldn't tell, but it was dark out, so at least half a day had passed.

Pinpoints of pain radiated over the front of her body, caused by the tiny brown speckles dotting her legs. Splinters. In her mind's eye, she pictured herself diving onto the wooden dock and cringed at the memory.

Ned's voice echoed in her mind—*Be careful*. Seeing that someone had tranquilized her and trapped her like an animal, she hadn't been careful enough. Though who would have expected such a brazen attack to occur in daylight in a public area?

Victoria took a deep breath to further quell her fear and regret, reminding herself that dwelling on her mistakes would not get her out of the situation. Easier said than done, but she needed to do it. She started by assessing her surroundings.

Victoria was fully clothed, except for her bare feet. Someone had taken her running shoes and socks. She glanced down at her waist, though she already knew her running pack was gone. And with it, her phone and her knife.

Her fear intensified and her breathing became erratic.

Calm down.

Inhale. Exhale. Deep breaths.

Her reflection in the wall mirror revealed several coils of smooth, yellow rope surrounding her wrists. Familiar and frightening.

She scanned the room for a sharp edge and didn't find one amongst the sleek built-in cabinetry. She got off the bed, careful not to make a sound. With her back to a dresser, she pulled the top drawer open with her fingertips, then turned around to see what was inside. Nothing but neatly folded undershirts. The drawers below it were empty. One corner of the room held a small trash can. She turned it over with her foot and ran her toes through the contents on the floor. Used tissues. A candy bar wrapper.

An empty soda can. Empty baggies. None of that would help get her hands untied. Dragging the side of her foot across the carpet, she shoved the loose trash under the bed. Using her foot again, she tipped the trash can back up to its base.

Inside the custom closet, she found a built-in cabinet. She turned away from it and got on her knees, moving her fingers over the panel behind her. When she found a small depression, she gripped it and leaned forward. The panel seemed stuck, and her fingers slid off. She repositioned them and tried again. It opened with a slow sucking sound and cool air hit her. Turning, she found a row of beer cans, and below them, a row of sparkling waters in glass bottles.

She dropped a glass bottle on the bed and went back to the dresser, where she grabbed a T-shirt. She scanned the room again. The nightstand would have to do.

Wrapping the T-shirt around the glass to buffer the noise and protect her wrists, she gripped the neck of the bottle and jerked backwards, ramming it against the edge of the nightstand. The bottle cracked. Foaming liquid splashed her backside and spilled over her fingers. She held her breath for several rapid heartbeats, praying no one else had heard.

A noise on the other side of the inner wall made her freeze. The thumping sound again. And then a woman's voice, not much louder than a whisper. "Hello? Can you hear me?"

Victoria moved to the interior wall. "Yes. Who are you?"

"Avery Jennings."

"My name is Victoria," she said in a burst of excitement. "I'm with the FBI. I work with your aunt Payton. She sent me to find you." While she spoke, Victoria didn't waste a moment. She dropped to her knees and leaned to one side, sticking the broken bottle between her heels, pressing her feet tight against the neck to hold it steady.

"Victoria Heslin? Are you Victoria Heslin?" Avery asked.

"Yes," Victoria answered as she leaned back into a camel pose and carefully, gently at first, moved the ropes over the sharp-edged glass, aware a false move might sever an artery. The task demanded a precision that made her thighs quiver and shake. She quietly grunted, straining to hold the pose and keep everything perfectly still except for the slight movement of her wrists.

"I know who you are," Avery said. "My aunt talks about you, and I read about you after that plane crash. Thank God you're here. Thank you for finding me."

"Uh...yes." She had found Avery, which was the goal all along. Victoria tried not to beat herself up about the less-than-ideal execution of her search.

You're not a victim. You're where you need to be. Avery is close.

"Are you still there?" Avery asked.

"Yes." Victoria carefully applied more pressure against the jagged glass. One loop came apart, dropping over her wrist and palm. "Are you hurt?"

"Not really. I'm okay. Just...I'm terrified of what's going to happen to me if I don't get off this boat soon."

"It's okay to be afraid," Victoria said, which was something she needed to hear, perhaps as much as Avery did. "We might have to hang in here a bit longer. Are you tied up?"

"I'm not tied. But I'm locked in a cabin. Are we still in Mexico?"

"I'm not sure. How many people are on the boat?"

"Five men that I know of. There's another girl here. At least there was. They were torturing her. I think...I think they might have cut off her toes."

An image of the corpse floating below the pier flashed before Victoria's eyes. Had that woman been on this boat before she died? Were there others? Was the same fate awaiting Avery if they didn't get out of there soon?

Victoria's thighs shook violently and sweat rolled down her face and into her hair, but another loop of rope fell away. One last coil surrounded her wrists. A few more sawing passes over the razor-edged glass and her hands would be free.

"I heard them arguing about you," Avery said. "They know you're with the FBI."

*How did they...*Victoria remembered her bag also contained her identification.

She felt a sharp sting and then wetness on her wrists. Drops of blood trickled out. Not a gush, which brought a measure of relief, but with another slip, she might not get so lucky. She had to slow down. Focus.

"Who are they, Avery? Do you know?"

"I don't know. The man who took me...I haven't seen him since I woke up in this room. One of the guys is a total psycho, the one who owns the boat. Watch out for him. What are we going to do now? Wait...shh...shh." There was silence before Avery whispered, "They're coming."

Victoria held her breath, horrified that harm might come to Avery when Victoria was so close to helping her. Footsteps came closer and stopped outside her door. Still gripping the broken bottle, Victoria kicked the T-shirt and remaining glass under the bed. She made a split-second decision to let her captor think she was still unconscious. She could harness the element of surprise when the time was right.

"Is Uno back?" a man with a deep voice asked from somewhere very close to her cabin.

"Yes," another man answered.

Victoria collapsed across the bed, assuming her earlier position. Rope still surrounded her wrists, but only a bit of it remained. She interlaced her fingers, cupping them around the loose rope and the broken bottle, and pressed her bleeding wrist against her shirt to stop the bleeding.

The cabin door opened. Someone crossed the room. Warm, meaty hands surrounded her ankles and dragged her roughly off the bed. She didn't resist, letting herself get scooped into a man's heavily muscled arms.

"You peed yourself," he mumbled with disgust, mistaking the sparkling water that splashed over her backside for urine.

With her arms behind her back, the way he carried her caused stabbing pains to radiate through her shoulders. She gritted her teeth and remained limp. He seemed to move effortlessly, carrying her down a corridor and up a set of stairs. A few more steps, feet clomping against wooden floors, and he stopped. The air warmed as they emerged onto one of the boat's upper decks.

"Is she dead?" a man asked from a few yards away. There was no emotion in his voice. He didn't care if she was alive or dead.

The man who carried her responded with animosity, "No. She's alive."

"No way I could have known she was FBI," the other man said.

"You didn't know because you don't think."

"How is this so different from what you did?"

The man carrying Victoria huffed. "I created an opportunity for us. Your screw-up might destroy that."

Their exchange reeked of hatred for each other. Victoria could use that knowledge to her advantage. She peeked through one eye. A vein throbbed in the man's thick neck and his face twitched with anger. A prominent scar cut through one thick eyebrow. There was no tattoo on his arm, but it definitely was the man from the bonfire photo. The man who took Avery.

It was now or never. Summoning every bit of strength, Victoria tore her wrists apart, ripping through the last threads of rope and freeing her hands. As she did so, the broken bottle fell and hit the deck.

With a grunt of surprise, the man gripped her squirming body tighter. His reaction was instant, and his strength shocked her. He lunged toward the side of the ship and heaved her body over the railing.

Victoria flailed her arms, grasping for something...anything,

With dark skies above her, black ocean below, and nothing to stop her descent, she twisted in the air, falling and falling.

CHAPTER 33

V ictoria slammed into the ocean and sank fast.

After a few seconds of pure shock, she kicked hard to stop her downward plummet, propelling herself against gravity with powerful, desperate strokes. Her lungs were bursting to breathe when she broke through the surface and gasped. A wave of salty water slapped her face and filled her nose and mouth. A burning sensation tore through her face and throat as she choked and coughed up seawater. Treading the cool water with frantic movements, she kept her head above the rolling waves. When she could finally breathe again, she tried to get her bearings.

The lights of the yacht glowed a mere twenty or so yards away. Large black letters crossed the transom. *The Untouchable.*

No spotlights scanned the ocean. They weren't looking. They'd underestimated her. Probably believed her hands were still tied. At the moment, that seemed to be the only element working in her favor.

The yacht's motor began to purr, its propellor churning up the ocean behind it. It moved away, slowly at first, then gained speed, leaving her utterly alone.

Treading water with one arm and desperate kicks, she lifted her injured wrist to her mouth and sucked on her cut skin to stop the bleeding.

The pitch-black water and dark sky blended, making it impossible to tell where one ended and the other began. She tilted her head up to keep the waves from crashing against her face. How far was the shore? And in which direction?

Still treading, she closed her eyes and tried to picture the shape of the constellations she needed to find. The big dipper or the little dipper. Cassiopeia if the others were too low on the horizon. When she could see them clearly in her mind, she opened her eyes and studied the sky, scanning for the seven stars that made up the little dipper. She found it, or thought she had, then identified the big dipper to confirm her discovery. The North Star, Polaris, would be the brightest star at the end of the little dipper's handle. She dropped her gaze directly below Polaris. That was due north. To the left would be west, the direction that would take her back to the coast.

The theory was sound, but staring up at the sky, at hundreds of tiny lights, with her life depending on getting it right, it no longer felt like an exact science. The constellations blurred together. One could easily look like another.

She wanted to cry, but she had to choose. Indecision would kill her. Or was she already so far from the shore that she'd never make it back no matter what direction she traveled?

Thinking that way will get you killed.

She couldn't allow fear and doubt to creep in. There was more than just her life at stake. She'd screwed up, but as long as she survived, they had a good chance of getting Avery back safe and sound. *If* they could quickly get back to the yacht.

The Untouchable.

We'll see about that.

The arrogance of the yacht's name fueled her. She started swimming west, in the opposite direction of the moving yacht. She paced herself, conserving energy for what might be hours and hours of swimming.

Keeping her mouth closed to prevent the salty water from splashing in, she breathed in and out through her nose. Applying a method to her current madness, she counted her strokes. Three hundred freestyle, three hundred breaststroke, three hundred backstroke. Then a rest. She was fit and athletic. She knew how to swim. She'd participated on the swim team at her family's country club until middle school. That's what she told herself. But a little voice crept in...*That was then. This is now. You're not a swimmer.*

Ned, who could easily power through a 3.9-kilometer swim during the first leg of an Ironman, had taken her swimming with him recently at an indoor pool. Smiling, she'd bragged about the box of blue ribbons in her old bedroom at her father's house that would prove her butterfly prowess. She showed off her rusty strokes, surprised at how familiar they felt. He said her form impressed him. He'd also had a nice laugh when she got out of the water after less than twenty minutes of laps, and sat on the side, watching him finish.

Water is water, whether an indoor pool, a lake, or an ocean.

Not true.

The ocean has a strong current. Whether it aids me or works against me...only time will tell.

Freestyle. Breaststroke. Backstroke.

My father never wanted me to quit swimming. Thought I had such talent and determination. He'd be proud of me now. Victoria let a laugh escape, but it was morbid humor.

She floated on her back, kicking her legs but resting her arms. On any other occasion, the enormous expanse of stars above might be beautiful. Instead, they intensified the humbling sense of oblivion surrounding her. How frighteningly insignificant she felt, staring up at the black sky, second guessing the constellations and fighting the panic that resulted from doing so.

She had to pull herself together again.

The best response to fear is strength.

She turned over and put her arms back into action.

Freestyle. Breaststroke. Backstroke. Rest.

Though she tried to stay focused on swimming, the concept of her own death circled her thoughts like a vulture. Working with her family attorney, she'd already filed instructions for handling her affairs. Most of her assets went to charities and to her brother, with a substantial fund set aside for the care of her animals. Ned would keep them as his own...wouldn't he? She hoped so. She wished she'd asked him and put it into her will. Knowing for sure...that would bring comfort.

She'd contemplated her own death before, vowed to be brave in the end, grateful for the life she had lived. Death was inevitable. Everyone knew it was coming. She'd already cheated her own several times. But she'd never expected to be totally alone when it came. Not like this. Not with her world suddenly becoming so huge and empty, as if she was the only living person left.

Was her mother alone when she died? And did she know her death was coming? Victoria would never have those answers, but she was certain her mother died bravely.

A random, distant memory hit her. She was standing in the corner of the room against the wall at the family vet and wishing more than anything she'd stayed home.

"Try to calm down," her mother told her in a voice that was gentle but firm. "We need to be peaceful."

Her mother sat cross-legged on the tiled floor with Jasper's head resting in her lap. Tears streamed from her mother's eyes too, but her voice gave nothing away as she leaned close and whispered to their dog. "Such a good boy, Jasper. The very best boy we could ever have. The most loyal boy who loved his walks around the pond. You always make me smile when you pull the pillows off the couch and bring them into the office. And remember when you stole the Thanksgiving turkey off the counter? No one will ever forget that, Jasper. I can absolutely promise that you'll be remembered forever for that day, and for so much more."

The vet entered the room then and asked, "Are you ready, Mrs. Heslin?"

"Not quite," her mother answered, stroking Jasper's side. "I need a few more minutes, please."

Freestyle. Breaststroke. Backstroke. Rest.

Victoria didn't want to miss her brother's upcoming wedding.

I will not drown out here. I will make it to shore...or something or someone will rescue me.

Rivera. He'd searched relentlessly until he located her downed plane in Greenland. Did he know she was missing yet? *Watch yourself. Be careful,* he'd said only that morning, sounding a lot like Ned. And look what she'd gone and gotten herself into.

Freestyle. Breaststroke. Backstroke. Rest.

Between each stroke, Victoria added long stretches of swimming on her side. Granny style, she'd called the stroke as a child.

Victoria couldn't remember how many sets of strokes she'd completed. She did not know how long she'd been swimming. The floating and resting periods came more frequently and lasted longer. Her exhausted limbs grew heavier in the cool water. Her teeth chattered.

She stared up at the sky again, blinking as water splashed into her burning eyes, and what she saw gave her hope. The moon was now slightly in front of her, setting in the west, which confirmed she was swimming west. *Thank God!* Her relief was palpable. She'd gotten something right. Something incredibly important.

She forced herself to flip over and breaststroke again. Her body was still following directions, doing what she told it to do, her arms stretching out and pulling to the sides...she knew this...and yet she could no longer feel her limbs moving.

You're not giving up out here. You might not make it, but it won't be because you quit trying. The shore might be close. Very close.

And then Victoria allowed herself this: *If you die trying, giving it your all, then that is the best you can do.*

The thought brought a choking sob to her throat. She didn't want to die. And they had to rescue Avery. Victoria knew what it was like—waiting to be found. Praying. Thinking you're so close...you have to be, because the alternative is unimaginable...until yet one more unbearable day goes by. Victoria would never forget her horrific experience in Greenland. Hope ebbed away with each passing hour, replaced by a deep and dark despair. Not everyone made it. Yet she and Ned had survived.

Left. Left. Left. Right. Left.

The mind-numbing rhythm popped into her head. It didn't match her breaststrokes, but it continued, establishing itself as the backtrack of her thoughts, keeping her going. Until...something bumped her right leg.

Victoria screamed as fear exploded inside her.

Squinting in the darkness, she treaded water in a tight three-hundred-sixty-degree circle, scanning for a fin, needing to eliminate the terror of a surprise attack. She saw only the constantly churning waves and the ripples made by her own frantic movements. Like a scene from a horror movie, from the perspective of an ocean predator, she could picture parts of her body underwater. Her terror surged to a new peak.

She screamed inside her head. *Calm down! Pull it together!*

Closing her eyes, she turned on her back and floated. She made herself as still as she could, despite her racing, pounding heart. Cringing, squirming inside with terror, she braced for the piercing pain of the bite that would pull her under and finish her off forever.

Sharks were the scent hounds of the ocean. They could detect a drop of blood from a mile away. Maybe a quarter mile. She couldn't remember exactly. It hardly mattered. If she'd been bumped by a shark, it wasn't a mile or a quarter mile away. It was right there.

You don't know that it's a shark.

Could be a dolphin.

Could be a turtle.

You might be so exhausted that you're hallucinating.

Eventually, she would have to force herself to flip over and swim again. But not yet. Not until she gave the creature more time to lose interest in her.

Might only be a dolphin or a turtle.

She prayed for strength and courage.

The fear-fueled adrenaline began to ebb from her system. A sense of calm spread inside her. The water wasn't so menacing once she stopped trying to fight against it and let it have its way, let it move her motionless body in its powerful current. She stopped worrying about predatory sea creatures and didn't lift her head when the ocean water covered her face. Victoria was more tired than she'd ever been before. She needed to sleep.

CHAPTER 34

Four days ago

A very opened her mouth and exhaled, fogging the large portholes. She slid her finger through the condensation and wrote HELP ME backwards. The letters didn't last long. She'd formed them dozens of times because it would only take one boat passing at the right time to bring the help she needed.

She'd been drugged and couldn't remember anything that happened between leaving her room at Azure Cove and waking up in a fancy bedroom on a boat with a tray of food beside her, more frightened than she had ever been before.

What sort of bedroom locked from the outside?

She'd always been a rule follower. This time, being respectful and following what she had assumed were legit instructions proved to be a terrible mistake. The whole Covid quarantine thing must have been a lie. She didn't know what was going on but had enough knowledge about the fate of abducted young women to be scared out of her mind. She'd seen a movie where wealthy men bid tens of thousands of dollars to buy young virgins. The auctioning took place on a yacht. Is that what this was about?

Her parents had to be freaking out, especially her mother. Were they in Mexico looking for her? Would she ever see them again? Graduate from college? Start her new job?

When Avery heard someone outside her door, her whole body tensed.

Next came the scrape and click of a key.

The door handle moved.

From the corner of the cabin, she watched a man enter. He wasn't the man from the resort. He looked to be only a few years older than her. He carefully closed the door behind him, letting the latch clink in slow motion, as if he didn't want anyone to hear.

Standing with his back to the door, he stared at Avery. His unnerving grin and tiny pupils told her he was high on something. If they were anywhere else, a party on campus, a bar, she'd have to admit he was handsome, in a cocky, full-of-himself way, though she'd never fall for a guy like him. Too much of an arrogant, bad-boy vibe. She recognized his T-shirt, a brand that cost several hundred dollars, and the tattoo of a heart and crown on his arm, which reminded her of one she'd seen somewhere before. Maybe on the guy from the resort who told her she had Covid.

"Hey. I'm Eric," he said. "This is my yacht. Welcome aboard."

So that's how it was going to be? Acting like everything was normal. Avery lifted her chin and glowered at him. She tried to keep her voice steady though she was trembling. "Why am I here?"

He didn't answer.

"My name is Avery Jennings," she said, to make herself as human and relatable as possible. "I'm twenty-two. A student at The University of Virginia. People are looking for me. My family. My friends. My aunt is with the FBI. And for the record...I'm not a virgin. You're a few years too late for that."

Eric didn't seem phased by what she'd said. Maybe he thought she was lying about her aunt. She went on, forcing herself to be brave, trying to keep her voice low so it wouldn't quiver and give away her fear. "You haven't hurt me, but I don't want to be here, so just take me back to Azure Cove and I'll forget this ever happened. Deal?"

He was still grinning, staring down at her feet. "Take your socks off."

"What? No."

"I can take them off for you. I can take off your whole foot. But I told you to do it, so you're going to." He came closer.

Avery held her ground because she was already in the corner. There was nothing for her to grab and swing. The cabin held no makeshift weapons—no lamps, clocks, vases. But that didn't mean she was going to let him have his way with her.

In her years of taking kick-boxing classes, she'd done thousands of jabs and right hooks, but never a poke-his-eyes-out or smash-his-balls lifesaving move. It was time to improvise. Shaking with fear, Avery shot out her leg, delivering a kick that connected with his groin.

Eric groaned and bent forward. His grin disappeared and his eyes narrowed at her, but he never looked away. She expected her well-placed kick to hurt him a lot more. Maybe he was too high to feel pain. As he straightened, she kicked again, harder this time, adrenaline strengthening her. He grabbed her ankle before it connected and jerked it over his head, yanking her other leg off the floor. She fell on her back and watched in horror as his boot came down. She turned her head to the side as it slammed into her chest, pinning her against the floor.

Pain tore across her torso as she thrashed and screamed beneath him. His hand clamped tighter around her ankle and his terrifying grin returned, growing wider by the second.

Avery suddenly understood. She stopped screaming and flailing. She wouldn't give him what he wanted.

The cabin door burst open. A man charged in, his face red, with a murderous expression. It was the man who told her she had Covid.

Paralyzed with fear, Avery watched, helpless. He was going to kill her.

"Get the hell out of here!" her abductor shouted at Eric, grabbing his arm, and throwing him toward the door.

Eric smashed into the wall before righting himself and stumbling out of the cabin, muttering, "Watch your toes, girl."

The other man pulled her onto her feet with surprising strength. He didn't look at her face, but he scanned her body. "What did he do to you?"

"He...he...nothing, he almost..." She jerked away from him and back to the corner of the room as her shock receded. "Why am I here? You can't get away with this! Let me off this boat."

"You should take a shower. You reek," he said, leaving her alone and terrified.

Avery heard the door lock behind him.

A few minutes later, from somewhere nearby, a woman's anguished screams pierced the silence.

Avery had already been on the yacht for three days when someone knocked on her cabin door. The handle rattled. Avery prayed it wasn't Eric. But if it was, this time, she would jab his eyes out. No hesitation. But even if she incapacitated him, how would she escape the boat? She'd have to worry about that when the time came. If she got free from her cabin, her first plan of action would be to find the other woman. Avery would not leave her behind. Though she hadn't heard any screaming or crying in over a day. What that might mean made Avery sick with worry.

The handle turned.

Just do it! It's now or never!

The door opened and Avery raced forward, two fingers extended like pokers.

It wasn't Eric. Eyes wide with surprise, the young guy jumped back. A plastic tumbler of liquid fell from his hand and splashed over the blue carpet. A grilled cheese sandwich and chips slid off a paper plate and hit the floor. "Whoa!" he shouted.

Avery stopped short. He wasn't her enemy. He was probably around her age, with a sad, tough edge she'd never seen the likes of in her University of Virginia classmates. That *edge* told her he'd led a dangerous life and was just trying to survive. He'd been kind to her. If she could call it that. He hadn't been cruel, anyway. Intuition told her he was the cook or the cleaning person, perhaps just as trapped as she was. She couldn't maim him. She wouldn't.

"It's just me," he said. "Bringing you food."

"Please, let me use your phone. Please," she begged him.

"I told you, I don't have one. And if I did, and I let you use it, I'd be a walking dead man."

"If you help me, I'll make sure the right people know. I'll make sure you won't be held responsible for any of this. Please."

"Told you, I can't."

"Yes, you can." Suddenly she felt desperate. She had so many questions and he was the only one responding to her. The only person on board who was treating her with any measure of normal behavior. The only one who didn't pretend he couldn't hear her. "Why am I here?" she shouted. "What is going to happen to me?"

"I don't know. I really don't."

"What about the other girl? What are they doing to her?"

"I don't know," he said, looking down at the sandwich and chips, making her think he knew and that's why he couldn't look her in the eye any longer.

"Who are these people?" she asked.

"You're better off not knowing." Still avoiding her gaze, he grabbed the empty tumbler and left the room.

Avery picked the grilled cheese and chips off the carpet and wolfed them down, wanting to keep her strength. She had to stay sharp and strong if she were going to get off the boat.

She went back to a porthole and peered out, praying her living nightmare would soon end. But in the ensuing silence, the sound of the other woman's tormented screams pierced her memory, making her skin crawl. Avery worried the worst might still be coming.

CHAPTER 35

P ayton needed a break but couldn't take one. She had to be back in court first thing in the morning with revised documents. Barely taking her eyes from her computer, she lifted the mug of lukewarm coffee from her desk and brought it toward her lips.

With a sharp and sudden woof, her dog leaped up from his bed beside Payton's desk, startling her. Brown drops of liquid spilled over her mug and onto the floor.

"Jeez, Sydney," she said, as the dog ran toward the front of the house.

Between barks, Payton heard a scraping sound. Someone was coming up her porch steps.

She wasn't expecting a package. With her current workload, weeks had passed since she'd had time to shop for anything except dog food and takeout meals. As she hurried to the kitchen to grab a towel to wipe up her spill, she braced for a knock or the doorbell's ring.

It never came.

Sydney let out one last bark, trotted back to her bed, and curled up again. Whoever was outside had left.

Payton wiped up the spilled coffee and sat back down at her desk, but her concentration was now broken. She slid her glasses off and frowned at the smudged lenses. After wiping the edge of her shirt over each lens, they seemed no cleaner. She checked the time, wishing she could set the clock back an hour or so and discovered it was even later than she realized. Much later.

So...why had someone just come onto her porch?

Payton got up, sliding her glasses back on before opening her front door. Wearing a thin blouse and cardigan, she wrapped her arms against her body to guard against the chill. One of her porch lights needed replacing, something she intended to do after she bought a new light bulb. The other cast a faint glow. There was no one in the nighttime shadows that hovered over the front path. No one on the sidewalk heading away from her house in either direction. No one getting into a nearby delivery van. Aside from the wind whistling through the barren tree branches, silence reigned on her street.

She was closing the door when she spotted the plain manila envelope on the steps. Her name was scrawled across the front in black letters. In the top corner, someone had written GLHA—short for Green Laurel Home-owner's Association, her neighborhood's board of volunteers. Under that, IMPORTANT was written in large letters. They were probably raising the monthly maintenance fee again. Or did it contain the proxy papers she forgot to sign to elect new board members?

She tossed the envelope on the kitchen counter.

And then she changed her mind. Because if it only required a signature, she should get it over with rather than add to the growing pile of bills, glossy catalogs, and junk mail she needed to sort through. She didn't want to be the neighbor whose indifference made life harder for the others. Everyone was busy, right? Maybe they weren't trying to put a murderous cartel in jail for a litany of crimes too long to document, but everyone had things in their lives that were more important than reading and signing the homeowner's proxy papers. That didn't make it okay to ignore the request.

Still standing in front of the counter, she folded the envelope's metal clasp together and lifted the flap. She slid out the single sheet of white paper and read the handwritten message related to her current case.

An icy chill snaked through her body and made the paper shake in her hand.

She stuck her hand inside the envelope again to see if she'd missed anything. That's when she found the photograph.

Her phone vibrated on her kitchen counter, and Dante Rivera's name appeared on the screen. Payton watched the phone through four more rings before she lunged for it, suddenly afraid she'd missed his call.

She tried to sound normal, but she barely recognized her voice when she answered breathlessly with, "Dante, please tell me you found Avery."

"No," he said. "We haven't found her. Not yet. And I'm not sure what's going on here."

Payton felt sick, her skin clammy. She read over the note one more time and didn't know what to do. In her panic, she didn't pick up on Rivera's strange tone, the worry in his own voice, and it took a few seconds for what he said next to register.

"Victoria is gone. I don't know where she is. I traced her phone to a field about ten miles inland. There was no trace of her, and her phone had been wiped clean."

CHAPTER 36

A very tapped her fist on the cabin wall, just loud enough to be heard from the other side.

No response.

She put her ear against the partition and whispered, "Victoria? Are you there?"

Still no answer.

The yacht was moving, and Avery hadn't heard anything from Victoria in a very long time. The FBI agent had said they might have to hang in there a bit longer, but hours had passed.

During that time, Avery heard yelling—only male voices—and other footsteps in the corridor, but nothing more.

She worried about Victoria, though convinced herself it was unwarranted. An FBI agent would know how to handle herself. She wouldn't have come alone.

Avery couldn't stop thinking about seeing her parents, her aunt Payton, and her friends. She imagined throwing her arms around them, overwhelmed with gratitude to be off the boat and returned to her real life.

Another hour passed. Avery told herself to be patient. It couldn't be much longer before help arrived. She only had to stay safe in the cabin until then.

She paced the room, stared out through glass windows into the darkness, and sat on the bed facing the door. Any minute now and she'd hear, "This is the FBI! Get down on the ground," just like in the movies. Then agents would crash through her door and deliver her to safety.

Avery made a mental list of questions she couldn't wait to get answered. Were Brie and Haley all right? Were they still at Azure Cove looking for her, or had they gone back to Virginia? Would she be famous when she got back home? Who were the people who took her? Why did they do it? Who was the woman they had tortured and where was she now?

More time passed. It had to be two or three in the morning. And she was still locked in the cabin. With each passing minute, Avery struggled more to keep her eyes open.

She dragged the mattress off the bed and stuffed it between the door and the bedframe. No one could open the door now, not without considerable effort. It wasn't an impenetrable barricade, but if Eric came back high as a kite, he might not go through the trouble required to get the door open. It would buy her more time and keep her safe if she failed to stay awake.

Weak morning light streamed through the portholes. Thick clouds had whitened the sky. The yacht was quiet.

Avery sat up on the mattress. She could hardly believe it was the next day, and she was still there.

Someone knocked, startling her onto her feet and away from the door.

"Who is it?" she asked, hoping whoever it was had come to rescue her.

"Hey. Morning. I've got food for you."

Recognizing the sad voice of the cook who had been kind/not cruel to her, Avery peeled one end of the mattress off the floor and onto the bed, pulling it up far enough so the door could open partway.

He handed her a plate and plastic bottle of water from the doorway. "Here. My specialty, or so I'm told," he said, casting his eyes over the mattress that hung half on the floor, half on the bed. "Let me know if you want seconds because there's more."

She took the food and water, and he left, closing the door behind him. He hadn't acted as if anything was different; he gave no sign the FBI was on the yacht and Avery was about to be free.

What was going on? What happened to Victoria? Despair rocked Avery's body, making her feel more desperate than she had since she woke locked inside the cabin days ago.

CHAPTER 37

V ictoria groaned.

She was lying on her stomach, one cheek pressed into the sand, the sun warming her back and shoulders. She didn't move for a very long time.

Increasingly aware of extreme discomfort, she finally pulled wet strands of hair away from her burning eyes and pushed herself up. She tried to spit out sand, but her mouth was bone dry, her tongue thick inside it. Her lips were so painful and swollen she couldn't close her mouth. She blinked in the sunlight, wanting only to close her burning eyes and collapse again.

Reality crept back, though it hardly seemed real.

First—*I made it!*

Then—*Avery!*

She didn't know how much time Avery had left. They had to get to the yacht fast.

Victoria tried to get up, but a sickening wave of nausea overpowered her, wracking her insides. Pain seared her throat as she heaved and vomited. She dabbed at her mouth with the back of her hand, scraping sand across her cracked lips and igniting fresh sparks of pain.

Weak and shaking, she remained on her side in the wet sand. Moving her head brought another sickening wave of dizziness to push through. Shielding her eyes with her hand, she took stock of her surroundings.

A beach. Rows of chairs. Between them, a boardwalk leading to white flags and a sign—Playa del Sol Resort. Pushing herself up on rubbery legs, Victoria stumbled toward the boardwalk, forcing her legs to move one after the other. Like nightmares of her past, she was in trouble, but her body couldn't respond. When her stomach cramped again, she dropped to her knees and retched so violently that muscles tore under her rib cage. The pain was so real; she wasn't dreaming.

After a few seconds, she got to her feet again, fighting another wave of nausea, and resumed her slow-motion stagger. It took her several miserable minutes to reach the boardwalk; it seemed much longer. She rested, swaying with her hands on her knees. In her peripheral vision, she caught movement ahead of her. She lifted her head.

A boy was staring at her. He couldn't have been more than twelve years old. Unable to stand much longer, she lowered into a crouch and hoped she didn't scare him off.

The boy hadn't moved, couldn't take his eyes off her, which made her realize how frightening and near-death she must look.

"Um...do you need help?" he asked. "Do you want me to get help?"

"Your phone," she said, her voice hoarse and her throat painfully raw. "Need your phone. It's an emergency."

"Ah...I can't make calls on this while we're here. I don't have the international plan." The boy hadn't moved, but his voice sounded far away. "But I can get help and they can call an ambulance for you. I think you need a doctor."

"I'm FBI. It's an emergency. Please, give me your phone." She turned away from him as she dry-heaved again. When she lifted her head, she wasn't sure if the boy was still there.

"You're FBI? You don't look like it. What happened to you?"

"I need your phone." Her vision blurred. She was going to pass out.

"I'll go back to the hotel and get you some help."

"No. Wait. I'm going to have to arrest you for interfering with an investigation."

"Why? And how are you going to do that? You can't even stand up."

She didn't have the time or energy to convince him. "A hundred dollars to use your phone."

"A hundred? I don't know how much it costs to make calls from here."

"Five hundred dollars to use your phone," she croaked. "I promise. I'm good for it."

"Seriously? Yeah...okay," he said after hesitating. "I hope you're not lying because otherwise my parents will kill me. Um...I better do it for you. Cuz, you know, you look really bad and...your hands are....um...what's the number?"

Eyes closed, shoulders slumped forward, she recited Rivera's number. Her ears were ringing.

"Do I dial a one first? Is that what I do?"

"I...I don't know..." she rasped, unable to think straight. She repeated Rivera's number, though she was unsure she'd gotten it right. When she opened her eyes, the sky and ground spun around her. She let her forehead drop to the wooden planks in a crumpled child's pose.

"I got it," the boy said. "Here. Or a...you want to take it, or you want me to do the talking? Never mind. I'm just going to put it right in front of you, okay? Here it is. It's ringing. You have to be quick about it. Don't stay on the phone long."

She heard a small clunk as he set his device on the ground. Then the phone rang and rang.

Pick up, Rivera. Pick up.

Finally, he answered. "Hello? Who is this?"

Hearing his voice gave her the last ounce of adrenaline she needed. "Avery is alive. Might be others with her. She's on a yacht. *The Untouchable.* You have to find it quick."

She heard the boy murmur, "Cool," but she didn't hear Rivera's response.

Everything went black again.

CHAPTER 38

"Victoria!" Rivera shouted, causing guests in Azure Cove's reception area to turn his way.

Alejandro Fuentes and two of his security staff stared at Rivera as he gripped his phone, willing Victoria back to the line

"Victoria! Where are you?" Rivera shouted again as the phone went silent. A chill coursed through his body, prickling his skin.

He called the number back. A 201-area code. New Jersey.

The person who answered sounded like a child.

"Victoria Heslin just called from this number. Are you with her?" Rivera asked.

"I don't know her name," the boy answered. "She said she's in the FBI. She was wandering toward my hotel like a zombie. I think she just passed out or...I don't know."

"Where is she? Where are you right now?"

"Uh, at the Playa del Sol Rio Hotel. Outside. On the beach. Oh, I see my parents. They're walking down the boardwalk right now. Dad! Mom! Over here!"

"Have them stay with her. I'm calling an ambulance. Tell Victoria I'm coming. Tell her Rivera is on his way there."

"Hey, can you hear me?" the boy said, presumably to Victoria. "I'm talking to the guy that you called. His name is Rivera. He said he's coming. Okay? There. I told her, but I don't think she can hear me. She hasn't moved."

The boy sounded panicked, which sent another flash of cold fear through Rivera. All the while, the resort manager and the security staff hovered around him listening. "You found the agent?" Alejandro mouthed.

"Stay with her," Rivera said to the boy before hanging up and calling 911. He requested an ambulance and told the operator Victoria was an American with excellent insurance they could bill in case that helped them get there faster. Still on the phone with Mexico's national emergency number, he raced through the resort's foyer and into a cab waiting out front. "This is an emergency. Take me to the Playa del Sol Rio Hotel," he told the driver. "Do you know where it is?"

"Sure. Just a few miles away."

"Hurry, please," Rivera said.

Palm trees, flowers, and bamboo flashed by outside the cab's window, yet he wished the vehicle would move faster. He couldn't imagine what had happened to Victoria to make her "wander like a zombie." Thinking about her in that condition made every muscle in his body tense. And in her dire state, she'd seemed to use the last of her strength to communicate that she'd found Avery. He didn't know how Victoria had gathered the information, but he trusted her enough to act on it immediately.

He called Sam in the FBI's D.C. office. "Sam, I need your help."

"Hey, Rivera. Sure. I'm just finishing a report for Murphy. Can I call you back in about an hour?"

"It's urgent. It has to be now." As one of the best intelligence analysts in the office, Sam received requests like that all day. Everyone's requests were top priority or an urgent emergency, at least in their minds.

"Is it about Payton's niece?" Sam asked.

"Yes. Victoria has been missing since yesterday afternoon. She just showed up a few miles away, apparently in bad shape. I called an ambulance and I'm headed there now."

"Oh, wow. Do you know what happened?"

"No. The only thing I got from her is that Avery is on a yacht called *The Untouchable.* She sounded certain. Can you locate it?"

"Sure. What other info do you have besides the name of the ship?"

"Nothing. That's it."

"Okay." Sam drew the word out, which meant he had a challenge but was already thinking about it.

"I'm assuming it's somewhere off the coast here," Rivera said. "Victoria told me she was heading back to the marina, where the tracking dog led us when I lost communication with her. Can you access a maritime registry database? Contact U.S. Customs and Border Protection. The Coast Guard. Maybe Immigration?"

"Yeah. Yeah. I'll get on it. Let us know as soon as you find out more about Victoria."

"I will."

When the cab reached the Plaza del Sol Rio Hotel, an ambulance was already waiting in front of the entrance. "Wait here," Rivera told the cabbie as two people wheeled a gurney toward the back of the open ambulance.

Rivera jumped out of the car and was next to the gurney before it went inside the emergency vehicle. Victoria was pale as a ghost and her eyes were closed. But the oxygen mask covering her nose meant she was alive.

"Where are you taking her?" he asked them.

"St. Mary's hospital."

"Can I ride with you? She's my partner. My colleague."

"You can't ride with us. You can meet us there. But hold on. She wasn't conscious when we got here. We need some information on her."

Rivera gave them a summary of Victoria's full name and age and told them she'd been missing but had no known health issues. Though her mother had a heart condition. He returned to the cab. "St. Mary's Hospital, please."

CHAPTER 39

C onversations in serious, professional tones roused Victoria. Something important occurring.

What are they saying? Something happened. Someone needs help?

Hands grasped her shoulders.

It's me. I need help.

They lifted her from the sand. Placed her on something firm but soft.

They're moving me. But...who are they?

A man with a strong accent, "Can you hear me? We've got you. You're
going to be okay."

In her mind, she nodded at him, though she didn't have the strength to
move her head or open her eyes.

A woman's voice penetrated Victoria's dreams. Kind, firm, and persistent,
eventually drawing Victoria from the depths of slumber. She smelled rubbing alcohol and bleach.

Is she talking to me?

The voice came again, closer now. Very close. Something nipped at Victoria's side.

Must be talking to me.

"No hablo español," Victoria whispered.

"Ah, si. We're going to take excellent care of you."

"Thanks," Victoria mumbled, as a sharp needle pricked her arm.

Hushed voices poked through the thick haze of Victoria's consciousness again. Words she didn't understand buzzed around her like mosquitoes.

"Asegúrese de que duerma,"

"Permanecer dormido."

"Si, si."

Another stinging prick.

Rivera stepped out of Victoria's hospital room and into the hallway to accept a call from Sam.

"How is she?" Sam asked.

"Not sure. She's been sleeping all day. Mumbled some stuff but hasn't been really coherent yet. The nurses are giving her a lot of attention. They said she's dehydrated and they're running other tests."

"Keep us posted, okay? Everyone who has heard the news is worried."

"Yeah. I will."

"In the meantime...I found the ship," Sam said.

"You did? Where is it?"

"Not the location, but the yacht we're looking for. Based on what I've found, I'm pretty certain it's the one. It hasn't checked into any ports in over a month."

"Can you send the ship's profile to the Coast Guard?"

"Doing it right now. It will be easy to confirm once it's spotted. It's a 2022 Italian-built semi-custom mega-yacht. One hundred forty-seven-feet of steel and aluminum. A really striking and unusual vessel. Looks more like a contemporary naval ship than a pleasure cruiser. It's got a six thousand nautical mile range."

"See if the Coast Guard has any maritime patrol aircraft that can begin searching in the Gulf off the coast of Mexico. They would be able to get there fastest."

"Yeah. Murphy is going to get that approved."

"Good," Rivera sighed. "Did you tell Payton?"

"Not yet. I wanted to see if we could locate the yacht before I told her. See, *The Untouchable* is flagged under the Cayman Islands. It's registered to an independent holding company. Coconut Transports."

"And?"

"Coconut Transports is a suspected laundering drug transport front for the Salazar Cartel."

"Oh, crap."

Something warm encompassed Victoria's hand.

"You've got to wake up. We've got a hundred questions for you," someone said in English. That voice she recognized. Rivera. She opened her eyes and stared at his blurred image as it came into focus. He stood above her. Holding her hand.

"Hey," she said, looking around. She was in a bed the width of a cot, wearing a hospital gown. A harsh fluorescent light ran across the ceiling. The windowless room wasn't much bigger than a storage closet. Beeps and electronic whirring came from a machine behind her. She raised her free hand toward her dry, cracked lips. Before her hand got there, something tugged it back with a painful pinch. An IV was threaded into a vein.

"How are you feeling?" Rivera asked, letting her hand go.

"I don't feel much of anything," she said, trying to sit up. "What's in this IV?"

"The nurse told me they're giving you IV fluids. You're not hurt, they don't think. You're extremely dehydrated. I've actually seen you look much worse." He offered a quick grin before his seriousness returned. "I should get the nurse. No one has been in to check on you in a while. Whatever is in that bag is almost empty. We were going to have you evacuated back to the states, but you begged us not to...you probably don't remember, but you were adamant about not leaving Mexico yet. Murphy's breaking protocol for you, Tori. So first... tell me what happened."

"Nothing. And I'm fine," she whispered, her throat still raw though the pain had dulled. She felt a little dazed, though details from the previous night pierced her memory. With them came a deep chill through her body.

"How long have I been sleeping? What time is it?" she asked, looking around the windowless room and pulling the sheet around her waist.

"It's Friday night. Five p.m. You weren't gone for long. But long enough to have me extremely worried."

Only a day had passed since she returned to the marina to search for clues. But it felt like she'd been in the ocean for days. And she'd been sleeping since then? It didn't seem possible, though she still felt groggy, like her brain wasn't firing with all cylinders. "Did you find Avery?" she asked.

"The U.S. Coast Guard located the yacht via helicopter and they're going to board it soon. You're sure she's on it?"

"I'm a hundred percent sure."

"How do you know?"

If she told the truth now, she'd probably get pulled from the investigation. The FBI would evacuate her to a secure medical facility with a protection detail. She wasn't ready for that. "I'll tell you later. Just trust me, please. Avery might not be the only captive. The woman who washed ashore with the missing toes...I think she came from the same yacht. There might be others like her. Do you know anything about her?"

"No. And if the Federales know who she is, they aren't saying. They haven't told us anything. Though, according to the hospital, Leo called here to see how you were doing and spoke to your nurse directly."

"What about Teresa?" Victoria asked. "Is she still missing?"

"As far as I know...yes. So, are you ready to talk about what happened? Why you disappeared and then seemed to crawl out of the ocean like a mermaid emerging from a war zone? And why you're sure Avery is on *The Untouchable*?"

Victoria didn't want to be difficult, but for reasons she didn't fully understand, she wasn't ready to talk about it. "Would you believe I snuck off to get a massage?"

"The massage from hell? No."

She pressed her cracked lips together and thought about what she could say. "To make a long story short, I went to the marina using a pretense to find the man who took Avery. I ended up on a yacht. I found Avery, and then couldn't get back to her."

Rivera cocked his head. "I've got time for the long story. You should tell me before you tell Murphy. Sounds like you might need a practice run through."

Rivera was right. She would have to explain everything eventually—how she'd ended up in a compromised position, more likely to die than to survive. She would have to share every single detail and answer a thousand questions. Rivera was probably the best person to sort through the events with her and make sense of everything. And if she were being honest, he would help her analyze and accept the mistakes she'd made. He'd probably rationalize her decisions and make her feel so much better about it. She could count on him for that. But not yet. She wasn't ready. Strangely enough, she could barely keep her eyes open and was fighting to stay awake.

"You feeling okay? Should I get the nurse?"

"No. I'm okay...just..." She shook her head to clear her thoughts and wrapped one arm around her waist, pulling the baggy gown tighter against her. "For now, can we please just focus on Avery? *The Untouchable* is a luxury yacht. It probably cost upward of twenty million. The people who took her aren't small-time criminals."

"No, they aren't. *The Untouchable* is registered to a holding company that most likely belongs to the Salazar Cartel."

"Oh, my God." Victoria's hand moved to her heart, pulling her IV again. Eduardo Salazar was the head of the Salazar Cartel. The knowledge shocked her, and yet it shouldn't have. The head of a cartel owning a mega-million yacht with abducted women aboard should surprise no one.

"We think his son Eric is on it," Rivera said. "Evading the warrant for his arrest."

"Can you show me an image of Eric Salazar?"

"Yeah. I'll find one. And...we have on record that Eric has the tattoo Brie described." Rivera slid his thumb up his phone and tapped the screen until he had a photo to show Victoria.

Victoria studied the photo. Eric was thinner, his face more angular, less thug-like than the man who abducted Avery and had thrown Victoria overboard. Wearing a perfectly fitted dark suit and a rakish grin with his thick hair slicked back, Eric looked like an extremely privileged young man. It was Eric who had driven the speedboat into the marina and shot her.

"From what I've heard, Eric Salazar is a playboy who is every inch as brutal as his father, without being half as smart. That makes him more dangerous. He might not cooperate with the authorities, even if it's in his best interest," she said.

"I know. The Coast Guard knows."

The Salazar Cartel's yacht. That explained so much. What happened with the Federales at the marina made sense now. They must have discovered the cartel was involved, and that changed everything. They'd quit investigating. Quit cooperating. They were either paid to ignore the cartel's activities or were too afraid to go after them. All those silver watches...gifts, maybe, but also constant reminders of who was in charge and what they could do to those who crossed them.

And only then, because her brain was still foggy, it finally hit her—what Rivera had certainly been thinking already. Payton currently played a key role in the case against the Salazar Cartel. And then they abducted her niece. How could that be a coincidence?

CHAPTER 40

A middle-aged woman wearing pink scrubs and a blue mask entered the hospital room. "Hola," she said to Rivera before focusing on Victoria. "Hola. You're awake. I'm Maria. Your nurse. I'm taking care of you. How are you feeling?"

"Fine, thank you," Victoria answered. "Do you know what happened to the clothes I was wearing when they brought me in?"

Maria shook her head. "I don't know. But I'll find them for you."

"Thanks. As soon as you can, please. I have to go."

"No. No. Not yet. We're still running tests. You're very dehydrated. You need more rest." Maria took the empty bag down from the IV pole. "But don't worry. You're in expert hands. I promise. I've got you." She turned to Rivera. "I need to examine my patient. Could you excuse us?"

"Wait, don't leave yet," Victoria said to Rivera. "Maria, could you please come back a little later? Thirty minutes? We're sort of right in the middle of something."

Maria hesitated before responding. "Sure. I'll give you your privacy just as soon as I finish this. Then I'll come back for your exam." She changed the IV bag and wrote some notes while Victoria silently urged her to hurry up.

"Okay for now," Maria said. "You stay put. Don't go anywhere. You need to rest. I'll be back."

"Thank you," Victoria said, scanning the items on the bedside table.

"What do you need?" Rivera asked.

"I was looking for my phone. I forgot it's probably at the bottom of the ocean with my gun."

"Actually, it's not. While you were gone, I traced your phone to a convenience store along the highway. Twelve miles inland."

"I was never there. I'm certain of that." She filed that knowledge away to deal with later. "Do you have Brie's number?"

"I do," Rivera said, taking out his phone.

"Can you call her and put her on speaker?" Victoria asked, followed by a yawn which made her wonder how she could possibly still be tired. She tapped her cheeks to wake up and thought about what she wanted to say once Rivera got hold of Brie.

"Brie? Hello," he said. "This is Agent Dante Rivera and Agent Victoria Heslin."

"Have you found Avery?" Brie asked immediately.

"Not yet," he answered. "We have some more questions for you."

"Oh. Okay."

"Did Avery ever mention her Aunt Payton?" Victoria asked.

"Always. She's so proud of her."

Victoria expected to hear something like that. "Did Avery tell you anything specific about her aunt's current case work?"

"Um...yes...sort of," Brie answered.

"What did she tell you?" Rivera asked.

"Um...well, that she investigates financial crimes. White-collar crimes, mostly. And that Payton is heading up something really huge that's going to put big-time criminals in prison. Something about evidence of their financial crimes."

Victoria felt her heart drop. She saw the same sentiment in Rivera's expression.

"Did Avery tell you who she was prosecuting?" Rivera asked.

"Yeah. Um...a cartel. The Salzar cartel? Is that right?"

That was close enough and hearing it gave Victoria a chill. "Do you remember if Avery mentioned the Salazar Cartel to you while you were in Mexico?"

"Yeah, she did. She talked about Payton's case on our trip."

"Were there other people around when she told you? People besides her friends?"

"Um...yes. I think so. Yes." Brie's response came out sounding very much like an apology.

On Saturday night, day three of her vacation, Brie could hardly look away from the mesmerizing bonfire. The fire seemed wild. Frightening. The flames shot skyward, rippling in the wind, sending dancing shadows across the sand. What was keeping those flames from leaping out of the elaborate stone pit and catching someone's hair? A woman with a long trailing scarf seemed oblivious to the potential danger. With her back only inches from the roaring fire, she tipped her head back in a laugh. How quickly a single spark could catch her scarf and set her ablaze.

Feeling a little rattled by her dark thoughts, Brie backed slowly away from the heat.

The crowd grew as more guests gravitated to the fire and lined up at the bar. The resort's entertainment staff mixed amongst them. Near the bonfire, the resort had set up a display of smoked meats with carving stations. Brie couldn't imagine why anyone would see an animal rotating over a grill and think the sight was festive or appealing. Talk about primitive. She wasn't a vegetarian, but the sight repulsed her. She suddenly wanted open space to fling her arms out and dance in the sand.

Moving farther from the others, she slid her sandals off and tossed them on an empty chair. As she headed down the beach, she twirled around with her arms outstretched and her head tipped up to the sky. Purple liquid spilled from her fluted glass, the bottom of her dress swirled around her legs, and the ocean waves wrapped around her ankles. "Twenty-two years I've rotated around the sun," she said. "Happy birthday to me!"

"Brie, come back," Avery called after her.

"We only have two more nights left," Brie yelled back, squishing her toes into the wet sand. "Let's walk."

"We can't leave the resort," Avery shouted.

"Yes, we can. We can do whatever we want." Brie strolled away from the bonfire's light and the tropical rhythms, singing, "Happy birthday to me. Happy birthday to Brie."

She heard panting and the shifting of sand just before someone grabbed her arm and spun her around. She gasped and her mouth fell open, but it was only Avery.

"Remember the guys who got murdered on spring break in Cancun a few years ago?" Avery asked. "They left their resort just to take a night walk on the beach."

"That's not going to happen," Brie said, but she looked over her shoulder more than once as she and Avery headed back to the resort.

They found Haley at the bar, standing between two counter height stools. Brie edged in front of a few people to reach her.

"Still waiting on my drink," Haley said, a blue strip of light casting a cold glow over her skin. "Where did you go?"

"I just needed a little space," Brie answered. "But Avery nixed my walk by bringing up those two guys who got murdered in Cancun. Remember them? They were hacked to pieces. Did the police ever find out who killed them?"

"I don't think so," Avery answered. "There's not much about it online. But I can ask my aunt. She would probably know. I think the FBI was involved."

"Has your aunt ever been part of a serial killer investigation?" Brie asked as she tried to remember where she'd tossed her sandals.

"Not that I know of, but maybe. She can't tell me everything she's worked on, you know. A lot of the FBI's cases are top secret. Mostly she does financial crimes, since she's the head of the forensic accounting division. She's working on something huge right now. The biggest case of her career."

"What's the big case?" Haley asked. "An investment banker CEO embezzlement Ponzi scheme thing?"

"No. But she's done something like that before. Right now, she's the lead on an investigation that is going to put the whole Salazar Cartel in prison."

"Who is the Salazar Cartel?" Brie asked. She considered ordering another drink, but her head felt a little woozy already. She wanted to get away from the bar and the people pressing into her personal space from behind her.

"They're organized crime, responsible for a ton of illegal activity," Avery said. "Counterfeiting. Money laundering. Murders. Payton is providing the evidence and testimonies."

"I've got mad respect for your aunt," Brie said.

The bartender delivered Haley's cocktail just as someone elbowed Brie in the back.

Brie frowned and said, "Come on, ladies. Let's go sit by the pool. There's practically no one there."

"Wait, I want to get some pictures around the bonfire." Haley held her drink in one hand and pulled her phone from her purse. "Let's go back over there. You two stand together."

Brie and Avery walked back to the bonfire and stopped in front of it for the photos.

Haley got in the middle and stretched her arm out, holding up her phone. "Say Hola!" She took some photos, then pulled her phone back in to check them out. "Hold on. These are terrible. The flash didn't go off. It's supposed to know when it's needed, and it never does! Let me try again. Just you two."

Haley moved a few yards away. Brie and Avery thread their arms around each other and hit poses.

"Are those good enough?" Brie asked.

"Not really," Haley said as she slipped her phone into her purse. She looked to her right and frowned. "See that lady?" Haley whispered to Brie. "That's the Zumba witch we told you about."

The old woman had a full-on glare aimed at one of the male guests. The guy had no idea the lady was scowling at him because he was focused on Avery. He had nice clothes, but there was something hard about him, and not just his body. A look that made him seem like a thug. Maybe it was the scar running through his eyebrow. Brie stared right back at him and gave him her best leave-us-alone-face before spinning around and grabbing Avery's hand. "Help me find my sandals, then let's go to the pool," she said, laughing. "This is our next-to-last night here. We gotta make the most of it."

She half expected the man to follow them and offer a creepy hook up line. But he didn't.

———————

"Oh, my God...that was the guy from the photo," Brie said to the agents. "It was! I don't know why I didn't remember his scar before. I mean, I guess I never got a good look at him. But I remember him now. I didn't really think anything of him that night. Guys checked us out and hit on us while we were there. I just didn't think...I'm so sorry. It was him, wasn't it?"

"We think so, yes," Rivera said.

"I'm sorry," Brie said again. "Let me know when you find her, please."

"We will," Rivera answered. He put his phone away and looked up at the ceiling.

"The trial is public knowledge," Victoria said. "It's not a secret. But in talking about her aunt's role, Avery could have made herself a target. I mean, you know as well as I do that the cartel's power and control comes from intimidating and terrorizing people. Only one method is more formidable and more effective than those. It works time after time, no matter how brave and committed someone is; no matter how impressive their pain threshold..."

"Threatening to hurt loved ones and family members," Rivera finished for her.

"Exactly. Payton is someone they'd love to control, especially right now. Threatening Avery's life would be the way to get to her. Thank goodness we know where Avery is now...and the Coast Guard is on their way, right?"

"Right," Rivera answered.

The agents were silent for a bit until Victoria said, "We should call Payton and tell her what Brie just told us. She needs to know."

"Yeah. I'll tell her." Rivera dropped his head. She couldn't blame him for not looking forward to delivering the news.

The Jennings had expressed gratitude for Payton and the FBI's involvement. Now it might turn out that Payton and the FBI were the motivating factors behind Avery's abduction. If it weren't for them, Avery would have traveled home safely with her friends and be at the University of Virginia right now.

The truth was going to hurt. And much more so if permanent harm came to Avery.

CHAPTER 41

R ivera had left the door to Victoria's hospital room open when he left to call Payton. Conversations traveled in from the hallway. Mostly Spanish, but some English. Something about a big storm brewing. The staff wanted to leave their shifts early before it hit.

Jennifer's anguished face appeared in Victoria's mind as she clasped her hands and prayed the Coast Guard would get to Avery in time. She imagined Jennifer's expression changing if they could find Avery unharmed and bring her safely home. Delivering that joy and relief—that's why Victoria had joined the FBI, trained her heart out, and sometimes risked her own life. She wanted to make a difference like that in someone's life. And yet, experience had taught her not everyone got happy endings.

Over ten years ago, a storm was brewing on the night that changed Victoria's life forever. The FBI had set up shop inside her parents' house, waiting to hear from Abigail Heslin's abductors. They said the call would come at seven p.m. with the amount of money they wanted and where to wire it. They'd instructed her father to write everything down and follow every instruction if he wanted to see his wife again.

The FBI had moved a land line phone onto the dining room table. Victoria stared at it every time she walked past, willing it to ring and give them a solid connection to her mother.

At the Heslins' kitchen table, the lead agent, the one calling the shots and organizing the searches, stared intently at his laptop.

Someone had spread a variety of takeout foods over the large kitchen island. Pizzas, boxed salads, cookies, and drinks. The coffee machine hissed, brewing a fresh carafe. The FBI went in and out of the house, making calls, monitoring computers, and providing updates on their search.

The initial excitement of strangers inside their house had worn off for the dogs. They gathered in one of the front rooms, peering out the rain-spattered windows toward the driveway with a singular focus, patiently waiting and expecting their main person, Abigail Heslin, to come home.

"She'll be back. It shouldn't be too much longer," Victoria told them, stroking their heads, before taking a seat on the couch next to her younger brother, Alex. He was trying to be brave, taking cues from their father, who kept telling them everything would be okay. Victoria couldn't wait for the ordeal to end, for everything to return to normal. She wanted to be back at school focusing on the stuff that seemed so important to her earlier and hardly mattered now. She wanted her mother safe and sound at home.

"Dad says she doesn't have her medication with her," Alex whispered.

Abigail was an avid hiker and skier who seemed more active than any other mother. Victoria was only vaguely aware that her mother had to take medication for a heart issue.

Each minute of each hour passed slowly as they waited for the time to arrive. Outside it poured. Inside, Victoria felt like she was suffocating.

"Can I do anything to help?" she asked the FBI agents.

They shook their heads.

Long before seven p.m. her father moved to the kitchen table and sat in front of the phone, surrounded by agents and a host of recording devices.

No call came.

Much later, Victoria, her brother, and the lead agent were in the family room. The storm had worsened. A boom of thunder sent one of the family dogs running to Abigail's room, where he would hide inside the closet. A few seconds after the crashing boom came the unexpected music. A bar of Beethoven's Ode to Joy. The agent's ring tone. He scooped his mobile phone off the kitchen table and brought it to his ear. Victoria and Alex turned around on the couch to watch him.

He listened for a few more seconds. Victoria counted them. One...two...three. His voice rose when he said, "You found her?"

Victoria and Alex sprung from the couch.

The agent swung around to face them. His mouth formed a surprised O. He'd forgotten they were nearby. Victoria would never forget the look he gave them next, a look filled with apologies. A look that made her heart freeze.

There was no happy ending for the Heslin family. No flood of relief and gratitude. No opportunity to do a better job of appreciating her mother. Under the stress of her captors and without the medicine for her heart condition, Abigail Heslin had died only a few hours before the FBI located her.

Victoria wiped a tear from under her eye. From her windowless hospital room, she couldn't see the lightning or the driving rain, but she heard drops lashing the roof.

The thunder came ten seconds later, loud but not too close.

Was Avery still on the yacht? Were they too late?

CHAPTER 42

The yacht rocked between the swells, and a lightning bolt streaked across Tony's window, followed by a deafening clap of thunder. He turned over in his bed and pressed a pillow over his ear. He wanted to wake up when the storm was over, but that wasn't going to happen. There was no way he could fall asleep. The violent sounds captured nature's savage power and reminded him how easily it could kill them out there. Their weapons couldn't save him. They were useless against the raging sea. He wondered how long the FBI agent had lasted before perishing. So far from shore and with her hands tied, she had zero chance of surviving.

At first, Tony thought the banging on his door was another tremendous wave slapping the hull. Then it came again. A quick pounding followed by the captain yelling, "Tony! We have a problem."

Tony jumped out of bed and grabbed his gun from the nightstand. "What happened?"

"Coast Guard helicopter," the captain shouted back from the other side of the door.

Tony yanked his pants off the floor. A Coast Guard boat could mean nothing more than a routine inspection to find out who was on board and what they were doing. A helicopter meant they already knew something about the yacht's passengers. Did they know Eric was on board? Were they here for him? Keeping Eric hidden from the authorities was the only reason they'd spent weeks on the yacht, and yet, Tony felt strangely excited about the possibility of Eric handcuffed and hauled off to prison.

Zipping his jeans, Tony raced into the corridor. The captain was there, wearing a life jacket over his shirt, which made Tony wonder if he should be more concerned about the storm than the Coast Guard.

"You're sure it's just the Coast Guard?" Tony asked, sticking his gun between his waistband and lower back.

"Yes."

"Do they need permission to board?"

"No," the captain answered, the lines on his wrinkled face deepening. "Not like police. They don't need permission or probable cause to come on board."

"Then get the girl and bring her to the hole below the office." Tony pointed a finger at him. "And don't say a word about her. Not one word. She's not here and Eric's not here."

Beads of sweat dripped from the captain's brow and rolled down his unshaven face as he bobbed his head before hurrying off.

"Wait!" Tony shouted, making the captain freeze in his tracks.

Tony ran back to his room and slid a box out of his closet. Silver watches and bundles of cash—some real bills, most fake. Tony shoved the box at the captain. "Take this, too. Hide it with her. "

As the captain rushed away again, Tony turned and ran to the end of the corridor, thinking about the weapons and stacks of drugs stored in different custom-made hiding places on the yacht. Outside Eric's cabin, Tony rattled the handle, then rammed his fist against Eric's locked door. "Eric! Get up and get to the office. Now!"

No response.

Smashing his fists against the wood and kicking the bottom of the door, he yelled, "Eric, get up!" He imagined Eric sleeping inside with his headphones on.

A microphone-boosted voice came from somewhere near the ship. "This is the U.S. Coast Guard. Come onto the deck with your hands up. I repeat. This is the U.S. Coast Guard. Come outside with your hands in the air."

Tony couldn't stay down there pounding on Eric's door any longer. There wasn't time to break it down. The Coast Guard might already be boarding.

"Get up and get into the hole right now, Eric, you stupid ass!" Tony shouted through gritted teeth as a final warning before bolting up the ladder. "And don't mess with the girl!" He didn't trust Eric in a hiding spot with the girl for more than a few minutes.

Tony raced outside. The driving rain drenched him immediately. He edged against a wall to assess the situation. The yacht's floodlights illuminated the surrounding sea. A large boat approached. Close enough for Tony to spot more than a dozen people aiming rifles. *The Untouchable* was outmanned and outgunned.

Beams of light suddenly flooded the yacht in blinding brightness. Squinting to see through the glare and rain, Tony wrapped his hand tightly around a railing. The Coast Guard and their rifles presented a real problem, but they had a protocol to follow, which made them predictable. Tony was more afraid of the storm. Until it calmed, he wanted to be anywhere but outside.

An amplified voice said, "This is the United States Coast Guard. Put your hands up and keep them there."

With a frightened reluctance, Tony let go of the rail and raised his hands over his head.

A commotion of shouting came from the corridor outside Avery's cabin. With the storm raging, it was hard for her to make out the words. A few terrified heartbeats later, her cabin door burst open with such force that the mattress buckled on the floor and folded in on itself.

A man with deeply tanned and leathery skin stood in the partly open doorway aiming a gun at her chest. "What the hell is this?" he growled, kicking the mattress. "Get over here. You have to move! Hurry!"

"Where am I going?" she asked.

He pushed his way in, grabbed her arm, and hauled her out of the cabin. With the gun pressed into her back, he shoved her down the corridor to a set of stairs.

"Climb down there!" he shouted. "Go!"

"No. Tell me where you're taking me!"

He shoved her forward. She tumbled down the stairs but managed to land on her feet and twist an ankle. The pain made her gasp.

Keeping his weapon trained on her, the man climbed down and forced her to limp into a fancy office with bookshelves, two leather chairs, and a desk that sat strangely off center. He twisted a small sculpture on a shelf and a piece of the floor silently slid open only inches from Avery.

She hopped backward on the foot that wasn't throbbing painfully and tried to get a look into the dark space.

"Get into the hole! Now!" the man shouted.

"Please, please, don't make me go down there."

"It won't be for long. You won't be there long, but you have to get down there now!"

"Can't I just stay in this room? Please."

"I won't kill you, but I will shoot you in the hand or foot or shoulder. It will hurt like hell. Get down there!"

Avery limped backward into the corner. He grabbed her and threw her into the hole.

She fell, smashing one side of her body at the bottom. The hole was no larger than a bathtub, but deep enough that she couldn't reach the door overhead. She stood on her good ankle and tried to scramble up the slick walls as the door slid shut above her, encasing her in complete darkness.

The desk moved across the floor and thumped down.

She tried to swallow around the fear constricting her throat. Her heart thudded wildly. She'd never been so terrified before. If the man didn't come back for her...no one would ever find her there.

She lowered herself to the floor and wrapped her arms around her legs as the yacht rocked violently in the storm. Her back rested against a pile of plastic packages filled with packed powder. Obviously drugs. Avery felt nauseous and the throbbing in her ankle had intensified, but she was too afraid to let discomfort be her primary concern.

CHAPTER 43

The Coast Guard crew scrambled aboard. Tony counted seven or eight armed men wearing body armor and Kevlar helmets as if they were about to battle an angry mob. The person commanding them was a beast of a man over six and a half feet tall. He seemed oblivious to the swell's stomach-churning lifts and drops as he stood with his legs wide apart and barked commands at the others. Looking every which way, they aimed their weapons, as if Tony had booby-trapped the yacht with hidden snipers.

"How many people on the vessel?" the leader shouted at Tony.

Tony took a deep breath and answered, "Four."

A powerful wave made the boat lurch. Tony's bare feet slid on the slick deck. He grabbed for the railing.

"Get your hands over your head! Now!" the leader shouted.

Tony widened his stance to resume his balance and lifted his arms again.

"Who else is here? Names!"

"I'm Tony Barerra. There's a captain. Two deckhands. There's no one else."

"We know Avery Jennings is here," the team leader said, aiming his weapon at Tony's heart.

Tony tried not to let his surprise show, but they might as well have sucker punched him in the gut. Somehow, they knew about her.

"The best outcome for you is to hand Avery over right now, unharmed. Where is she? And where is the rest of the crew?"

"I don't know," Tony said.

As if on cue, the captain came outside with his hands up. Marineros Uno and Dos followed, tucking their chins and turning their faces aside in the slashing rain. They lined up next to Tony, their backs against the wall and their hands in the air.

"Just keep your mouths shut and you'll be fine," Tony told them, blinking into the rain. He was confident they'd never be able to find her.

A massive wave made the ship rise on one side. When it slapped down, Tony fell, slamming his face against the railing. He scrambled to stand up again, clutching the railing as blood filled his mouth.

As the yacht steadied, four Coast Guard men left the deck and marched inside the yacht. The rest stayed behind, their guns trained on Tony and the crew like a firing squad itching to pull their triggers.

The leader pointed his rifle at Marinero Uno. "You. Come with me."

As Uno moved forward, Tony tried to cast a warning glare. A reminder that whatever strategies the Coast Guard used to make people talk, they were no match for what Tony would do if Uno betrayed him.

Uno kept his eyes fixed straight ahead, avoiding Tony's gaze.

"Hey," Tony hissed, but the deck hand didn't turn around.

Tony ground his teeth. He was devising ways to make Uno suffer when shouts of "U.S. Coast Guard!" and "Clear!" rose from below deck.

A voice boomed, "Open the door!"

Tony cursed under his breath. The only locked door on the floor below was Eric's. He still hadn't left his cabin.

"This is the U.S. Coast Guard. Open the door now!"

A solid, smashing sound came from below. Wood cracking and splinting. An eruption of frantic shouts and commands followed. No gunfire, but it sounded like the Coast Guard had lost control. Had Eric surprised the intruders and gotten the better of them? The streak of resentment that coursed through Tony was more powerful than the blow he'd just received.

The boat suddenly rose. It hovered in the air, suspended between swells before it plummeted down and crashed into the water. Dos fell against Tony as he grabbed for a handrail.

A uniformed man burst outside carrying a lifeless-looking body. "Is this Eric Salazar?"

Tony didn't answer.

"What is he on?" the leader shouted.

Tony and the rest of the crew remained silent.

The leader stormed forward. He stopped inches from Marinero Dos's face and resumed his shouting. *"What is he on?"*

"Heroin," Dos said.

"Shut up," Tony snapped, right before beast-man stepped closer with his gun.

"Get him on our boat," the leader told the man carrying Eric. "And radio ahead for Narcan!"

Tony should have been angry. Soaking wet in his bare feet on a lurching ship in a God forsaken storm and unable to retaliate. He was going to lose the FBI lady's niece—his precious leverage. And he'd failed to do his job. He'd failed to keep Eric safe. But he temporarily forgot all that when he heard someone on the ship behind him shouting, "Get the defib machine! Hurry! We're going to lose him!"

Anticipation buzzed through Tony's body and his next thought came before he could stop it.

One less fool.

Between claps of thunder, Avery heard shouting and heavy footfalls.

She jumped up, pounded on the sides of the confined space, and screamed her lungs out.

The footsteps went away.

Avery slouched against the wall in tears.

The footsteps returned. They were directly overhead. She resumed pounding and screaming. The desk thumped down again, but not directly overhead.

The door slid open above her, and a bright light shone down into her face.

She blinked up at two people who looked to be wearing full riot gear with U.S. Coast Guard written on the front.

"Avery Jennings?" a uniformed man asked.

"Yes! Please get me out of here!"

"We will. Are you hurt?"

"Just my ankle. But there's another girl on board. She's really hurt. I don't know if she survived. Please find her," Avery said as the man pulled her out of the hole.

The chef who had been kind to her stood by the bookshelf, his hand near the sculpture. "You're going to be okay," he said right before another Coast Guard member yanked him away.

A female from the Coast Guard led Avery from the room and up two levels. Avery stepped outside for the first time in days, right into a torrential downpour. The howling wind whipped rain into her eyes. She could barely see where she was going, even as lightning slashed through the sky and lit up her surroundings.

The ship lurched up and down between gigantic waves.

"We're getting off this yacht," the woman said. "Can you walk? Or do you want us to carry you?"

"I can walk," Avery said, gripping the woman's arm tightly for balance and reassurance. So close to safety, yet Avery feared something terrible might still happen. She couldn't leave her abductors behind fast enough and only let herself start to relax once she'd made it from the yacht to the Coast Guard's ship and out of the wind and rain. Wiping drops from her face, she looked around the larger vessel. A group of people hovered around a table under a bright light.

There he was, in the center of the others. Eric. The arrogant, drugged-out man who had toyed with her like she was a mouse in a cage. He was lying face up on a table with his shirt ripped open and his arms hanging lifelessly off the sides. Someone stuck a needle in his arm. Defibrillator paddles pressed against his chest. Avery watched in horror as electricity shot through his body and made him leap from the table. She didn't look away until someone pushed her in the other direction, away from the morbid scene. She hoped that was the last time she'd ever see Eric again.

CHAPTER 44

When Victoria woke up, she peeled off the tape holding the IV in place and withdrew the tiny catheter from her vein. Drops of blood slid over her skin. She pressed it against her hospital gown to stop the flow.

Something wasn't right.

Why am I still here? No hospital in America would keep someone for more than one day for dehydration. And in a private room, no less. Are hospitals in Mexico that different?

Whatever sedative the hospital staff was giving her, enough was enough. She had to leave now, regardless of any tests they continued to run. She needed an update on Avery's situation and to find out if Teresa was still missing. Her work in Mexico might not be done.

On the corner chair, someone had left sandals and the clothes she'd worn on the plane. Underneath her folded blouse, she found white panties and a sports bra. Rivera must have brought them from her room at the resort. She wasn't sure how she felt about him selecting her undergarments, yet she was grateful they were there. She lifted the entire pile and found a phone on the chair. Recognizing the blue case as her own, she turned on the device. It was already eight a.m.

She called Rivera. "Thanks for the clothes and my phone," she told him. "I can't believe it's in one piece and working."

"You're welcome. It was clean. No prints."

"Did you just bring these? Are you still at the hospital?"

"Yes. I'm grabbing a coffee downstairs. Do you want one?"

"No, thank you. I've got to get out of here before they stick me or fill me up again with whatever is keeping me asleep. Do you have a car?"

"Yes. I got one from the FBI's field office yesterday."

"Good. I'll meet you downstairs in the lobby...if there is one. By the front entrance."

"You're ready now?"

"Five minutes."

In the cramped bathroom with dim lighting, she splashed water on her face and brushed her teeth with the travel set someone had left there, being careful not to bump her swollen lips. Her stomach growled as she took off her hospital gown and got dressed, smacking her hip against the sink as she leaned forward to pull up her pants. Her body was slow to respond, but she felt little pain or soreness.

After combing her fingers through her hair, which was dry and in desperate need of conditioner, she pulled it back into a ponytail again and studied her reflection. Cuts dotted her lips and a greasy medicating ointment covered them. Her eyes were a little red. Otherwise, she didn't look much different from any other time she'd been overdue for a shower.

She paused in the doorway of her room and looked out into the hospital corridor. She could see outside through a window, and it appeared she was on the second floor. Why did it feel like she was sneaking away? The hospital had no legal recourse to keep her there. But she sensed she might be up against something or someone who had no regard for the law. Or maybe, after all that happened, she was just being paranoid.

"Hey, where are you going?" a nurse called after her. "I was just coming in to check on you. You aren't ready to leave yet."

"I'm fine, thank you. I have to go. Send me the bill and I'll take care of it." Without breaking stride, Victoria headed toward an exit sign.

"No, no. Wait! You can't leave! Someone stop her!" The nurse's high-pitched shouts confirmed Victoria's suspicions. The hospital staff were keeping her drugged and asleep.

Victoria picked up her pace, speed walking down the corridor. The irony of civilians chasing an FBI agent down a hallway didn't escape her, but she wasn't in America where she enforced the laws. She needed to get out of there and understand what she was up against.

"Help, stop her!" the nurse yelled again.

Victoria broke into a run, her sandals flopping off and smacking the tile floor with each stride. She passed a fire alarm and, for a split second, considered pulling it. The ensuing chaos would buy her some time. It might also endanger the lives of other patients. She rushed past it, burst through the exit door, and hurried down one flight of stairs to the next landing.

Another voice behind her shouted, "Victoria Heslin. Stop!"

She pushed through an emergency exit to the outside and raced across the parking lot to a smaller building with a red cross on the front. Only once did she look back over her shoulder. No one had followed her out of the emergency door.

Ducking into the trees on the side of the building, beside a large puddle, she called Rivera back. "Change of plans. There's a clinic to the right of the hospital. I'm on the side of it. There's a white bus near me."

"What are you doing there?"

"Uh, I'm waiting for you."

Rivera didn't answer right away. He was probably trying to figure out what was going on. "I'll get the car. It's a blue Nissan sedan. What did you do?"

"Nothing. I swear. Can you sort of hurry?"

"I am. Wait there. I'll come around."

Catching her breath, she watched for the blue Nissan while also keeping an eye on the hospital exits.

When the sedan pulled up alongside her, she quickly got into the passenger side. Rivera hit the gas while she buckled her seatbelt.

"What was that about?" he asked.

"They didn't want me to leave." She huffed, still unsure of her thoughts on what had just occurred.

Without coming to a full stop, Rivera turned right onto the main road. "I talked to a nurse this morning. She said the police called and told her to take special care of you while you were here. She said they were still running tests."

"What? Well, that explains things. There's nothing to test, Rivera. They were drugging me. Aside from that, I'm fine."

"Hard for me to confirm that when I don't really know what happened to you while you were missing."

She shook her head, not ready to talk about it. "I know the police don't want our help, but to try and keep me in the hospital, that seems desperate. Anyway, any update on Avery?" she asked, bracing herself for bad news.

"Yes. Avery is safe. She's with her parents at Azure Cove. They had a doctor check her there. She's okay. That's about all I know."

Victoria leaned back against the cloth seat. Warmth spread through her chest. She was beyond thrilled. Except...Avery wasn't the only missing person. "And Teresa?"

"Still missing, as far as I know," Rivera said. "Now that we've been *uninvited to assist*, we don't have direct information on either investigation."

"The police don't want our help, but the Jennings did," Victoria said, checking the side mirror to see if anyone was following. "Let's get back to the resort and talk to Avery. She's as direct a source as we're going to find. I want to know what's going on."

CHAPTER 45

V ictoria hadn't talked to Ned in almost two days. She couldn't wait to connect, though she still wasn't sure what to share with him about her recent ordeal. After taking a much-needed shower in her room, she called him.

"Victoria?" he said. "I'm so glad you called. Are you okay?"

"Hi. Yes. I'm fine." Hearing his voice, full of love and concern, she wanted to fall into his arms and stay there for a long time. Instead, she shoved down an odd urge to cry and said, "I lost my phone yesterday, so I didn't get your messages until now."

"Oh. I left some. I was just calling to talk to you, and then to make sure you were all right."

"I am. I'm fine. What's going on there?" she asked as she pulled on a clean shirt.

"The dogs are well. It's been raining so we haven't walked much, lots of muddy paw prints all over your house."

"There was a huge storm here." After all that happened over the past two days, she could hardly believe she was chatting about the weather.

"It's..." He blew out a loud breath. "It's fantastic to hear your voice. You wouldn't believe the things I imagined...maybe I overreacted, but it's hard not to."

"I know, but I'm okay. Really." She had to swallow the lump in her throat and was still surprised how much overwhelming relief came from speaking with him.

"So, how is the investigation going?"

Victoria combed her fingers through her wet hair. "Well...Avery was abducted from the resort and brought to a yacht. The Coast Guard got her back last night."

"Wow. That's...incredible! I'm glad you weren't the one rescuing her from a yacht. Right off the top of my head, I can think of too many ways that could have gone wrong."

His comment elicited discomfort that came from hiding the truth. People dealt with trauma differently. After the plane crash, the other survivors made the morning and late-night talk-show rounds and were on the cover of different magazines for weeks. Sharing their story helped them cope with the tragedy they endured. Victoria, on the other hand, had barely talked to the press. She had her career to fall back on. She also had Ned. They helped each other heal. But telling him about her real-life nightmare in the ocean would only make him more worried now. Doing it just to comfort herself seemed selfish. Maybe when she got home...she could tell him then.

They talked for a few more minutes, until eventually Ned said, "The dogs miss you. But not as much as me. I'm glad you're safe. I love you and I can't wait for you to get back."

"Same. I love you, too. I should be home tomorrow or the day after," she said. "There are a few more things I want to wrap up here before we go. I'll talk to you soon. Goodbye."

She couldn't wait to get back to Virginia, and yet, despite the irrational feeling that a nurse might show up and try to drag her back to the hospital, she wasn't ready to leave Mexico. As she slid her shoes on, the open-ended pieces of the investigation troubled her. Teresa. The dead woman with the missing body parts. The Salazar Cartel. She wondered how Payton and her family had reacted to that news. She'd find out in a few minutes when they talked to Avery and the Jennings.

Tom met them at his bungalow. He lit up at the sight of Victoria. "Hello. We heard you located Avery. She said you were on the yacht with her. We can't thank you enough."

"I'm just so glad she's safe."

"How did you find her?" Tom asked. "She doesn't know. None of us know."

"We can talk about that later," Victoria said, her voice kind but firm. "We'd like to speak to Avery. If that's okay with her."

"Come on in. You can ask her yourself."

As they followed Tom into the bungalow, Victoria spotted a flyer on the foyer table. It had Teresa's picture and the words, *missing, have you seen her?* written in several languages below it. The resort must have delivered one to every room.

"These are the FBI agents. Your aunt Payton's friends. Victoria and Dante," Tom said.

With her feet up on an ottoman, and one ankle looking swollen, Avery rested on the couch next to her mother. There was something fiercely protective in the way Jennifer sat so close that they were touching from their shoulders to their knees. Avery wore shorts and a loose blouse. Victoria recognized the outfit as the one Jennifer wore when they first met with the Federales.

Avery didn't get up from the couch, but she scooted to the front edge. "Ms. Heslin! I owe you my life. I can't thank you enough. But...how did you get off the ship?"

"We're going to save that for another time," Victoria said, wanting to move the conversation away from her. "I'm just sorry that I had to leave you, and I'm very grateful you're here now."

"Believe me, no one is more grateful than me. Thank you for finding me. I can hardly believe it's over." Avery shivered, her shoulders rising toward her ears. Her mother pulled her closer.

"Now we'd like to learn what happened to you, how you ended up on that yacht," Victoria said, taking a seat across from the couch. "It might help us find another missing person."

"Yes, of course. The other girl. And I heard about Teresa," Avery said. "Do you think the same people took her?"

"I do," Victoria answered. "Teresa paid attention to things. She saw the man who abducted you. He was at the bonfire on Saturday night."

"He was? I mean, when he took me, he was wearing a mask and a cap. I could barely see his face. But still, I didn't think I'd ever seen him before. I don't remember him."

"He didn't want you to," Victoria said. "He wasn't a guest or a staff member, and I think he did some disguising to confuse everyone. A fake tattoo from a California-based gang. Filling in a prominent scar. Either that, or he's got a twin. Can you tell us what happened after he told you to pack your things and you left your room?"

Jennifer took hold of her daughter's hand and squeezed it. "You don't have to relive any of it if you don't want to. It can wait."

"No. I want to help," Avery said. "I mean, mom...can you imagine if this was yesterday, and you were trying to find me and someone told you they could help, but they needed more time first? The FBI has to find Teresa and the other girl who was on the yacht with me."

Jennifer gave Victoria and Rivera hard stares, imploring them not to mention the girl under the pier.

Avery crossed her arms and began her story. "I still don't know his name. After we left my room, I had my suitcase, which I guess is gone now—my laptop and everything." She bit her lower lip. "I know that hardly matters. I can get new ones. There are far worse things. I'm just telling you everything that happened." A few beats of silence passed before Avery continued. "I followed him to the health center. He must have drugged me there because that's honestly the last thing I remember. Next thing I know, I'm waking up on the yacht. All my clothes were on. I smelled strange. I had seaweed tangled in my hair and under my clothes."

"Did they hurt you?" Victoria asked, casting her gaze to the scabs covering Avery's knees. It might be a sensitive topic, but Avery needed to get used to answering it.

"No, not really," Avery answered. "I sprained my ankle when they pushed me down the stairs to get me into the hole. And Eric crushed his boot into my chest. I don't know what he might have done if the guy who took me didn't stop him. But that was all. I was mostly alone, locked in a cabin the whole time. I had my own bathroom. One guy brought me food. He even apologized but said he couldn't do anything to help me, or he'd get killed. He's the reason the Coast Guard found me. He told them where the others hid me." Avery screwed up her face into a tight grimace. "It was Eric's yacht. He's a psychopath. The other girl...I heard her screaming. Begging and pleading in Spanish." Avery curled her lips inward as she recalled the memory. "I think he was torturing her. You haven't found her?"

"They're working on it," Jennifer said quickly, again shielding her daughter from the truth.

"Did you ever see the woman you heard?" Victoria asked.

"No. I never saw her." Avery took a deep breath before telling them everything that happened, ending with the Coast Guard pulling her from the hole and escorting her to one of their ships, where she saw medics working to revive Eric. "So did Eric Salazar die?" she asked.

"We're not sure," Rivera answered. "We don't have that information yet. We're just glad you're okay,"

Victoria hoped they would soon find Teresa and tell her the same thing.

CHAPTER 46

T hough no one else was around Victoria kept her voice low as she and Rivera headed down the boardwalk.

"Avery and her parents didn't seem angry that Payton's role might have put their daughter in jeopardy," she said. "I'm sure that helps Payton feel better."

"I haven't had a chance to talk to Payton since you went missing. She's been so busy. But if Avery knew Payton was working the Salazar case, I'm sure her parents knew also. Unless this experience has completely scrambled their brains, they've put two and two together. Like you said, it's either a huge coincidence that the cartel abducted Avery...or it's not."

"I didn't say that. I think you did."

"You don't know what you said, Tori. You were out of it for a while."

"Like I told you...drugged. But I don't have evidence of that, I don't want to get tested right now, so let's just keep it to ourselves."

"And like *I told you*, without knowing what happened to you while you were gone, I couldn't tell if you needed all that sleep or not."

Victoria avoided his eyes, gazing out at the ocean beyond the water sports pavilion instead. When she arrived at the resort, the sound of the waves lapping the shore had relaxed her. Now it grated on her nerves. Without warning, a violent shiver rocked her core as she remembered falling into the ocean. For an instant, she couldn't catch her breath and felt like she was drowning all over again.

She turned back to Rivera and refocused her thoughts. "If we figure out what happened to Avery, we have a chance of figuring out what happened to Teresa. I know we're supposed to let the Federales handle things, but after they pretty much gave up on Avery's trail at the marina, and tried to keep me in the hospital, I don't trust them."

"I don't either. And the longer we wait for information, the less likely we are to find Teresa alive." Rivera ran his hand down the side of his face. "Avery doesn't remember how she ended up on *The Untouchable*. Before, we thought she'd been carried down the beach in that stolen paddleboard bag. Now that we know she's alive, I'm not sure if it's possible."

"I think it is. They might have sedated her, knocked her out like they did with me."

Rivera jerked his head around. His eyes widened. "What was that? Do you mean when they drugged you in the hospital?"

"No. Before that. The man who took Avery is strong."

"He looks strong, you mean."

"No. He is. He carried me effortlessly up a set of stairs and dumped me overboard."

Rivera's mouth dropped open. He stopped walking. "What? Dumped you overboard? And you swam to shore?"

Victoria offered a curt nod but kept heading down the boardwalk.

"How far?" Rivera asked, catching back up to her.

"I don't know. It was dark."

"It had to be far because you were in rough shape when the medical team got to you. You were barely coherent or conscious. I just didn't realize...Damn, Tori. You're lucky you've got nine lives, you know that? Did they know you were an FBI agent?"

Without actually deciding to do so, she told him the rest—everything that happened to her. *Happened to her*—those were the keywords. Getting shot, captured, thrown overboard, drugged. Those things had happened to her. She hadn't been in control. "I let my guard down at the marina. And pretending to be unconscious rather than striking first...that was another mistake. I really screwed up."

"No. You didn't, Tori. They were dangerous, armed men with a lot of experience in killing people. It's likely if you struck first, you'd be dead. Maybe the way it played out wasn't ideal, but you found Avery, didn't you? She's safe. And so are you. That's all that matters."

"I hope so. Don't tell anyone yet. I don't want to be taken off the investigation."

Rivera pressed his lips together and didn't say anything for several strides. "What did Ned have to say about what happened? How much did you tell him?"

"Nothing...I told him nothing. It wasn't my proudest moment, you know."

Rivera frowned and dipped his head. "Okay. You're entitled to that." He was quiet for several strides. "I guess I'm surprised you didn't mention a thing about the swim or recovering in the hospital. It's not good to have too many secrets between you. So much of what we do each day doesn't make for good shareable conversation, you know? Intimate details from murders and rapes, and the mindset of psychopaths. I think that's what makes it so hard to have a relationship with someone who isn't in the law enforcement business. We probably shouldn't share those stories. But we should share our own. I'm sure Ned would want to know what you went through."

"You the relationship expert now?"

"I'm no expert. Obviously not or you and I...well, never mind. No point in bringing that up now. I do know relationships get stronger when you share important things. And if I can be blunt here, you aren't great at letting people get close to you. Ned seems to be changing that dynamic. You seem to be letting him. Don't chicken out now."

"Chicken out?" she asked, though her mind was replaying Rivera's unfinished comment, something about the relationship they almost had but didn't.

"It takes strength to let yourself be vulnerable."

Victoria gazed up at the swaying palm fronds above the boardwalk and thought about ways to refute what Rivera had just told her. She had her reasons for not telling Ned. She wasn't proud of what happened. There was that. But even more important—she didn't want to freak him out. She didn't want him worrying what might happen to her every time she left the house to go to work.

They'd reached the camouflaged area with the seaweed truck and came to a stop there.

"You should tell Ned," Rivera said.

"Fine, thank you for the advice," she said, with a little snark to her tone. "Can we get back to the investigation now?"

"Sure. I already have. Let me summarize where we're at. We think they sedated Avery with whatever they gave you and put her in the seaweed truck. Then they waited until dark and moved Avery down the beach to the marina in the stolen paddleboard bag. Which makes sense, if they wanted to abduct Avery and keep her hostage as some bargaining chip," Rivera said. "But with Teresa, assuming they took her because of something she knew or saw...did they have a reason to keep her around?"

"None I can think of. They only had a reason to shut her up."

"So they might have put Teresa in the seaweed truck also, since that worked out for them. But why bother carrying her down the beach, right?"

"Probably not the best use of their time if all they want to do is get rid of her."

The agents stood above the seaweed truck and looked down into the back of the cargo bed.

"They have to dump this thing at least once a day and it looks almost full right now," Victoria said. "We need to find out where this stuff goes. But before we do, if we're going to pay a visit to the local dump, we should change out of work clothes into shorts and a T-shirt, so we don't look suspicious."

"Because that worked out so well for you at the marina?" Rivera asked, a grin playing at the corners of his mouth.

She gave him a firm punch in the arm, but she was grateful he was already joking about what happened to her. It helped. "We better change fast," she said. "The truck could leave any minute."

CHAPTER 47

Inside her room, Victoria whipped off her travel outfit and put on her remaining exercise clothes. The drugs the hospital had given to her had long worn off. Now it hurt to bend at the waist, to raise her arms, to walk. Every muscle in her body ached. She popped two Ibuprofens into her mouth and stuck some evidence bags, gloves, and water bottles into her backpack before meeting up with Rivera again.

The seaweed truck hadn't left, so the agents parked their car in a spot along Azure Cove's deserted maintenance road. The truck would have to drive right past them when it left the resort. They planned to follow it.

With the sun dropping in the western sky, Rivera lowered the windows all the way, letting air flow through the sedan. "We could forget about following the truck, ask Alejandro where the dumping ground is, and head straight there."

They didn't have to decide on Rivera's suggestion because the truck brimming with seaweed came rumbling down the service road. Rivera started the engine and followed the pickup out of the resort and inland through the city. As they drove farther from the ocean, the breeze disappeared. The air grew stagnant. Rivera shut the windows and turned on the air conditioning. After about twenty minutes, the truck stopped at a gated dumpsite.

A man jumped out of the truck's passenger side. He opened a padlock on a rusty iron gate and pulled one side open. The truck drove through.

The agents waited while the workers dumped the load of seaweed and drove away with an empty cargo bed, locking the gate behind them. They waved at the agents as they passed. Victoria pulled the brim of her cap down over her eyes and waved back. She held her fingers tight together so they wouldn't look out of the ordinary.

When they were alone again, the agents got out of their car and walked to the dump site. Large signs with NO PASAR in bright orange letters were posted every few yards along the chain-link fence. They walked the perimeter, confirming there was no way for them to get inside except to go up and over. The fence was eight feet tall, but luckily for the agents, there was no barbed wire on the top.

After glancing back to search for approaching vehicles, Victoria shoved the toe of her leather flats into the fence's metal slots and hoisted herself up.

"You aren't wearing the best shoes for this."

"Yeah, well...apparently the cartel liked my running shoes. They took them, which left me with the option of wearing cute sandals or these sensible work flats."

"Ah," he said, climbing the fence a few yards away from her.

On the other side, giant piles of garbage were on the left, and piles of seaweed and brush to the right. The rotting seaweed piles rose from the ground like small brown mountains with dark tendrils strewn between them. The agents would need a small army to sort through it all. At home, they could have called forensic techs to complete the task, but here, it was only the two of them.

"Smells like rotten eggs," Rivera said. "That's hydrogen sulfide. Prepare to have a headache. You sure you want to do this?"

Victoria pulled two masks from her pocket. "These might help mute the stench. Here," she said, handing one to Rivera.

Two pitchforks leaned against a nearby utility shed. Rivera grabbed one for himself and held one out for Victoria. Digging her pitchfork into the smelly mess behind the recently dumped pile, she tossed aside clumps of rotting brown algae, broken shells, and sand with the occasional colored wrapper, plastic bottle, and dead sea creature. "One forkful at a time," she said, altering a phrase Ned often used for encouragement,

"This one is going to go down in the records, won't it?" Rivera said, digging in across from her.

After only a few minutes in the sun, perspiration trickled down her face and back and pooled between her breasts. Her arms and legs still ached from her swim and protested as she tried to toss the seaweed around.

"You know what I was just thinking?" she asked.

"That we most likely won't find a darn thing at this dump?"

"No. This reminds me of when I was a kid and I used to clean stalls in the barn where we kept my horse. The first time I picked up a pitchfork, it was taller than me, and I could only get one stall done. Then two, then three, and pretty soon I could clean ten without taking a rest. I think they paid me a dollar per stall, but I was so proud of myself because it was hard, physical work."

"*You* had a job cleaning out horse stalls? You?"

"Yes. I had jobs every summer. None of them were what anyone would call *cushy*. My parents wanted me to know the value of hard work. But my point about the stalls is that your back gets used to the work, eventually."

"Yeah, well, I hope we don't get to find out if that's true. There might be a fine line between appreciating hard work and being a glutton for punishment." Sweat had darkened Rivera's shirt in several places. He pulled it over his head, hung it on the fence, and returned to digging. Muscles across his arms and back glistened in the sun as he plunged the pitchfork into the side of his pile. He looked like a movie star, aviator glasses shielding his eyes, and considering that he was sorting through rotting seaweed, the thought made her laugh.

After a few more minutes, Victoria stopped digging and leaned against the handle of her pitchfork. The sun was dropping fast on the horizon. They were running out of daylight. "What are we doing?" she asked, shaking her head.

Rivera held his pitchfork upright and wiped the back of his hand over his forehead. "I believe this was your idea."

"What? No. This was your idea."

"That's not how I remember it."

They stared at each other until they both laughed.

"You thirsty?" he asked.

"Not enough to climb back over the fence yet."

"You have water bottles in your backpack, right? Warm, probably hot, but better than nothing. I'll be right back," Rivera said before leaving.

"Get the evidence bags, too. Just in case," she called after him.

Victoria dragged her pitchfork in lazy circles around the edge of a seaweed pile. She heard the fence clang as Rivera scaled it. Her eyes stung from the methane, and she was rubbing them with the back of her wrist when she spotted something orange and white in the pile. Just as suddenly as she'd seen it, she lost it again. She blinked a few times and refocused, scanning the mass of brown tendrils. There it was, barely visible, peeking out from between the seaweed. A splash of white and orange thicker than just a food wrapper. It looked like fabric. Familiar fabric.

She trudged up the filthy pile, sinking in and ignoring the disgusting feel of the rotting vegetation on her ankles and shins. She nudged debris away from the object. It was a headband, crusted in dirt and slime, but recognizable.

Rivera returned carrying two water bottles.

"Hand me an evidence bag," she said. "I found a Chanel headband. Teresa had one like it. I want to get to the bottom of this pile."

Rivera handed her two evidence bags. She used one to pick up the headband and deposit it inside another.

"Here," Rivera said, tossing her a bottle. "Drink this."

After pulling off their masks and drinking, they set the almost empty water bottles down-and resumed their search with renewed motivation.

Between her labored breathing and Rivera's grunts, Victoria heard the hum of a car engine growing louder as it approached.

Victoria no longer had her FBI identification. Even if she did, the agents had no jurisdiction there. They were trespassing.

"I'm going to see who it is," Rivera said.

Victoria grabbed evidence bag with the headband and rolled it underneath the hem of her shirt. She tucked her shirt into her waistband before following Rivera toward the front of the dumpsite. A car marked *Policia* idled on the other side of the locked fence.

Leo got out of the driver's side. He locked eyes with the agents, then stormed toward the gate, yelling in Spanish. Victoria didn't have to understand the words to know he was angry.

"Leo said he got a call about trespassers. But now that he sees it's us, he said he's not surprised," Rivera told her.

"I don't trust him," Victoria whispered, certain Leo was responsible for her extended hospital stay.

From behind the fence, she wasn't sure if she felt safe or trapped.

She went to reach for her gun, again forgetting it wasn't there.

CHAPTER 48

L eo stared from the other side of the chain-link fence, his hand resting on his weapon. "Heard you found Avery and you were in the hospital," he said to Victoria.

Yes. And I heard you told the staff there to take *special care* of me. Thoughtful of you," she said, through gritted teeth.

Not even attempting to deny the implication, Leo shrugged as he moved closer. "How did you find her?"

"I got lucky," Victoria said.

"And what are you doing now?" he asked.

"We're looking for something. We think Teresa Middleton, the other missing resort guest, might have been killed and dumped here," Rivera said, apparently deciding the truth was the best way to proceed.

"You need to get out of there now, before I arrest you for interfering with an investigation," Leo said, unholstering his weapon.

Victoria had no intention of leaving. Not yet, when there might be more than just Teresa's headband to find. And she didn't trust Leo with the evidence she'd found. He could be on the cartel's payroll. Or perhaps the cartel had threatened to harm his family. In either case, if she handed the evidence over and it traced to the Salazar Cartel, he might bury the truth.

Rivera stood his ground but pulled Victoria behind him. "We're not finished here," he said. "Teresa is an American and we'd really appreciate your cooperation."

"You found Avery. Isn't that enough? How much will you risk to get to the bottom of this?"

"Whatever it takes," Victoria answered without hesitation.

Vince got out of the car. "Hey, Leo, let me handle this. If they think she's here, I'll have a look. You can go. We'll keep you out of it."

Leo frowned at his partner but lowered his gun. "You don't know what you're getting into, Vince."

"I do. I know what could happen. Just let me have a look around with them and then I'll make sure they leave."

Leo grumbled and shook his head. "Don't do anything stupid. Not if you value your life, Vince."

The officers walked back to the car together. Vince grabbed a plastic wrapped evidence sheet from the trunk. Then Leo drove off, leaving Vince alone with the agents.

"Thank you for helping us," Victoria said.

Vince eyed the locked gate. "How did you get in?"

"Up and over," Rivera said.

Vince eyed the fence. "Let me make a few calls. See if I can get someone to open the facility and put those spotlights on for us."

After Vince tracked down the city workers who could help them, the agents waited on one side of the fence and Vince on the other.

"We confirmed the identity of the girl from under the pier," Vince told them. "It was exactly who I thought it was. I met with her family this morning to deliver the news."

"Hardest part of the job, isn't it?" Rivera asked.

"It is," Vince said. "At least they have closure."

"Would be nice if they also got justice," Victoria said, still unsure if she could completely trust the officer.

"I agree," Vince answered.

It didn't take too long for someone to come and unlock the gate and turn floodlights on. At Vince's request, the city worker stayed and moved the debris around with a small tractor.

Victoria studied the progress, watching for anything other than seaweed.

Vince was the first to say, "Wait. Stop the tractor. Look!"

Victoria followed his pointed finger and saw it, too. A solid pink shape under a mass of brown. They climbed through the pile and pulled seaweed away from the shape with their hands. After only a few seconds, they knew they'd found a corpse.

Vince and Rivera carried the slight body out of the refuse and laid it over the blanket. They gently lifted away more debris, but Victoria already knew who it was. Teresa. The inhuman angle of her neck, her face too far to one side, almost turned backward, made her look like a broken mannequin. Her wig had come off and gray tufts spotted her otherwise bald head. Victoria moved closer. Signs of petechial hemorrhage in Teresa's eyes and the dark bruises on her neck strongly suggested someone had strangled her. And Teresa had put up a struggle. Her pink nails, perfectly manicured a few days ago, were now broken. Victoria hoped they would find her perpetrator's skin and DNA under the cracked nails.

Victoria scanned Teresa's hands and bare feet. All fingers and toes were intact, but her diamond ring was gone. So was her fiery personality. Only an empty shell left behind. No more post workout drinks. No more journal entries.

Victoria looked away, not trusting her voice. Her heart ached for the lonely woman who had died a violent death. What if they hadn't kept digging? What if Leo had forced them to leave? Teresa might never have been found.

Vince wrapped the blanket around Teresa's corpse, just as he'd done with the girl they'd found under the pier.

"Wait," Victoria said. "Can you assure us your department will do a thorough forensic investigation?"

Vince just stared back at her. His lack of response told her all she needed to know. If the Salazar Cartel was involved, there were powers beyond Vince's control calling the shots. It wouldn't surprise her if evidence implicating the cartel was "accidentally" misplaced.

"Then let us scrape under her nails," Victoria said, grabbing another pair of gloves and an evidence bag.

"Let me do it," Rivera whispered, so only she could hear him. "Evidence collected by an FBI agent who was recently under physical duress, drugged, and escaped from a hospital might not stand up so well in court."

He had a good point. She handed Rivera the bags and gloves.

Unlike Vince's sister and so many other people who disappeared in Mexico, Teresa would not become another missing person statistic. That was something. But it wasn't near enough. Whoever killed her needed to pay for what they'd done.

CHAPTER 49

The agents were almost back to the resort, driving down Azure Cove's main entrance road under the giant archway, when Rivera got a call from Murphy.

"Hey, boss. Good timing." Rivera sounded energetic despite hours of shoveling through seaweed. "I'm with Victoria. We just found Teresa Middleton, the resort guest from Pennsylvania who disappeared. Unfortunately, someone murdered her. The Mexican authorities took her body, but we collected a scraping sample from under her nails. We'll mail it to the lab in the morning."

Victoria expected Murphy to have questions. Instead, he grumbled, "Just got another call from the Chief of Police there. I need both of you to book flights to come home as soon as possible. Consider yourselves on vacation until then."

Victoria and Rivera exchanged confused looks.

"Uh, what's going on?" Rivera asked. "Because we were working with a Mexican police officer when we found Teresa."

"It was Leo," Victoria whispered.

"You both did great work there," Murphy said.

"Then...why do you sound like we royally screwed up?" Rivera asked.

Murphy sighed. "You stirred a pot that we can't stir right now. I know that's hard for either of you to accept, but you have to follow orders now. I can only take so much rebellion in one day."

Victoria mouthed, "What is he talking about?"

Rivera shook his head.

Murphy cut off the call before the agents could ask him if he knew what happened to Eric Salazar and the rest of the cartel crew on *The Untouchable*.

"What just happened?" Victoria replayed the conversation in her head.

"Someone used one of his Georgia Bulldogs mugs," Rivera joked, parking the car in the resort's lot.

"Call Payton and see if she knows what happened. I'll call Sam. I guess there's no need to mail the fingernail scrapings sample to the lab now. You can deliver it in person as soon as we get back to Virginia."

Victoria felt almost like a new person after taking a shower. Wearing Rivera's sweatshirt again, she curled up in a chair and called Sam's personal cell phone.

When he answered, she filled him in on everything that happened, ending with the call from Murphy. "I don't know if he's just angry because he thinks we messed up the relationship with the police chief here, or if something else is going on there."

"Something is going on. But I don't have the direct story. I don't want to spread rumors...if that's all they are."

Though Victoria respected Sam's stance, he'd left her more confused than ever. She hoped Rivera would have better luck getting information from Payton.

With her hair still damp, she went to the room next door to see Rivera.

His solemn expression told her he'd learned something.

"What's going on? And don't say nothing. I've known you and worked with you long enough to know something happened. You finally got to talk to Payton?"

"Finally," he said, his shoulders rising and falling with a sigh.

"She feels terrible about Avery, doesn't she? Did you tell her it's not her fault? I should call her."

"It's not that."

"You're making me nervous, Rivera. Tell me what's going on. Did you find out why Murphy was so angry?"

Rivera dropped his head and huffed. "Secrets. Let's just say you aren't the only one good at keeping things to yourself." He turned away and stared out the balcony window. "She knew."

"Who knew what?"

"Payton knew the cartel had Avery."

"Huh?" That didn't make any sense.

"Someone delivered a handwritten note to her house. A threat. It said if she didn't get the evidence against Salazar thrown out and get a mistrial somehow, she'd never see Avery again. It included a time stamped photograph of Avery."

"When did she receive the threat?"

"Two nights ago. When you went missing. Payton didn't know where Avery was obviously, but she knew the cartel had abducted her."

"That information could have helped us find Avery sooner. Why didn't anyone tell us?"

"Because Payton didn't tell anyone."

"Oh...wow...okay." Victoria stayed quiet, thinking about what Rivera had told her and what it meant. The threat probably instructed Payton not to tell anyone, or she'd never see Avery again. But Payton knew better.

"After she got the threat, Payton didn't show up for court. She claimed to have an emergency health issue. She didn't tell anyone what was really going on. Not even me."

"Well...she must have been terrified...confused..." Victoria struggled to come up with excuses for what Payton had done—withholding information and jeopardizing the investigation.

"She confessed to Murphy. She said she never would have sabotaged the Salazar case. She just wanted to give us more time to find Avery. And she was scared out of her mind and didn't know what else to do." Rivera crossed his arms. "What she should have done is trusted us with the information, particularly me."

"I know, but we can't really understand what was going through her head. She was under so much stress already, with the Salazar case, before any of this happened with Avery. And what matters is that we found Avery. She's okay."

"We could have found her sooner. And if we'd known the Salazar Cartel was involved, we might have saved you from almost dying."

He was right. If they'd known who they were up against, the FBI could have gone straight to searching properties owned by the cartel and their suspected holding companies. They might have tracked down known cartel members and brought them in for questioning. And they wouldn't have done it alone.

CHAPTER 50

With help from Alejandro, Victoria scheduled a quick memorial service for Teresa on the beach before leaving the resort. It was a pleasant surprise when hundreds of guests and staff showed up to say goodbye and share memories of Teresa. She had annoyed, amused, and inspired many. None of them would soon forget her.

"While her death should not have occurred," Alejandro said. "The FBI assured me that Teresa's astuteness and attention to detail, something we can all testify to and appreciate, helped them locate Avery Jennings and will help bring the perpetrators to justice."

The media was there to capture the short but sweet ceremony. They'd surrounded the resort, wanting stories about Avery and Teresa. The reporters had learned Victoria and Rivera were involved with finding both women. As the agents left the resort, they could barely escape the barrage of questions.

"I covered the story about the plane crash," a reporter said to Victoria. "I know Dante Rivera was one of the people who found you and the other survivors. Our network would love to have the two of you come on as missing persons experts."

"I'm honored, but no, thank you," Victoria said, giving the same answer she'd given to other reporters and networks who had made similar offers. She valued her privacy and peace and quiet when she could get it. "I'd rather be finding people than talking about finding them. And anytime I'm not working on that, I want to get back to my real life. I'm just glad Avery is safe. I'm sad about Teresa Middleton, and eager for the people responsible to see justice."

"Same as what Agent Heslin said," Rivera told them.

The agents pushed through the crowd of reporters and climbed into the FBI vehicle that would take them to the airport. For security reasons and to minimize the agents' media exposure, the Department of Defense had a small private aircraft waiting to take them back to Virginia.

From the back seat, Victoria peered out her window. Amidst the reporters, Carlos stood a few yards from the shuttle, watching her leave. She hadn't seen him in days, but there he was, in his housekeeping uniform, staring at her in that strange way that still made her think he had something to tell her. She met his eyes and waved to him. He waved back. He wasn't wearing a mask and he offered what looked like a sad smile.

"Can you imagine if the media learned about your middle of the night jaunt in the ocean?" Rivera asked in a whisper, sitting next to her. "Then they'd really be all over you. Offering you a small fortune for your story."

Victoria turned away from her window to face Rivera. "Which reminds me...that number I called you from, when I told you to find the yacht, I need it."

"That phone belonged to a boy. You want to thank him?"

"I have a vague recollection of promising him something."

Rivera switched his phone on, unlocked the screen, and handed it to her. "Here you go. Look for the number with a 201-area code."

Victoria scrolled through and copied the number. She planned to trace it and anonymously send the boy five hundred dollars in cash. Personal cash, in no way endorsed by the FBI. Though her primary memory of their interaction involved the boy being difficult, a promise was a promise.

Rivera made a phone call as soon as he had his device back. He'd been in a funk since finding out Payton withheld critical intelligence from the investigation. He was probably worried about the repercussions she'd face at work. And he had to be upset that she'd withheld the information from him. The irony of what he'd told Victoria about sharing big moments with Ned wasn't lost on her. She wanted to talk to him about it on their ride to the airport, help him clear his thoughts. Instead, he remained with his phone to his ear, mostly listening to the person on the other line, for the duration of the trip and their walk through the airport.

His call finally ended as they headed across the tarmac to the awaiting plane. "I got confirmation that Eric Salazar is dead," Rivera said. "Died of an overdose. Just like Avery told us. Looks like he won't have to pay for his crimes."

"I don't doubt that he's responsible, but do they think it was actually him who killed Teresa and the girls with the missing parts? I didn't think Eric would have to do any of the actual dirty work."

"We think it was him. The other crew members are talking."

"That's a little convenient since Eric isn't around to refute their stories."

Victoria glanced at their small aircraft. She took a deep breath, preparing for the flight, then remembered something.

"Oh, you probably want this for the plane, right?" she held up his hoodie. "Thanks for letting me wear this the whole trip. I should know better by now. Always pack a warm sweatshirt or sweater."

Rivera stared at the hoodie then met Victoria's gaze. "That's not mine."

She wasn't sure what he meant. "But...yes, it is. You were wearing it at the Jennings' house before we went to Mexico."

"I was wearing one like it. Not that one. Here, I'll show you." Stopping near the plane, he unzipped his carry-on, letting the two sides fall open, and pulled out a black hoodie. It was darker than the one Victoria had been wearing and it had a silver zipper rather than a black one.

Victoria looked down at the hoodie in her hands as if it had taken on a life of its own. "Then whose is this? I've been wearing it for days!"

"Where did you get it?" Rivera asked.

"It was on the balcony after we checked into our rooms. I thought you left it out there. I asked you if I could wear it. Don't you remember?"

"Yeah, I do. I thought you wanted approval or my opinion because it's not really business attire. I said go for it, we can be casual here, or something like that."

Heat spread over her face, flushing her cheeks. "Oh, my God. It must belong to Carlos. He was cleaning rooms in our corridor when I took it."

Rivera smacked his leg in a laugh. "Well, you said he kept staring at you and that he wanted to tell you something. There you go. Mystery solved."

"I can't believe it. I wore it right in front of him so many times. He must think I'm crazy. Why didn't he say something?"

"Maybe he was too embarrassed for you. You did kind of steal it. And don't forget, at Azure Cove, the guests' needs come first." Rivera chuckled. "You can mail it back to him with a thank you note and a big tip. Tell him how much you appreciated it."

"I will. I absolutely will." Victoria dropped her head into her hands. "So much for my gut instinct, huh?"

CHAPTER 51

On the tarmac in Virginia, the wind blew strands of Victoria's hair into her eyes. "See you later, Rivera," she said.

"See you later. Get some rest," he said.

She laughed because she'd had more than enough rest in the hospital. "You, too," she answered before parting ways.

"Tori, wait."

She stopped, let her suitcase settle on its bottom, and turned to see what he had to say.

"You should tell Ned what you went through. He'd want to know. He'd be proud of you. And keeping secrets from someone who is supposed to trust you isn't a good idea."

Rivera gave her one last, long look before walking away, leaving Victoria feeling sad for him and unsure of what she would say when she saw Ned.

Ned's SUV was in her garage when she arrived home.

She put her phone away and went in through the side door. "I'm back," she said, though her announcement was unnecessary. Her dogs were going crazy with the frenzied, bursting-with-joy response they delivered every time she came home.

Wearing a faded blue T-shirt and jeans, Ned met her halfway across the kitchen. They embraced, holding each other tight.

He pulled back to smile at her.

She didn't realize she was crying until his expression changed and he asked, "What's wrong? Why the tears?"

Her swim had left no scars, no broken bones, no missing appendages. Just blistered skin that could pass off as a sunburn. He didn't need to know anything about it. She didn't want him to worry. And yet...it had been one of the most terrifying experiences in her life, and she didn't want to keep it from him.

There was a tightness in her throat. She was still deciding if she would say anything at all. Rivera's words came back to her, about not letting people get too close. He was right. She needed to do better. She didn't want to keep Ned at a distance.

He caressed her back, and suddenly her emotions took over. She told him what had happened. Getting shot. Waking up on the yacht. Finding Avery. Failing to save Avery or herself and getting thrown overboard like garbage. And then the swim.

"I was so determined at first. I knew if I didn't make it to shore, it might be Avery's death sentence as well as my own. After hours of swimming—I think it was hours—I still didn't know if I had a chance of making it to shore. I was floating, trying to be still in case there was a shark circling... ...I think I fell asleep. I swallowed water. I was choking. I couldn't breathe and that woke me up real quick. I thought it was the end. I was dying." Her tears flowed freely. She pressed on. "I was so sad that I wasn't coming back to you. So, so sad. I didn't want to die because I wasn't going to see you again."

"Oh, Victoria." He held her against his chest. "How did you get back to shore?"

"I heard your voice in my head. You kept saying, one stroke at a time. You know how you say that about so many things? One step...one breath...one day?"

He nodded, gazing into her eyes.

"And I kept swimming. I'm not talking about Olympic efforts. Granny-style on my side. Away from the moon. And it was getting farther and farther away, dropping. I kept reaching, again and again, until my feet hit something, and this time, it was the ocean floor. I'd made it. I still can't believe it." Sobs shook her shoulders. "I didn't want to die alone. And now I'm so grateful to be here. You have no idea."

She buried her head against his shoulder, feeling very safe and exactly where she wanted to be.

"That's an amazing story. Terrifying...and yet incredible. You know, experiences like that...they either crush you or strengthen you. You've got a long list of things that have made you stronger. Your mother's death. Your training and your cases. Surviving a plane crash. And now, an all-nighter in the ocean. Just...wow. You're a strong woman, Victoria. It's one of the many things I admire about you. You're incredible. Maybe you should do the next ironman instead of me." He chuckled. "I'd say you more than qualified."

His reaction surprised her. She thought he might freak out. She hadn't expected him to be in awe of what happened. She lifted her head from his shoulder. "I'm going to ask you something, and I need you to be honest with me. After hearing what happened, do you want me to quit my job?"

"What? No. I would never. I...I want what's best for you. If your job is important to you, and I understand why it would be...I want you to be happy and fulfilled. That's what I want. More than anything."

How could there be a more wonderful answer to her question? She took a few steps backward and sunk into a chair. Ned followed, kneeling on the floor in front of her, taking her hand and staring at her with so much love and concern.

And for an instant, because of the way he was down on one knee, looking up at her, she imagined he was about to propose. She felt a warm rush of joy. The moment passed when he stood up, pulling her up with him and into his arms, but she realized that if he had asked her to marry him, she would have said yes in a heartbeat.

CHAPTER 52

Two weeks later

T he Coast Guard had arrested Tony in international waters, and the
U.S. could prosecute crimes against U.S. citizens no matter where
they were committed. As a result, Tony found himself in a Washington
D.C. detention facility, waiting for the case to "play out" in the federal
court system.

Two guards unlocked his cell and led him into the hallway.

Tony's current residence wasn't luxurious like his cabin on *The Untouchable*. The food looked and tasted terrible. They could learn a lot in
the cafeteria from Marinero Uno. But at least Tony felt safe. He wasn't
surrounded by ocean. And anyway, he didn't expect to be there much
longer. The cartel's attorneys were working behind the scenes. They'd
already discovered that Avery's friend, the girl who identified him, had a
major drug trip on the day she claimed to have seen him. Her recollection
could hardly be trusted. The United States prosecuting attorneys wouldn't
call an unreliable witness to testify against anyone.

The guards moved him into a small room with concrete walls, a metal desk, and two chairs on either side. Two FBI agents stood behind the prosecutor chick, who was already seated.

"Sit," she said.

Tony lowered himself onto the metal chair and set his handcuffed wrists on the table. He knew an entourage from the U.S. Government watched from the opposite side of the mirrored glass.

Tony's attorney came in, wearing a suit that probably cost more than what the prosecutor made in a few months, and took the seat next to him.

"Ready to get started?" the prosecutor asked them. "We're going to need Tony's story one more time."

"Sure," Tony said. He'd been extremely cooperative since his arrest. Why stop now?

She opened her file folder and gripped a pen between her fingers. "Start from where Avery Jennings is still at the resort."

"Yeah. Right. So, Eric told her she had Covid and had to go with him for another test."

"Eric Salazar, correct?"

"Yes."

"Why did he tell her she had Covid?"

"He said he wanted to buy some time...so no one was looking for her right away. They'd think she was in quarantine."

"And then what did Eric do to get Avery off the resort property?"

"He said she went with him to a health office. A medical office? And that's where he drugged her, behind the building. He carried her to a truck...where the place piles the seaweed... and hid her there. Once it was dark, he stuffed her in a huge bag...left it unzipped so she could breathe. He never intended to kill her. At least, that's what he told me."

"And no one saw him carrying a bag with a body in it?"

"No. I guess they didn't, or they would have stopped him, wouldn't they? He stuffed seaweed around her to get rid of any strange bulges. The bag had wheels on it, so he half dragged it down the beach, I guess. At the marina, he put Avery on a speedboat and took her to the yacht. His father's yacht."

The marina staff had seen Tony. That was after they accepted watches and bundles of cash from him. He'd told them his name was Eric. He'd also told them what would happen to them and their families if they talked. If they were called to testify, which they wouldn't because they valued their lives too much to admit they'd seen anything...but if they did...they would say Eric did it. Dead Eric. They would be too afraid to pin the crime on a man who was very much alive and could retaliate.

Eric's death had done Tony more favors than he'd imagined. It wasn't Tony's fault that Eric had overdosed. Tony wasn't a babysitter. He was supposed to protect Eric from the authorities, not from his own pathetic self.

"And regarding the death of Teresa Middleton?" the chick asked, now tapping her pen on the metal tabletop.

"All I know about that is Eric said he took care of an old lady who was harassing him. He didn't tell me what he did with her, or to her."

The prosecutor set her pen down and leaned forward in her chair. "And that's the story you're sticking with?"

"That's right," Tony said. It was easy to cling to the facts because they were all true. Except for a few minor details. The more times he had told the story, the more he believed it.

"The Coast Guard found a bucket of body parts in formaldehyde on *The Untouchable*. Fingers, toes, an ear. From two different people. Both of whom went missing recently in Mexico and turned up dead. Can you tell us what that was about?"

VANISHED ON VACATION

Tony snorted. "Anyone who was on the yacht can tell you."

"I'm asking you."

"Well, that was Eric's thing. He got messed up when he was a kid. Like six years old. He saw something he shouldn't have seen."

"Tell us what happened."

"I don't know," Tony lied.

Everyone in the cartel knew Eric's story. Wandering his father's estates, he'd hear strange sounds coming from the basements. Shrieking. Blood-curdling howls. Often, he'd put his hand on the basement doorknob and stand there listening. Usually the door was locked, but one day, it turned under his hand. Eric crept down the stairs and sat there, watching. The guy was tied up and screaming, begging them to stop. They went toe by toe, using an old rusty bone saw, then moved on to the fingers. It took hours. Eric didn't move from the stairs until they were done.

Tony had heard Eric's father tell the story more than once, and with a sense of pride. Most of the cartel members got desensitized to that means of doing business. Not Eric. It continued to fascinate him.

As for Eric's tattoo—obviously Eric had never been part of a gang in San Francisco. He'd copied the design from someone who had. One of his father's most heinous torturers. Young Eric's idol.

The prosecutor kept staring at Tony, and suddenly she was looking too self-satisfied for her own good.

"Considering what you've told us, I think you're going to be very surprised with the new charges we're filing," she said. "Maybe your attorney will, too."

Tony's attorney stiffened beside him. "What new charges?"

Tony swallowed hard, but he didn't let his expression change. He wouldn't give her the satisfaction of knowing she'd made him curious. He'd been so careful. So clever...even down to the temporary tattoo, a near match to one Eric had. He thought back to the yacht, the olive oil lifting the green ink from his skin, blending it into a dark fluid, destroying the crown and the swords. He could have scrubbed the hell out of his skin in the shower, but how would it look if someone questioned him, and his skin was raw and strange exactly where the tattoo had been? Not good. Tony was smarter than that. Eric had lived with the smug certainty that he could do whatever he pleased and get away with it, but Tony didn't take chances.

Once he'd erased all traces of the tattoo, he'd wiped away the dark eyebrow pencil liner that filled in his scar. The scar was cool and distinctive; a constant reminder of the fist that tore through his face during a street fight and almost claimed his right eye. He'd won that fight with his bare hands. Every time he looked in a mirror, the scar bolstered his confidence, providing a stark reminder of who he was. Usually, he wanted people to notice it. Except for when he didn't.

He'd been so very careful.

The prosecutor was just screwing with his head. She had to be.

"We've got air-tight evidence that doesn't match up with your story," she said. "We found out Miguel Barrera is your cousin. You stayed with him the night before Avery disappeared. He gave you the wristband you wore to mingle with the guests at Azure Cove. You stole his paddleboard bag and his uniform shirt as part of your abduction scheme."

Tony kept his mouth shut, but he could hardly believe what he'd just heard. Miguel was family. Family had each other's backs, no matter what. Had Miguel really told the police those things?

The prosecutor put a check mark next to a line on her paper and looked up again. "Teresa Middleton put up a fight when she was strangled. She managed to cut her assailant and get his DNA under her nails. That DNA matches yours, Tony. Maybe Eric helped you, but you're the one going down for Teresa's murder."

Tony kept his face passive, but inside, he was furious. He never should have stuffed that scrawny broad into the seaweed truck and left her behind.

"The best deal we can offer you is life in prison without parole," she said. "And your attorney would be wise to convince you to accept that deal, or you're likely to get slapped with the death penalty. Juries don't tend to favor men who strangle eighty-seven-year-old women. The evidence is clear. You're a cold-blooded killer. Fortunately for Agent Heslin, the FBI agent you threw overboard in the middle of the night, you aren't a very good one."

Victoria Heslin hadn't died in the ocean! That seemed impossible. Was she the reason the Coast Guard had found them? Was this her fault?

Tony clenched his hands into fists. If he ever got a chance to kill that deformed agent again, he'd see it through to the very end.

CHAPTER 53

Victoria had done a lot of thinking since the day she returned from Mexico and told Ned everything that had happened there. She had an idea for some changes, and she was excited. She wasn't a super creative person, but she'd done her best to come up with something cute she thought Ned might appreciate. The time had come to showcase her efforts.

Her stomach fluttered as she opened the small package with the new dog collar tags she'd ordered. She slid one tag on Myrtle's collar and the other on Oliver's.

Victoria went into the kitchen, where Ned was opening a bag of tortilla chips. The dogs followed her, their new tags jingling.

Ned looked up but didn't notice the dogs, who were heading toward the dog door to go outside.

Victoria had wanted this to happen organically, to catch Ned by surprise, but now her impatience got the best of her. She called the dogs back inside. They swung around quickly, expecting a treat.

"What do you think of their new tags?" she asked Ned.

He glanced at the dogs. "I thought you didn't like the jingle those tags made?"

"I don't. But these were too special to pass up."

"Oh," he said, attaching a clip to the top of the chip bag.

"The dogs want to ask you something," Victoria said, grinning. She hadn't expected this to be so hard.

Ned pursed his lips. He'd finally caught her silly grin and realized she was up to something. "What do they want to ask me?"

"You'll have to see for yourself."

"Oliver, come here, boy," Ned said.

Oliver trotted over to him.

Ned lifted the heart-shaped tag and read it aloud. "It would be so great if Ned lived with us."

Not willing to let Oliver have all the attention, Myrtle butted her face into Ned's hands. Ned lifted her new tag and read it, too, "Ned, will you please move in with us?"

Ned laughed. "You did this? I mean, obviously you did." He went to Victoria and wrapped her in his arms. "So, the dogs want me to move in, but what about you? I mean, it's a big step. Are you sure it's what you want?"

"I know it's a big step and I'm very sure. If you want to."

Ned smiled.

"Okay, so is that a yes?"

"I think so. But can I have a day or two to give you my answer?"

Victoria's smile froze in place. She hadn't expected that. She was totally embarrassed and felt the heat of her face growing red. "Yeah, sure. Of course. Take all the time you need. And I mean, it's not like we have to be in my house, but my animals...and you have a condo."

He chuckled. "My condo would not work for your crew, that's for sure."

Ned put the bag of chips back in the cabinet and opened the fridge.

Victoria crouched down to pet her dogs and take off their new tags. How quickly she had gone from feeling giddy to feeling stupid.

"Want some?" Ned asked, moving the bowl of chips toward her.

"No, thanks. I'm good." She tried not to let her hurt show and chided herself for not anticipating that he'd need time to think through such a huge decision. He'd said he loved her, and she believed him, but that didn't mean he wanted to move in with her. Maybe he wasn't ready. Maybe she should have waited for him to bring it up, since it was his life that would change the most.

"I have to go back to my condo for a bit," he said.

Her stomach dropped. He wanted to leave. "Okay. Um, are we still going to watch a movie or whatever tonight?"

"Yeah, this won't take long." He scooped his keys off the counter and was in the mud room putting his shoes on when he said, "Why don't you come with me?"

"Oh, okay. I just need to grab my purse."

Sitting next to him in his SUV, she felt strangely uncomfortable, though she did her best to act natural.

When they got to Ned's condo, he got out of his SUV and walked around it to open her door. She followed him inside and into his living room, where she took a seat on his couch. He continued to his bedroom.

"Come here," he said.

She got up and went into his bedroom. Ned opened the top drawer of his dresser and moved aside a layer of undershirts. When he turned around, he held a small black box. He opened the lid.

Victoria's hand flew to her heart. "You...you already had a ring?"

"I sure did."

"But...when?"

"Let's just say I've known I wanted to marry you since the day I walked into your house, and you started telling me about each of your dogs. I've just been waiting for you to get that we are perfect for each other."

Victoria clasped her hands and felt her eyes brim with tears.

"I was waiting to do a whole big thing in the woods with the dogs. It was going to be an epic proposal, but now that you asked me to move in with you...I honestly couldn't wait."

Victoria stared from the beautiful ring to Ned.

"You haven't answered yet. I'm sorry, this isn't all that romantic, is it?"

"It's great. It's just, can I have a day or two to think about it?" She had to press her lips together to keep from smiling.

Ned's face fell.

"I'm kidding! Yes! Absolutely, yes!"

He slid the ring onto the remaining nub of her ring finger.

The ring really was beautiful and something about it seemed familiar. She'd never had much interest in jewelry, so she wasn't sure why. Then it came to her. "My mother had a stone like this."

"This was your mother's engagement ring, Tori."

"But...how?"

"Your father thought I should give it to you. He said your mother would have loved for you to have it."

"You already asked him about marrying me?"

"Weeks ago. So, even if you said no to me, the ring is yours. Or if you prefer, we could pick out a new one together."

"No. this one is perfect. It's really special. Almost like having my mother's blessing as well. I love it. And I love you."

That concludes this investigation. Read on for the first few chapters of *The Atonement Murders*, book seven in the Agent Victoria series.

EXCERPT - THE ATONEMENT MURDERS

CHAPTER 1

Two months ago, Charlotte, North Carolina

Sometimes the most unexpected things ruin what is supposed to be a perfect day. Real estate agent Paige Malloy was well aware of this and needed Wednesday morning's appointment to go exactly according to her plan. Stepping out of the elevator at Charlotte's Prestige View Condominium building, she said a little prayer that this property would be the one. Her clients would love the condo, and she would soon be free of them once and for all.

Philip and Tricia were challenging clients. Paige had taken them to three newish and nice listings yesterday, and several others the day before. They hadn't shown the slightest sign of excitement about any, though their criticisms were many and the hushed whispering between them almost constant. Buying a house was stressful...but still.

"You ready?" Paige asked, beaming at her clients from outside the door of the unit, just one floor down from the top of the building. "Two bedrooms. Two bathrooms. Floor to ceiling windows with absolutely amazing views of uptown. Hardwoods throughout. And it comes furnished."

Tricia scrunched her nose and scowled as she stared down the beautiful, clean corridor behind them. "Do you smell that? It smells like men's cologne out here. As if someone used way too much or just sprayed it right here in the hallway. Who would do that? Makes me wonder what they're trying to cover up."

Lord, give me patience, Paige thought, forcing a smile, though she smelled it too. Prepared to enter the code, she reached for the door, only to find it wasn't locked. It wasn't even fully closed.

"That's strange," she said, thinking perhaps the buyers from the previous showing hadn't shut the door all the way. Very unprofessional of their realtor. Except...Paige had selected the first showing of the day.

As they entered the condo, a phone began ringing from somewhere inside.

Tricia narrowed her eyes at Paige. "Do you think the owner is here?"

"He shouldn't be," Paige answered, stepping farther into the unit and calling out in her professional sing-song voice, "Hello? It's Paige with Carolina Realty Group. I scheduled a ten o'clock showing."

Paige waited for an answer. An apology really, because the owner wasn't supposed to be there.

None came.

Only silence.

The ringing ceased.

"There's no one home," Paige said. "Have a look around. See what you think. Take your time."

Her clients wandered toward the balcony, murmuring something Paige couldn't hear.

Dirty dishes in the sink and a glass on the countertop caught her attention. Even the smallest details mattered and contributed to an overall vibe. It really miffed her when a seller didn't clean up before a showing. After placing her business card on the stone countertop, she rinsed the used plates and glass and tucked them in the dishwasher. She wiped leftover crumbs into the sink with a paper towel and quickly scoured the basin. If she could prevent her clients from finding a single fault with the amazing condo, it was worth the small effort.

Finished with the cleaning, Paige turned to survey the space. The floor to ceiling windows were truly amazing. Very nice minimalist décor. Perfect for the unit. The owner, a man in his late twenties, must have used a high-end designer.

She eased through the living area with the comfy sectional couches and Carolina Panthers-themed bar and into the second bedroom, taking in the rest of the condo but staying out of her clients' way. Paige was admiring the view from behind a modern desk when she heard Tricia's blood-curdling scream and Philip's string of curses.

Hurrying to retrace her steps, Paige met Tricia and Philip in the center living area, where Philip leaned forward with his hands on his thighs, taking ragged breaths. Tricia's face was pale, her mouth agape. Unable to speak, she pointed down the hallway.

Paige moved past her clients and into the primary bedroom. She continued down a short hallway, her high heels clicking on the polished wood, and into the bathroom.

What she saw made her freeze in horror.

Submersed under a full tub of water...a naked man. His body was young and strong, but his skin had pruned and turned a grayish hue. His opened eyes stared upward. He was unequivocally dead.

On the polished Carrara marble tiles above him, written neatly in a thick red substance, were the words: THIS IS YOUR ATONEMENT.

Paige's scream was even louder than Tricia's.

CHAPTER 2

Present Day, Washington D.C.

First thing Monday morning, FBI Special Agent Victoria Heslin walked into her boss's office thinking she was about to get reprimanded. She'd thwarted protocol on her last investigation in Mexico, but only in pursuit of the greater good.

She loved her position as a special agent—specifically the opportunity to help desperate families who were often at their lowest point. Her professional accolades were many, and though she appreciated the credit, they usually came with a great deal of fuss she could do without. In almost ten years with the Bureau, she'd experienced few reprimands. Few in her entire existence, in fact. So the prospect of this looming admonishment did not sit well with her. Especially now, when everything in her life seemed fantastic. She'd been floating along in a bubble of happiness, and now her boss was about to burst it.

Stopping in front of Special Agent in Charge Murphy's desk, Victoria mentally prepared herself for what might come. Whatever it was, she supposed she deserved it. "You wanted to see me?" she asked her boss.

Murphy stood behind his desk with his phone in one hand and a Georgia Bulldogs mug in the other. The scowl on his face matched the mascot's. "Yes. Hold on."

She took a deep breath, wanting to get this over with. Instead, she had to wait while he set his phone down, sorted through a stack of papers, and selected one. His thick eyebrows pulled together as he scribbled a few lines in his messy penmanship. Finally, still holding his mug, he looked up at her.

"First, I hear congratulations are in order," he said, dropping his gaze to her left hand and the diamond sparkling on her finger.

"Thank you," she said, unable to contain her widening smile. After only a few days, Victoria wasn't used to the ring yet. Each glimpse ignited a spark of excitement inside her.

"You marrying a veterinarian makes sense. I'm happy for you, Victoria."

"Thank you," she said, thinking, *Is that all? Is that what he wanted to tell me?* Some of the tension weighing her down lifted away. Already she felt better about getting called into his office.

"That's not why I called you in here." Murphy's tone shifted to a more serious one.

So that's how this was going to go. He'd lowered her guard. Now he was going to hit her with a lecture, or worse.

"Did you hear Jerome Smith died over the weekend?" he asked, in what seemed a non sequitur because the topic wasn't anything Victoria expected.

"The NBA player?"

"All-Pro NBA player for the Celtics. It's all over the news. Twenty-nine years old and at the peak of his career. Although, who is to say what he might have achieved next?" Murphy looked away and stared out his office window while taking a drink from his mug. He sounded deeply sad, as though Jerome had been a close friend or personal hero.

"That's a shame," Victoria said. "Do they know what caused his death?" So young and healthy. If she had to make an educated guess backed by statistics, it was an unintentional overdose or a motor vehicle accident.

"This hasn't been confirmed to the public yet, but he was murdered inside his home in Boston."

"Oh, wow!"

"And we don't have a suspect. I just got off the phone with the Boston PD. We're going to assist them."

"Why is the FBI involved?"

"High-profile death, for one. But it's more than that. Jerome's death might link to an unsolved murder that occurred two months ago in Charlotte, North Carolina. A young man was found drowned in his bathtub. The same exact message was left behind at both crime scenes."

"A message?"

"*This is your atonement.* That's what the message said. We've either got a serial killer or a very big coincidence, and we've got to get a handle on it. The cops are already under tremendous pressure from politicians, the NBA, the Boston community, the victim's family, and every fan of Jerome's, of which there are millions."

Victoria nodded, imagining the urgency to find the perpetrator.

"You're going to catch the next commercial flight to Logan and see how you can help figure out who killed him."

"Why me?"

Murphy snorted and set his mug on his desk with a thunk. "That's something I've always liked about you, Agent Heslin. All that inherited money and you've never acted like you're above any of this." He shook his head. "How's this for why? You've got a reputation. An earned reputation. And you're very good at linking clues."

Victoria felt her face flush. She appreciated his words, but that was enough. If he continued, she'd be genuinely embarrassed.

"And besides all that, the Boston field office is slammed with casework. They need other hands and the detective working Jerome's case asked for you specifically. Her name is Suarez. Detective Lieutenant Lisa Suarez. She said she worked with you recently on your friend's case. That missing groom investigation."

"Yes. Of course. I like Suarez," Victoria said, picturing the native Bostonian with the grouchy personality. Suarez had proven to be an excellent and committed detective and a good team player. Victoria trusted her and welcomed the opportunity to work with her again.

Murphy picked up his mug. "What do you know about Jerome Smith?"

"Um...that he's a professional basketball player. An All-Pro. Plays for the Celtics. Twenty-nine years old. He might have been at the peak of his career when he died, but who is to say what else he might have achieved. He has lots of fans."

One side of Murphy's mouth curled into the slightest smile, the corner actually twitched, as Victoria finished repeating what he'd just told her. "That's what I thought," he said. "Your lack of interest in professional sports might give you an advantage. You can certainly be more objective than others. Right?"

"There's that. Yes. Objectivity."

"Grab your stuff and get to the crime scene while it's still relatively fresh. Meanwhile, I'm going to set up a task force here to support you. We'll work both atonement murder cases under one umbrella." Murphy was already turning to his computer as he gestured for her to leave his office. "Be on the lookout for the files on the Charlotte murder. We'll talk more once you're on your way to Boston."

"Okay. Thanks." Victoria left his office, thinking her meeting with Murphy hadn't played out the way she'd expected. Instead of an admonishment, she was on the hunt for a possible serial killer. Could an FBI agent ask for a better turn of events?

NOTE FROM THE AUTHOR

I f this is your first Agent Victoria Thriller, you might not know it's part of a series. I wrote the books so readers could read them alone without confusion. Each features a unique mystery investigation which resolves at the end. Victoria's personal stories continue from novel to novel. There is a list of her adventures in the back of this book.

I also want to thank you for being a reader, and for choosing my novel. Without you, I couldn't continue to write. Please consider leaving a review and recommending this book to others. Your continued support is appreciated more than you'll ever know.

Until my next novel,

Yours sincerely,

Jenifer Ruff

JENIFER RUFF

U SA Today bestselling author Jenifer Ruff writes suspense novels, including the award-winning Agent Victoria Thriller Series. Jenifer grew up in Massachusetts, has a biology degree from Mount Holyoke College and a Master's in Public Health and Epidemiology from Yale University. She adores peace and quiet, animals, and exercise, especially hiking. Jenifer lives in North Carolina and Virginia with her family and a pack of greyhounds. If she's not writing, she's probably devouring books or exploring trails with her dogs. For more information you can visit her website at Jenruff.com

a amazon.com/stores/author/B00NFZQOLQ

f facebook.com/authorjruff

[O] instagram.com/author.jenifer.ruff/

d tiktok.com/@jeniferruff.author

BB http://bookbub.com/authors/jenifer-ruff

Made in United States
Orlando, FL
15 February 2024

43680463R00189